COUNTRY ROADS

"Evil lurks in the small Irish countryside of Kilcross and Colin Leonard knows just how to deliver it. Leonard's ability to craft believable and complex characters while immersing you into the rich Irish landscape sucks you in and leaves you horrified at each twisted tree and bend in the road. A must read for fans of rural horror."
—Francesca Maria, author of *They Hide: Short Stories to Tell in the Dark*

COUNTRY ROADS

by Colin Leonard

Edited by Elle Turpitt
Proofread and formatted by Stephanie Ellis

Cover illustration and design by Elizabeth Leggett
First Edition: July 2023

ISBN (paperback): 9781957537672
ISBN (ebook): 9781957537665
Library of Congress Control Number: 2023940149

BRIGIDS GATE PRESS
Bucyrus, Kansas
www.brigidsgatepress.com

Printed in the United States of America

To Bonnie and my children

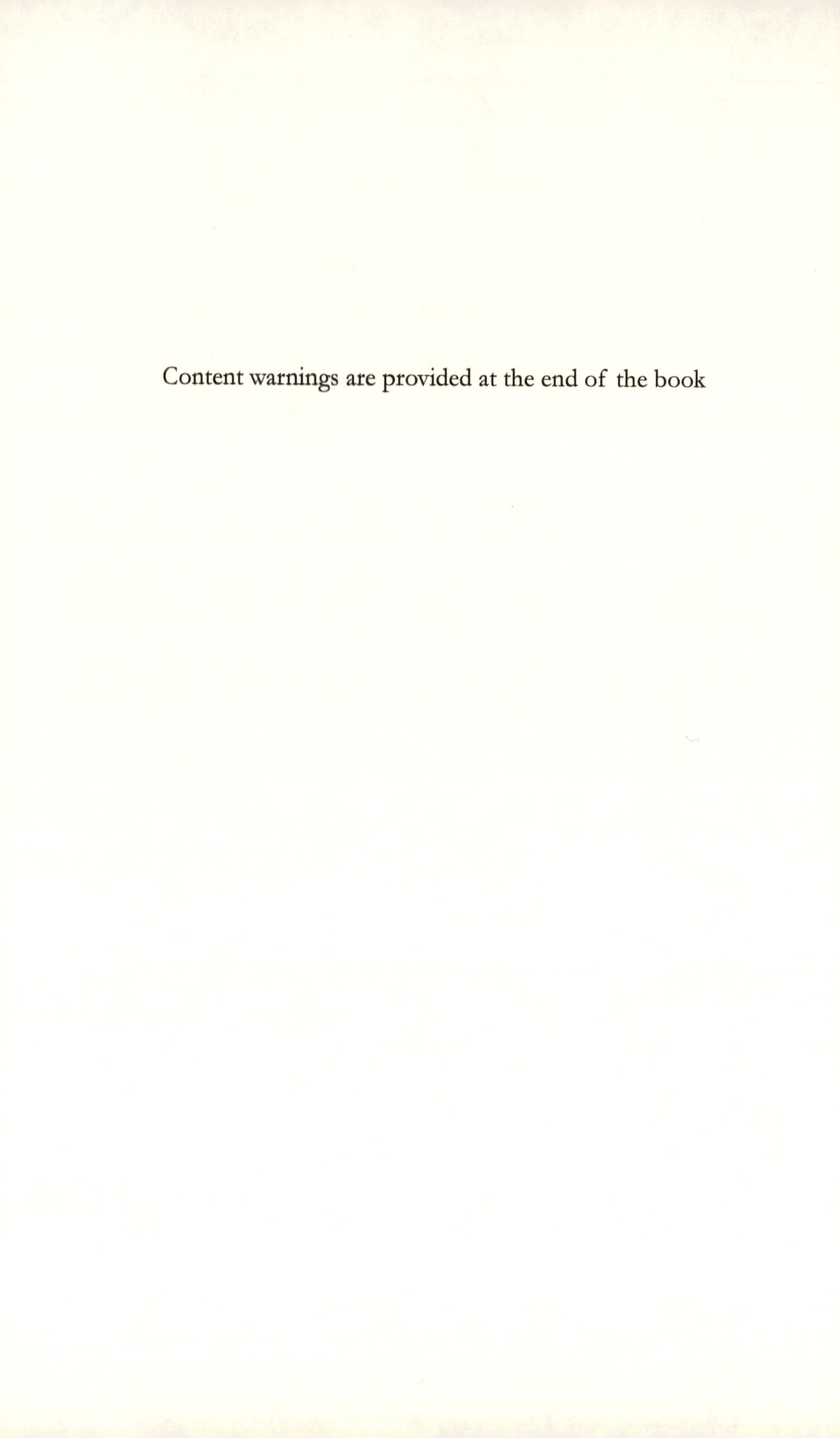

Content warnings are provided at the end of the book

CHAPTER ONE

See this gnarled and ancient hawthorn tree. Its fruits consist of knotted socks, sodden gloves, crumpled sleeves and stockings. These ragged offerings have rotted through the years with the weight of the prayers of the faithful, begging for recovery, for solace, for relief.

Sometimes angels and saints might attend here to answer those prayers. Sometimes other cruel creatures gather to laugh at human frailties.

This is one of those rare trees in Ireland attributed healing powers. They usually grow beside a holy well or some source of water. You can easily recognise them, festooned with brightly coloured rags and bits of clothing that flutter in the wind, hang damp in the rain and fade in the sun. This tree stands near the small, scattered village of Kilcross, just a couple of miles from the house where Declan Maguire found himself living with local girl Denise Weldon and their three-year-old boy. Declan didn't know when exactly his son was conceived, but he could narrow it down to one of the times they had sex on the night he first met her, fuelled with vodka and tonic, cocaine and recreational Viagra. Some of his friends laughed with him about a shotgun wedding. He didn't find that joke funny anymore.

The source of water from which this tree sprung had long dried up. It served as a well before running water became commonplace in houses. The remains of a ruined stone wall circled it, held together with moss and smothered with weeds. In a certain light, at a certain time of night, the gaps between the crooked roots appear as if they open to somewhere deep and forbidden. Cracks maybe, a split in the seams between worlds. Tradition claimed that this tree was particular for the healing of crippled limbs. Its branches curled and contorted round its trunk like it was being strangled by itself, long ago earning it the name the Twisted Tree. They said its twisted form came from taking on the deformities and pain of the supplicants who tied their offerings to it.

Declan drove past it every day on his way to and from work as a Garda in Cromuck, twenty miles away from Kilcross. It formed part of a landscape that he was growing more embittered towards the longer he lived there, surrounded by drab, insular neighbours with whom most of his interactions turned spiky. Like his neighbour, Brendan McGrath, a farmer who lived a little further on from the Twisted Tree. McGrath was the type who preferred a quiet, unassuming life and, for the most part, got to enjoy one. He rarely had cause to contact the Gardaí. If Declan was prompted to root through the records, he would only find three instances in the past thirty years.

Once, McGrath discovered a car crashed and abandoned in a ditch and he called it in. Another time someone had siphoned diesel from the tank in his yard and also vandalized his tractor. Nothing had ever come of that but a new lock on the tank and an insurance claim.

The third time—this time—McGrath wasn't quite sure what it was he was reporting. His wife thought she heard someone outside the house the previous night, someone laughing. In the morning, he found his household bins knocked over and a shed door open. Maybe it was just kids, nothing seemed to be stolen. He rang the station at Cromuck and reported it as a disturbance. Declan took the call and said he'd drop in on his way home, using it as an excuse to leave early.

Declan walked around Brendan McGrath's yard with him and searched around the shed. He took some notes. McGrath showed him the bins that had been toppled.

"Wind? Animals?" Declan suggested.

McGrath picked up an empty vodka bottle from beside the bins and let it dangle disapprovingly from his large hands.

"What about it?" said Declan.

"It's not mine," said McGrath. "Someone left it here."

"What about your kids?"

"They're away at college."

"Your wife?"

"My wife?" said McGrath. "What do you mean by that?"

The farmer's wife came out of the house just then and offered Declan a cup of tea. Emma was a tall, pleasant-eyed woman, as polite as her husband. Declan didn't want any tea. They told him they had also seen bottles littering the ground at the Twisted Tree near where he lived and other bits of rubbish dumped along the roadside.

"You should report that to a litter warden then," Declan said and shut his notebook.

When he left them, he drove in the direction of his own house, despite the fact he wasn't particularly bothered about going home. He toyed with the idea of heading back into Cromuck and hooking up with Cliona Casey, but she was beginning to be a bit too much work. He drove to the Twisted Tree. Might as well check it out while he waited for inspiration on how to entertain himself. The first thing he noticed when he pulled over were the black loops of tyre marks on the road. He didn't like the tree. It disgusted him with its rotten mob of filthy rags begging on its branches. It was amazing that in this day and age people still believed in that shit but, from the amount of material stuck there, it was obvious plenty of them did.

The tree was covered in snatches of colour, old sleeves and torn baby grows, as well as a scatter of limp grey tubes that were once socks. Broken glass nestled in the exposed roots of the tree. He hadn't liked the way the McGraths had mentioned the dumping here and on the local roads. He thought their tone was suggesting he was neglecting his territory by allowing rubbish to spoil the countryside.

Declan nudged a shard of glass with his shoe. A flap of feathers and leaves attacked the silence as a large bird broke cover from behind the tree. Lush brown and white flecked feathers housed a pair of intense orange eyes, as magical as childhood marbles. The bird passed over him and flew away across the fields on the other side of the road. Declan wasn't very good at identifying wildlife but the round face and short beak convinced him that it was an owl. *That was peculiar*, he thought, *to see that in the daytime.* Something must have disturbed it.

The area settled into silence once more. He lifted the piece of glass and recognised the remains of a Jameson label. There were also jagged necks of wine bottles separated from their bodies. Deformed beer cans hid in the trampled grass. He picked one up and unfinished lager sloshed around inside it. Then, in the distance, he heard the growl of a modified car engine and started to make connections. He got back into his car, taking the can of beer with him, and drove in the direction of the engine noise.

The roads around here were narrow. In many places, particularly in long stretches between houses, the ditches were left uncut. The spread of grass and the bullying thistles and nettles threatened to encroach onto the road if the trucks, tractors and commuters didn't keep up their daily work of forcing it back. Declan preferred roads where the bushes and trees were scalped back harshly and neatly. He didn't care about nesting birds or biodiversity. He'd rip them all out and install steel fences if it were up to him.

He came across the Honda Civic idling in the gateway of a field. Smoke and music drifted through the open window. Declan wasn't in a squad car, just his personal one, and the driver didn't realize who he was until he had pulled up right in front of him and blocked any attempt at flight he might think of making. Declan got out of the car, hoping he would smell the earthy scent of a joint coming from the Civic, but it was just a regular cigarette. The young man continued to smoke while attempting to screw his features into a defiant expression to overcome the worry in his face.

Declan stood close to the young driver and placed his hands on his hips. He held the half-full, battered beer can in his hand, saying nothing. The young man didn't turn his eyes to him and didn't speak either. He just stared uncomfortably out his windscreen while the music thumped from the car stereo. The cigarette burned down to its butt and he stubbed it out in the ashtray of the car, his defiance having not developed nearly enough for him to flick it out on the ground.

"Turn off the music," Declan said, finally.

The young man's narrow shoulders sunk and he obeyed the order.

"Noel Quirke," continued Declan. "This must be yours."

He waved the can at him. Noel Quirke had a large nose for the size of his weedy face and it crinkled away from the exhibit being presented before him.

"What do you mean?" he said through a dry mouth.

"You've been drinking up at the Twisted Tree and leaving your shit all around there. Have you been trespassing up at the McGrath's as well?"

Relief of the innocent relaxed the tightness in Noel's breath. "Not me, Garda. I don't even drink."

Declan's hand shot out and grabbed Noel by the chin. He squeezed hard and turned the boy's face upward.

"Don't you lie to me, you ugly little prick."

He took the beer can and poured the stale liquid over Noel's lips, twisting his grip to force open the resistant mouth. The yellow lager splashed off gritted teeth and down Declan's wrist.

"I could arrest you now for drunk driving if I wanted to. How would you like that? How would you like to lose your license?"

He poured the rest of the beer over Noel's face and into his eyes. Noel's neck squirmed and his weak hands tried to pull the Garda's fingers away from him. When the can had spewed its contents, Declan pressed it down across Noel's cheek and nose and spitefully crushed it, feeling the aluminium fold against his facial bones. A sharp point formed where the metal creased and it drew blood just beneath Noel's eye. Declan released his grip and from point blank range hopped the crushed can off the youth's forehead.

"I'll make your life a misery if I find you up to any more of your shit," said Declan as he walked back to his car.

Noel wiped his face with the sleeve of his hoodie, smearing blood and sticky lager together across his pallid skin. He spat out the window then leaned his head down, defeated, on his steering wheel.

"It's already a misery," he muttered to himself.

CHAPTER TWO

After a long day, it was usual that parts of Brendan McGrath ached. His shoulder had once gotten dislocated when a frightened bullock rammed it between his manic, twisting head and the pen gate as Brendan helped the vet ram a syringe into the animal's mouth. That shoulder would usually be the first to trouble him, even as he'd be pulling his boots off in the hall. His left knee was missing some cartilage since ten years ago when a giddy jump from a haystack while playing around with his kids led to a trip to the emergency room in Cromuck, a painful half hour away from their farm. That left knee might throb as he sat, still unshowered, at the kitchen table.

If he hadn't been wearing gloves on the farm, and he rarely did, then his hands might ache from cold, or cuts or fatigue. His back, the same as every fifty-three-year-old back, would always be sore from having to hold the rest of his creaking self upright. He didn't mind those aches. They were good aches, proof of hard work, proof of life.

This particular evening it was his head that ached. He sat back in the armchair of the sitting room and squinted at the nine o'clock news as if it was the serious blonde newsreader making him frown. His head ached, partly because of the disturbance last night and Garda Maguire's brusque visit, but mostly because he had spent some of the morning, a lot of the afternoon and most of the evening going over the accounts with his wife, Emma. He never remembered this being so complicated years ago. They had a good accountant. What Brendan used to do was gather all his receipts and paperwork up in a folder, hand it to his accountant and let him turn it into something that made sense so he could fill in what he needed to for their subsidies.

About five years ago, though, Emma had persuaded him to start rearing some free-range poultry for the Christmas market. Brendan was a cattleman, he always had been. He'd grown up with them on this very farm. He had no real interest in poultry but he started a small flock all the same. *At the very least*, he thought, *the geese would act as a mass, honking guard dog and they'd surely sell a few turkeys*. Emma decided on the price per kilogram and set up the social media side of things. He shook his head at how much she was charging for the birds but he liked the photos she posted up online and the little one-liners she wrote beneath them. She was a witty woman, his wife. They were having a good laugh, enjoying the new venture, and the birds weren't all that much extra work for a man like him who always loved to be outside doing something anyway. The kids helped out on the weekends of that first year but he really wanted them to be concentrating on school. Mark was doing his Leaving Cert back then and Siobhan would be doing it the following year. As November ticked along, the orders started to come in, and he thought that there must be some sort of mistake. After a week they had to stop taking requests. Emma was almost going to sell the turkey picked out for their own table as well but Brendan put his foot down about that.

"If we're going to be selling them again next year then we have to know what they taste like."

And they did sell them again the next year, much more of them, and again the year after, and the money from them was now putting the kids through college.

His wife brought him in a can of Smithwick's and a glass. She smiled as he poured the russet-coloured beer, creating too high of a head, and clumsily trying to stop the foam from spilling over the sides. He didn't drink often. He wasn't one to usually have beers in the fridge but Emma had got a few in especially as a reward for what she knew would be a tedious chore for him. She had been barraging him with questions all day about receipts and payments and forcing him to recall work done and trips made. The poultry farm operated under a different name than the rapidly shrinking beef side of the business but Brendan consistently found it difficult to separate the two. Work was work and money was money, what difference did it make which side of the business it was spent on? But it did matter apparently, and Emma interrogated him about each fence post bought and every fill of diesel, then, even when he remembered what an expense was for, she might say, "Well actually it might be better if we put that in the other accounts."

He worried they were cheating or being dishonest somehow but she assured him that they weren't and their accountant said the same. They were just maximizing their profits. He had a suspicion that the end game here would eventually be the wrapping up of his cattle farm and moving full-time into poultry. He just couldn't understand how they got such a good price for the turkeys and geese while they struggled to break even with beef.

"Firstly," explained his wife, "we have no middle man with the free-range poultry telling you what they're going to pay you and, secondly, there is no special occasion once a year when people will pay whatever it costs to put an extra special roast beef on the table."

He had grumbled at that and stuck his head back into an indecipherable list of invoices for casual labour.

"Thank God that's over till next year," he said now, as Emma went back into the kitchen to check on their dinner.

"Well, you're to keep on top of it in future. Organise things better so it's not like one big nightmare of a day before meeting the accountant and we're left eating this late in the evening again."

"Hmmmf," he mumbled, his mind turning guiltily to his cattle. He hadn't been out to check on them since early that morning. He took a sip of his beer and his muscles sagged with relaxation. The weather forecast came on the television and told him that, thankfully, it was going to be a warm night for September with little chance of rain. The sitting room window was on the same wall as the television and he stared through it while listening to the forecast, as if he needed to be convinced of the weatherman's soft and cautious predictions.

He heard his wife's voice from the kitchen.

"You know, I was reading a thing on the internet about how they're short of frog's legs in French restaurants …"

"Emma, we are not farming frogs. Anything smaller than a chicken is not farming."

He realised suddenly that while he had been settled in the numbing cloud of television and ale, he had been gazing out the window into the large round eyes of one of his cattle.

"Emma? Emma, one of the bullocks is out."

"What?"

"He's staring in the window at me here." Brendan stood up and moved carefully towards the window so he wouldn't startle the animal. He peered out past the bullock to their small lawn, ringed with sturdy shrubs and home to a wooden swing seat that they never got the time to sit on.

"Ah no, there's more of them out. Dammit, there must be a fence broken or something."

Emma sighed. "Do you want me to help you?"

"No, no." Brendan bustled into the kitchen and took a torch out of a drawer. "I'll round them up. Maybe it's just a gate left open. If so, I won't be long."

"Maybe you shouldn't go out there," Emma said. "What if it's intruders? Should you call someone?"

"Ah no, sure if that business last night was anything serious then they would have done more than knocked over some bins and left a vodka bottle. It must have just been kids, like Garda Maguire said."

"Unless they were scoping out the place to come back tonight."

"Well, if that was the case they definitely wouldn't have been knocking over bins and leaving things open. Sure, didn't you say you heard laughter? Someone scoping out a place wouldn't be laughing."

"I'm not exactly sure that it was laughter," she said.

He squeezed her shoulder. "I'll be fine. I have to put them back in the field before they go wandering."

She kissed him on his rough cheek. "Ok then. Dinner's almost done. Bring your phone with you and let me know how long you'll be. And if you see anything wrong, promise me you'll ring somebody. Don't go investigating."

He put on his boots and kissed her on the forehead before going outside. Brendan took a four-foot-long ash stick from where he always left it leaning near the door. It was smooth and straight. The parts where he had snapped off the growth of smaller twigs had healed and rounded.

"Here boy," he called as he sensed the arrival of their black and white collie, Jack. Jack trotted towards the cattle, knowing they shouldn't be there and perhaps knowing he should have played some part in not allowing them to get there. Brendan swung his stick by his side just to show the cattle there was a stick present and that it might be used. At the end of a deep sigh he rasped, "C'mon, c'mon now," more as noises than words. He wasn't bothered too much that he had to leave his evening of relaxation because he had seen so little of his herd that day. Brendan understood cattle. He enjoyed being among them. He felt no real affinity for the birds they farmed. The outside sensor lights on the farmhouse had come alive with all the movement and they brightened the grey haze of dusk to allow him to see the hoof marks and cowshite that bestrew the lawn.

"Ah no," he said to the wrecked lawn before marching the cattle away behind the house with a string of his 'C'mon' noises and Jack scampering around the backs of their nervous legs.

He marched them past the turkey coops where a few of the wrinkle-headed birds had come out to snoop at what was going on. He shook his stick at them. In his other hand he held his torch. It was dark enough now for him to need its light. He thumbed its switch and illuminated the ghostly white forms of three large geese inside the fenced-off run that housed them at night. He expected them to start honking and send the cattle into a run, but they were strangely silent in their observations.

The gate to the small field where the poultry spent their days had been left open and the cattle filed through it. Brendan examined it for damage from the wandering bullocks but there was none. He closed it behind him and ordered the livestock forward towards their own field. The gate to the cattle field was closed so he skirted round the small herd to open it, leaving Jack to guard the rear and keep their noses turned the way they should be going. He opened that gate and scanned the fence with his torch to see how else they might have gotten out. One of the fence posts a little way up from the gate had been uprooted and it had dragged a section of the fence down with it. Jack kept the cattle moving toward the gate and Brendan jogged awkwardly back behind them, swinging his stick lightly as a warning not to change course. The cattle trudged on, strings of dried cow dung matting the back of their legs, and Brendan realised he hadn't heard a noise out of any of them since he came out. There hadn't been a bellow or a grunt and they hadn't at any stage broken into a run. It was as if they were filled with a sadness or resignation about something.

"Jesus Jack, they must have missed me today, huh?" he said and chuckled at the thought. Jack stopped and regarded him, cocking his head to one side.

"You're fairly quiet as well, boy."

His phone broke the stillness of the night with a stern sounding text alert. Despite the broken section of fence, he still closed the gate behind the last of the bullocks to reduce their points of egress then read the message from his wife:

'Dinner ready. Shall I keep it in the oven?'

He replied to it, 'Yes pls. Broken fence.'

Another sound disturbed the silence but he couldn't tell whether it came from close by or from way across the fields. It was like a laugh, but he was sure it wasn't human. It went on for a good thirty seconds with a callous and cruel lilt. It was similar to the way a fox could sound like a crying child, but this wasn't the sound of a fox. He stood still and listened. Once, his son had shown him this

YouTube video with donkeys that sounded like humans screaming. They had looked weird, fake, even though he was aware that they could make those sounds. There was an otherworldly sense to the noise of those donkeys. This laugh was similar in that there was something off about it, like it didn't rightly belong to whatever it had come from. Or perhaps it seemed otherworldly because he couldn't guess at what might have made such a noise, even having spent his whole life in the countryside of Ireland, in close proximity to animals both domesticated and wild. Just in case it had actually come from a human—and that notion steeled his grip on his stick—he called out.

"Is someone there?"

The laughing noise came again but seemed to be trailing away from him.

A bird? he thought uncertainly before inspecting the fallen fence post. The electric fence had snapped where the post was knocked and he would have to repair it if he wanted the cattle to keep to their field.

"Stay here, Jack," he ordered the dog, and headed off to the sheds to get some tools. The shed closest to the house contained the switch for the electric fence. After he turned it off, he considered going in to Emma to let her know how long he would be but thought it best to get back to his canine sentry as quickly as he could. He grabbed his fencepost driver, a pliers, a hammer, and stuffed a few fencing nails into his back pocket. As he strode past the turkey coops and then the geese, he noticed again how quiet they were. The wandering light of his torch caught a hare, standing alert, staring at him from the middle of the field. On the branches of a gangly ash tree perched a crowd of birds and he shone his torch at them to see if he could recognise one that may have made the strange sound but they were all silent now. There was a mix of crows, thrushes, swallows, all together, all spying at him, a phalanx of beaks of diverse shapes and sizes like mercenary spear bearers. They weren't startled by the light of his torch.

When he reached the cattle field, Jack was sitting on his back legs facing the placid herd. There was barely a move from any of them. He sensed something dark and low in the grass about ten metres away and a sweep of his torch revealed a badger. It didn't scurry away at being discovered and Brendan thought it unusual Jack hadn't gone barking after it. The dog seemed out of sorts indeed. There was something else wrong. The gate was wide open. He had thought there was something odd as he had approached and now it landed with him like a weight of dread sinking down through his head and seeping through his body. He had closed that gate, he was sure. Even though the fence was broken he had closed the gate.

"Who's there?" he shouted. "If someone is there, you'd better leave. This is private property."

He walked over to the fallen fence post and laid his tools on the ground, but kept the hammer in his hand. As he stood up again something swiped by his face, grazing his cheek. He roared, as much in defence as from fright, and swung around. His hands went limp with panic. One of them dropped his hammer, the torch dangled from the other. He couldn't see anything. The animals hadn't bolted at his shouting, the birds hadn't dispersed from their branches.

"A bat," he muttered. "It must have been a bat. A fucking bat."

But a bat hadn't opened the gate, his racing mind told him. *No, he reasoned, the only explanation was that he hadn't closed it properly or the latch was broken and he hadn't noticed.* There was nobody here, there was nobody. He picked up his hammer and walked over towards the gate to check his theory about the latch, his legs tingling still from the recent shock but his heart rate gradually getting back to normal. A grassless patch close to the gate made him hesitate. There was a hole in the ground, about a metre deep and the same around. The clay was scattered beside it. He stood at its edge and shone his torch down to examine. It hadn't been dug with a spade or a shovel, the sides were too rough. He thought of the badger but it didn't appear like the work of a burrowing animal. It looked as if it had been dug out frantically by a gang of sticks. He felt a push in his lower back and stumbled forward. His left leg went into the hole, jarring his bad knee, but he had hardly registered the pain of that impact when a heavy and violent weight landed on the back of his calf, buckling that leg and forcing it down, twisted into the hole. He gasped and grimaced into the dark air.

The torch, lost from his hand, threw a beam of light across the unmoving legs of the cattle. He snatched it up and turned the light onto his own leg. The movement caused a dart of agony to shoot up his thigh. A large rock lay on his leg, trapping it in the hole. He tried to move it while the adrenaline of shock was still hot in his muscles but he couldn't get both hands around it from his awkward position and with one he had no chance of pushing it off. He took his phone from his pocket and swiped the screen to bring it glowing to life. Before he could complete the short sequence that would call his wife, a ferocious blow across the back of his knuckles sent the phone flying from his hand. He expelled a rough shout of anger and pain. The phone turned a small patch of grass to a ghostly blue, too far away to even tempt his reach.

"Jack," he cried. "Jack, go get help, boy! Jack, run home, Jack."

The dog just stood there. Brendan got a chill that superseded the pain in his leg and the hurt that pulsed from his bleeding knuckles. Something evil was there, something he had never known before, something ancient and knowing but at the same time juvenile and mean and he felt a terrible fear. The next thing he saw was the point of a stick in front of his right eye. It jabbed at him, short and hard. Blood streamed from his eye and it was like the moon had swung down and filled his sight with silver light. His head started to throb so hard it was like his heart had been stuffed inside it. He became aware of a buzzing. He thought it was inside his head until his remaining eye focussed a little and he identified horseflies gathering around him. They gathered on his neck and cheek, savouring his blood. There was the laughing sound from earlier, but this time it was all around him and from many sources, some deeper in timbre, some higher, all in a horrible harmony. He saw a shape coming towards him and tried to make sense of it through the pain that enveloped him, but in the dark, with the fluttering focus of one eye, it was impossible to perceive. Rough hands grabbed his face. Then he felt the biting.

Chapter Three

Luke Sheridan sat behind the wheel of a white rental Ford Transit van and tried to keep the pristine sides from getting scraped by the brambles and branches that encroached on the narrow country roads on his way to Kilcross. He wished they hadn't given him something so new. When he did the walk-around with the man at the rental company, he had been hoping to see a history of bumps and dents written in the bodywork that could disguise any future mishaps he might have in it. Never before had he driven a vehicle this big or this new. The car he owned was almost ten years old and had weathered those years badly. He was nervous enough driving this behemoth in the city, finding a parking spot close enough to their flat to load their belongings, but what he had forgotten to take into account was how tight the roads were on the way to his new house.

He wished he had just paid the extra money to hire a removals company but, he had reasoned, the meagre amount of stuff he and Sophie owned didn't warrant it. Even with all the baby paraphernalia there was barely a full van load and whatever Sophie was bringing down in the car. Despite the money saved, this part of the drive was really fraying his nerves. Every time another vehicle approached, he slowed down to at least a crawl, if not a stop, and made a vague and half-hearted signal of apology to the other driver. Invariably they glared at him for not moving in closer to the ditch.

Twice he pulled into convenient gateways to let frustrated tailgaters pass him by but gateways on these roads were sporadic and the traffic was strangely substantial for a Saturday morning in the middle of rural nowhere.

He had his visor down to shield his eyes from the sunny September morning. His windows were open so he could breathe in the fresh air he was hoping would help make up for both the length of commute from Kilcross to his job in Dublin and the scarcity of amenities out in the countryside. There would be no more arthouse movies on a random Tuesday evening for Luke, no more spur of the moment cafe brunches on a hungover Sunday. At least when driving in his own compact, well-worn Renault he wouldn't be quite as worried on these roads. The only good thing about having to go this slow in the van was that he could hear the stereo clearly compared to when he had been on the motorway. He was listening to Four Tet's *Rounds* and appreciating most of the intricate melodies above the noise of his drive. Since they closed the deal on the house, he had stopped listening to talk radio and only listened to music again, the old albums he had spent so much time and money on when time and money weren't such precious commodities to him, and a lot of new stuff he had missed while his mind had been consumed by the house purchase. For a while, it seemed to him and Sophie that every radio or television show produced in the year 2007 concerned property in some form or another and they couldn't stop themselves from listening. They were drawn into this unrelenting barrage of advice, warnings and woe concerning lending practices, location, housing supply, until at last one day it was all over for them. They finally managed to get that elusive set of keys and, on that day, Luke threw a bunch of his CDs into his car, listened to an old Aphex Twin album and let his mind think of nothing. It had seemed so long since he had nothing to think of. Before the all-consuming house hunt there had been the all-consuming pregnancy and the all-consuming first year of young Elliott's life. Of course, now there was the move, but he wasn't going to let that take over all his waking and sleeping thoughts like the other things had. The move would be over soon, one way or another, then it was time for a new phase of life.

However, he really did wish he had hired a moving company, especially when the low blue Honda Civic sped up behind him, getting too close as if it was nudging his van on the shoulder like a cynical football defender trying to make its presence felt.

"Slow the fuck down," Luke muttered. He tried ignoring the car but his eye kept drifting towards his wing mirror. It was all narrow, blind bends on this part of the road with nowhere for him to pull in. He couldn't see the driver through the car's tinted windows but he could hear a thud of bass above the sound of both vehicles. Suddenly, despite the fact that it was completely unsighted of the road ahead, the Civic pulled out past him with a loud thunk of its exhaust. It swerved rapidly back in front of the van. Luke swore and instinctively pulled the steering wheel towards the ditch. He heard the scratch of branches tear off the paintwork, and his heart sank.

"That fucker," he said to himself. "I should have got his number plate. I should have checked his number plate in the mirror when he was behind me."

Too late now. He sighed, sank back into his seat and turned up his music.

"Fuck it. I bet Declan knows that car."

Luke's old friend Declan Maguire might have been lazy, slightly corrupt and decidedly self-serving, but he was purported to be very effective in his job as a Garda. Luke suspected the main reason for his success was because he didn't have to travel far mentally to put himself into the mindset of a criminal, particularly the kind of low-level troublemaker that haunted Irish country towns. He probably knew what they were up to before they did themselves and he was adept at smelling out his own kind. Declan was the primary reason behind Luke buying a house near the village of Kilcross. Declan got stationed in nearby Cromuck around four years ago, and among the women he hooked up with in his frenzied invasion of the local social scene was a girl from Kilcross called Denise. First came the unexpected pregnancy. Then came the unexpected offer of a plot of land with planning permission from Denise's father,

Willy Weldon. That plot of land was beside Willy's house, the house Denise had grown up in. Later came Willy's unexpected death. The house Luke and Sophie had just bought was Willy's house.

Last year, Luke and Sophie had attended his funeral, despite having only ever met him at Denise and Declan's wedding. It was only right to show their faces, though, to give support to their old friend. Declan was glad to see them there, if only to lay the care of his then three-year-old son on Sophie while he circulated among the cigarettes and whiskey glasses that marked old man Weldon's reunion with his wife in the grave for eternal life, amen. Of course, now there was a house to be sold, and not just any house, but one that would contain Declan's neighbours for what would likely be the rest of his marriage to Denise, however long that might turn out to be.

Luke pulled the van up alongside an ornate, cast iron gate, its red paint flaking with age. He opened it and inexpertly reversed up the short driveway of his new home. Declan had first persuaded him and Sophie that this would be a lovely place to buy, a safe and healthy area to bring up children. Then he went to work on Denise and argued that a fair price and having decent neighbours they could trust and get along with was more important than squeezing the most money they could out of the open market. Denise's dormant sentimentality, aroused by her father's passing, got the better of her business mind and the usual slog through solicitors, estate agents and banks took much less time than if rival buyers had been allowed.

Sophie was reluctant at first but, even though a string of visits didn't warm her much to Denise, it did excite her to the design possibilities of the plain 1960s dormer bungalow. The soothing peace of the bushy garden enticed her and the spread of hills that filled the view beyond it made up her mind.

Luke put his key in the door with a little internal ceremony and exposed the hallway to the fresh morning air. He had been smart enough to keep the kettle, coffee and a cup separate from the myriad of boxes and bags in the back. He took them from the passenger seat and brought them through to the kitchen, where he opened the window blinds onto an overgrowth of green in the untended back garden. The cold tap spluttered when he turned it on and he wisely let it run for a few minutes before filling the kettle. When his coffee was made, he brought a dusty kitchen chair outside and sat there contemplating his frontage onto the quiet road, savouring the stillness and wondering how many cars passed per average hour on a day like this. He checked the time on his phone. No surprise Declan was late to help him unload. He didn't mind. The house where Declan lived was no more than a hundred metres away, downhill on the slight incline of the road. From his seat it was obscured by a bright laurel hedge that made it hard to tell if there was a car outside it. A loud bang and roar of an exhaust broke the silence, scattering crows from the trees. Luke saw the blue Civic from earlier speed by the house, screech to a halt at the top of the road and swing off to the right with another explosion of sound. He hoped this wasn't a regular occurrence. The barefaced aggression of noise and recklessness grated on him. He thought of the driver speeding on to spread his disturbance elsewhere with no regard for the annoyance he might have left behind. Or maybe that was the point, to disturb as many people as possible, like a spoilt child screaming for attention.

Luke knocked back the last of his coffee and brought the cup inside. He checked the time again. His expectation of Declan's tardiness hadn't accounted for him to be quite as late as this. He rang his friend's number but it went straight to voicemail. When he opened the back door of the van, he found that the rushed pack and the winding roads hadn't disturbed his load as catastrophically as he'd feared, but he really didn't want to start unpacking on his own. Sophie wasn't arriving until later in the day with their baby boy. Declan had promised he would be there at eleven to help Luke. It was quarter to midday now. Luke marched down his driveway and over to the gate of Declan's house. From there he could see there were no cars parked in front of the house. There seemed to be no sign of life, no windows open, no sounds of voices. He was about to open the latch on the gate and investigate further when he heard the scurrying of small canine feet across gravel, and he remembered Denise and Declan owned a diminutive but particularly vicious Jack Russell Terrier. The dog scurried down the driveway and leapt towards the gate, barking and snarling.

"Jesus Christ." Luke stepped back smartly, even though he could see the dog couldn't get through the mesh wire lining the gate and the wooden fence. Then, as the dog's war cries subsided to a low growl, he heard the sound of singing coming up the road. It was a song Luke recognised from last year's charts that had been ubiquitous on the radio and seeped into everyone's consciousness through an advertisement for an insurance company. He couldn't remember the name of the young band but he remembered hating the cheerful guitar chords and the annoyingly ungrammatical chorus. A girl on a bicycle pedalled strongly up the hill towards him. He guessed her to be in her early twenties. She was rosy-cheeked but didn't seem to be out of breath at all, as evidenced by the enthusiasm of her tuneless singing. The bicycle was slick and professional, every contour a work of finely crafted elegance. Her blue and black patterned cycling gear was impeccable. The girl smiled as she noticed Luke and stopped cycling and singing. She removed her helmet to reveal a short, neat bob of blonde hair, as if someone had spooned a serving of custard onto her head. Before she spoke, she extracted a set of earphones and Luke could hear a snatch of the song playing through them until she hit a button somewhere around her belt. A frown suddenly invaded her face.

"I hate that dog," she said.

The dog snarled and made a series of futile attempts to jump over the gate, causing Luke to step further away from it.

"The feeling seems to be mutual," he said.

"Are you looking for Denise?" The return of her smile permeated her voice. Her accent was quite broad, even more country than most he had heard from this area.

"Yes, I'm Luke Sheridan. We just bought the house next door, Denise's father's old place. I'm looking for Declan really."

"For Declan? Well, it's rare you'd find him here-"

He cut her off.

"I suppose I'd better warn you that I'm his friend before you say anything else."

"Oh," she replied, in a tone suggesting she wasn't worried about causing offence. "Are you a Garda as well then?"

"Me? No. I work in a museum."

Her eyes twinkled with laughter.

"What's so funny about that?" he asked.

"You're too young to work in a museum."

He didn't really know what to say to that. The midday sun was warming him up nicely for a haze of insects to visit. They didn't seem to be interested in the bicycle girl at all. There wasn't a drop of sweat on her skin or her hair, the only sign that she had been exercising was a blush in her cheeks, but he had a feeling that might actually be a permanent feature.

"I'm a, um, museum technician."

"That sounds interesting, what does that do?"

He hated explaining about his job so he didn't. He just rattled out a stream of words.

"It's interesting, yes, you get to learn all the time, and living out here it'll be useful because there's flexibility of hours, sometimes, you might have to work when the museum is closed, I mean, and my wife actually she can work from home mostly, she's a graphic designer." Until he wondered why the hell he was nattering on to this disinterested looking girl and finally asked her, "So do you know Denise?"

"Yes," she said. "They'll all be at Brendan McGrath's funeral. Everyone from around here is at it—" The bang of an exhaust interrupted her. "Apart from Noel, of course, you've probably heard Noel in his car."

"So, Noel is his name, is it? I've seen him as well, driving right up my arse. And you, of course, you're not at this funeral."

"I have to do my training," she said, her voice infused with a righteousness that stiffened her stance on the bicycle. She turned her head back down the way she had come. "You should go to it yourself, it'll be only starting now. You could meet all your new neighbours."

"Right," Luke replied unsurely. "Would that not be a bit intrusive?"

She nestled her helmet onto her head and started to tuck her earphones back in.

"I dunno. You wouldn't have to go into the church, you could just hang around outside. You have to find out who your neighbours are if you're going to live around here. Or maybe you don't, maybe you like to keep to yourself, I dunno."

"No, I … so what's your name, by the way?"

The girl pressed down nonchalantly on her pedals and moved away, the music filling her ears and raising her voice.

"Ah, you'll see me around. I'm always cycling around these roads. Training."

And she cycled off singing a different song that irritated Luke as much as her last one.

CHAPTER FOUR

Declan Maguire looked in through the door of the stuffy church, full to the brim with its sombre congregation. He looked at his wife, walking in ahead of him, and his son holding her hand. He didn't want to follow them. He looked at the auld lads skulking to the side of the church, sucking on their cigarettes, and he looked at the late cars circling the car park for a free spot that they wouldn't find; the distant relatives and friends who didn't know the parish so well. He was always looking. He'd stare barefaced at people on the street and peer into premises trying to sniff something out that might interest him or he might want to use at some later stage. That was one of the reasons why he was such an effective Garda, always noticing what was going on. He looked at the sunny September sky and he looked at the man who had just appeared at his side.

"Nice day for it, Sergeant Harris," Declan said to his boss.

"Yeah, nice day for the beach, or a barbecue."

"Yeah, a barbecue," said Declan. "Shame he didn't go for a cremation."

"I thought you might have worn your uniform, represent the force," said Harris without smiling.

"Represent the force?"

"I often wear mine when attending large church services. All you have to do is ask permission."

"Fuck that, I'm here to represent myself." Declan paused. "Why? Would I have gotten paid overtime if I had worn the uniform?"

"Ah yeah, Declan, always in it for yourself."

Declan's wife turned around to glare at him as she sidled into a pew half way up the church.

"You'd better go in," said Harris. "Denise and little Willy are looking for you."

"Bill," said Declan. "We call him Bill."

Declan stepped inside, his tall, athletic frame causing the loiterers at the back to glance up at him and nod muttered greetings. That was another reason he was an effective Garda, he had a presence, a presence of good-natured intimidation, he liked to think. He often counted up the reasons why he was an effective Garda, just in case he needed to list them off to a panel of his superiors in the future.

He nudged in beside his wife and son. She glared at him and he noticed tearstains around her eyes. The priest welcomed everyone on this sad occasion. What the hell was she so upset about? She wasn't close to the McGraths. *She had a right sour puss on her when she was annoyed*, he thought, *and the boy was starting to develop one too.*

"Bill," he hissed down to his son. "Stop pulling that face."

"Willy," said the boy, too loudly for the church's hush.

Declan sighed with exasperation. How long was this mass going to go on for anyway? He made a sneaky search for his phone as they were invited to kneel but then realized he had left it in the car. He gazed around the church while moving his lips to the words he vaguely recalled from childhood. Brendan McGrath's family sat in the front row. Emma, the wife, sobbed into her son's shoulder as he wrapped his arm around her. Ronan was the son's name, he remembered. He had caught him once outside a nightclub in Cromuck, smoking a joint, and Declan had taken it off him. He was probably eighteen then, a couple of years ago, and he had begged Declan not to tell his parents. Now anytime the lad saw him coming he gave him a polite nod of gratitude laced with fear. He supposed he had moved on to more interesting drugs now that he was in college in Dublin. That would probably come to an end for him now. Back to the farm with you, boy. Wash the cowshite off you at the weekend to search the nightclubs of

Cromuck for women. He counted the stations of the cross that decorated the walls of the church, frescoes painted in drab pastels of a startled Jesus on the way to His fate. When was the last time he was in here? It seemed like ages ago. Was it Bill's christening? No, surely not that long ago. There was the time he came out to investigate some petty vandalism in the graveyard but that was—oh, yeah, Denise's father's funeral. Shit, that must be what has her so upset. This must be bringing it all back to her. That was one of those things that made him not such an effective Garda, he didn't make connections between things all that quickly. That, and he was always getting distracted— who the fuck was that?

He watched the girl walking up to the altar to give the first reading. She was wearing a black pencil skirt and he watched it clinging to her thighs as she sombrely approached the pulpit. Her head was down and her hair brushed against her breasts with such a sad eroticism that even he was aware of the wrongness of the fact that he was salivating like a dog. She raised her head slightly to speak and he was struck by a faint recognition. She must be the daughter. Fuck, she had developed. Not particularly pretty, her nose was long, her cheeks shallow, but that figure! He could feel what he thought was a glare of disapproval at his leering from his left but, when he stole a glance at Denise, he could see it was outright disgust rather than disapproval that had contorted her face. *Well, who cares*, he thought. If she hadn't put a best before date on their sex life then he wouldn't have to be ogling grieving college girls, and he also wouldn't have to be sneaking around sleeping with other women.

He kept that logic in mind for the rest of the mass—that he was surely justified in whatever infidelities he might get caught up in— as he checked out any females in view and considered whether or not they were worth fucking. Weddings were usually much better for this game than funerals, he concluded, due to the dress code, but at least with it being a summer funeral it gave him a little extra visible flesh to kick-start his fantasies. He put manners on his erection before it was time to go in peace to love and serve the Lord.

He followed the congregation out of the church and towards the graveyard, not dallying for his wife and child, who were keeping a couple of spiteful steps behind him. Waiting at the gate to the graveyard were those who had either left the church early or else not been inside at all. His pulse quickened as a familiar face emerged between a cluster of sombre-suited shoulders. Cliona Casey, the woman satisfying his sexual urges on an increasingly regular basis. He hadn't expected her to be here. She didn't have any connections that he knew of to Kilcross. She hadn't mentioned to him that she knew the deceased or that she was going to turn up here.

Walking slowly behind the coffin bearers, he tried to watch her without catching her eye. She was wearing jeans and a white blouse. They weren't mourning clothes. Were they 'making a scene' clothes? Were they 'revealing your lover in front of his wife' clothes?

There was something out of place about the man standing beside her as well. He was wearing a faded blue T-shirt and old torn jeans as if he was attending a campfire on the beach rather than a funeral.

As he neared them, he could feel Denise closing in behind, and a nervous itch spread through the muscles in his legs as if he was unconsciously preparing to bolt away through a gap in the crowd. The coffin was carried through the gate and two seconds later he found himself alongside Cliona and, as her mouth opened to speak, he was startled to hear a male voice whisper his name. Cliona's mouth remained open as she turned in surprise to the man standing beside her, then back to Declan before slowly slinking back into the crowd.

Declan watched with relief over the heads of the mourners as she kept walking towards her car, parked clumsily with many others along the grass verge of the road. Only when the man in the T-shirt hissed his name again did he recognise him and realise all of a sudden that he was supposed to be helping him move into his house that morning.

"Ah shit, Luke, I forgot all about it," he whispered to his friend, sidling out of the procession to stand beside him. "This funeral, you see. Here come on, I don't have to watch him going into the ground."

Declan checked to make sure Cliona's car had driven away and he took Luke by the arm, leading him back towards the church as discreetly as he could. Denise watched him go but rooted herself to where she stood with a tight grip on their son's hand.

"Is Denise …?" started Luke.

"Ah, we'll wait for her back at the car," said Declan as they moved away from the crowd. "How did you know I'd be here?"

"There was a girl on a bicycle who told me."

"Oh, her." Declan's face twisted with distaste.

"What's wrong with her? I thought she seemed nice, a little bit odd maybe."

"Yeah, a bit too nice, a bit too goody-two-shoes, there's something unhealthy about someone who's that good."

"She might do you out of a job, you mean?"

"Ha, ha, no, there's plenty to keep me busy. I just don't like her. It annoys me even to look at her. I suppose she told you she was training."

"Yeah. She said I might meet some new neighbours if I came down here. She wasn't wrong. They're fairly chatty down this way, especially when I told them I was your friend. Before you all came out of the church everyone was having a right old discussion about how this Brendan McGrath person died. They were probing me for info in case you had said something to me. Some of the theories going around, I mean, I wouldn't want Sophie to hear them, what with her being in a new house, a new area, and being on her own with the baby when I'm at work."

Declan shook his head dismissively. "There's nothing to worry about."

"But"—Luke checked to make sure there was nobody within earshot—"they said he was tortured to death, that he couldn't have an open casket because of what they did to his face. If people as vicious as that are around then … I mean, you hear stories of rural attacks on isolated houses."

"There's nothing for you and Sophie to worry about, or anyone else."

"But, some of the things they did. Sticks and stones, like the old rhyme, but they did more than break his bones."

"Exactly, and what did they do then?"

"What do you mean?"

"Did they go up to his house? No. Did they harm his wife? No. She got worried when he didn't answer his phone and she called a neighbour. They went to look for him and they found him dead but there was no livestock taken, no machinery stolen."

"So, what does that mean?"

"It means it was personal, revenge or something. He wasn't killed because he lived out here, he was killed because … well, between you and me, we have absolutely no idea why anyone would want to kill him, but it wasn't a random rural attack. It's the safest place in the world out here in Kilcross. You have to go into Cromuck before anything exciting happens."

"Ok, ok," Luke conceded, flattered to be taken into Declan's professional confidence. "I guess that makes sense. I can explain it like that if Sophie is worried. You can give me some crime stats to back it up. So, it's boring for you out here? Country life isn't all you thought it would be?"

"Well, you know why I'm stationed out here, don't you? It's because it is so quiet. They stuck me out here because it would be harder for me to get into trouble and what trouble I do get in won't get as much attention."

"Ah come on, Declan, you don't really believe that."

"I do, they told me in those exact words! I was called in after my last … em … indiscretion and that was the decision they made. Remember, I told you all about it at the time but you wouldn't believe me then either. They just move troublemakers like me around when I fuck up."

"And have you managed to stay out of trouble down here?"

"Well, they were right on both counts." He smirked. "It is harder to get into trouble, and when you do manage to find some, it draws less attention."

"What are you smirking at?" Denise snapped at him as she joined them. "I can't believe you just walked away from the burial like that, leaving me and Willy on our own." Then her tone and her visage both softened. "Hi Luke, how are you? I told him last night to ring you and let you know we had to go to the funeral. A terrible thing."

"You did not!" protested Declan.

"But he probably didn't hear me. I think he had been drinking before he got in yesterday evening so who knows what he heard. He never listens to anything I say anyway."

"That's ok, Denise, sorry for your … eh … loss, I guess. Did you know the man well? I suppose it must be hard for you anyway, so soon after your father. And how's little Bill here?" Luke crouched down to examine the sulky-lipped child. He tried to make the boy laugh with a little routine of face pulling and shadow boxing.

"It's Willy," said Denise. "After his grandfather."

"It's Bill," said Declan. "How many times must we go through this? Do you want people calling him little Willy?"

Denise ignored her husband. "Is Sophie here?"

"No," replied Luke, getting no reaction from the boy to his playacting. "She's coming later on. She wants to give me a chance to get everything unloaded before she arrives with Elliott."

"Right, so," said Declan, "if that's the case we'd better get cracking. Here." He dangled the car keys towards his wife. "I'll go back with Luke. "

The rest of the afternoon cascaded away from them. When they got back to the house Declan realised his funeral suit probably wasn't the best gear for unloading a van, so he brought Luke over to his place while he got changed. Luke sat in the kitchen having coffee with Denise. Declan could hear them talking from upstairs. He hadn't spent that much consistent time with Luke since the two intense years of college friendship they shared before he finally stopped fooling himself that he wasn't going to drop out. In the second of those years Luke met Sophie and, if he hadn't done so, then he likely wouldn't have completed his degree either. Before meeting her Luke always deferred to Declan if a decision had to be made. Should we go to class or the bar? Should we take this drug? Should we vandalise this car? Declan's decision always followed a predictable irresponsible pattern. When Sophie became the main influencer of these decisions the waves of Luke's life became a lot calmer. Occasionally this new, more sensible sway marshalled Declan's life as well. Not that often, but sometimes. Not enough to keep him from dropping out.

After Declan surprised everyone by joining the Gardaí, the friends still kept in touch but only met sporadically, usually to mark life events like weddings and christenings, birthdays and a few, thankfully rare, funerals. Usually, at these occasions, Declan would look at Luke and muse that he might be like that now if the interesting and fun bits were removed. When he was feeling cruel, he might say it to him as well, but Luke generally didn't seem to take it as an insult.

He could hear good humour in Denise's voice so thought he'd better go down and ruin it with his presence. Surprisingly, she stayed chatty when he entered the kitchen in his old work clothes. Maybe Luke's amiable manner was reminding her that not everything to do with him was toxic. There was that short-lived time at the start of their marriage when they gazed at each other with desire, then for a while with fondness before this badly disguised spite took over. She even made lunch for them before they went off.

Before they got down to unloading the van, Declan wasted more time by having to make a private phone call to Cliona. After the call he still wasn't sure why she had turned up at the funeral or why she had turned on her heel before speaking to him, but he had managed to entangle himself into meeting her later that night, which filled him with a confused and apprehensive horniness.

They wandered through the house with the intention of planning where they should unload everything so they wouldn't be double handling, but this plan just had the effect of distracting them. Dodgy electrical fittings prompted examination and conversation; bad carpets led to debate about the best type of flooring. The greatest delay was when they went out the back and, after time spent staring into the generous but overgrown garden with hands on hips planning orchard corners, herb gardens and the best places for benches, they then went for an adventure in the shed. Here they found a vast exhibit of DIY tools and implements from throughout the ages, though not likely arranged in chronological order. Buckets were filled with metal parts whose provenance they couldn't even hazard a guess at. Old damp shelving gave long-term tenancy to powders, paints and poisons.

"Look at this," Luke whispered reverentially, pulling out an intimidating brush cutter and wiping dust from its harness. "This'll sort out that garden."

"Jesus Christ, you'll cut your legs off with that thing. What do you know about using things like that? Or this?" Declan laid his hand on a circular saw and ran his fingers over the teeth while baring his own canines in a trance-like smile. "I'll take this I think."

"What? Nope, you can't just take it. You can borrow it."

"Well, it belonged to my father-in-law, so it belongs to my wife, and I don't think she'll want it, hence it's mine. You can have the gardening crap and I'll take the power tools, how's that?"

"How about we share? I think I'd like to get into gardening now that I'm living out in the countryside. I think I'll be good at it."

"I don't think you will."

"Fuck you."

By the time Sophie arrived, shortly after five, the van had been emptied but very few boxes had. The two men trundled out of the house to greet her and the baby and Declan raised his eyebrows at how much had been packed into their Renault Mégane. The chassis worryingly hooded the back wheels.

"I'm afraid I'm going to have to pull you over on suspicion of a dangerously overloaded vehicle, madam. Licence and registration please."

"It still seems like a joke when you say things like that, Declan." Sophie greeted him with a hug. "Do people actually take you seriously or do they just not know you as well as I do?"

Declan was always struck by how pale Sophie was, a translucent beauty. It was like she was wrapped in rice paper, though he noted that now you'd need a little more rice paper to wrap her than the last time they'd met. The good weather never gifted her a tan but it had encouraged more freckles around her face and arms. She went to Luke and kissed him lightly on the lips. Declan made a childish 'ooo' sound and they laughed. She pretended to wipe her lips and spit his kiss away.

Declan noticed she wasn't wearing lipstick and her lips faded into the rest of her skin. Bare lips, barely there. He mused how entirely different to his own wife she was and had a sudden realisation that there was no chance at all of the two women becoming close, despite the proximity to each other that began today.

When they brought the baby inside, asleep from the heat and motion of the journey, Sophie was dismayed to find that the cot wasn't assembled yet in the nursery. She made Luke get the travel cot from the car and quickly set it up while she walked from room to room astounded at the lack of progress the two men had made.

"Well, there was a funeral, you see, Sophie," explained Declan.

"There's going to be two more," she replied.

Conversation finally took second place to unpacking. They concentrated on the immediate necessities: sorting out the kitchen utensils, finding the toiletries, spreading bedsheets, arranging the baby's room. Their own clothes, books, albums and ornaments could wait in boxes for another time. In a couple of hours there was enough done for the evening. By the evidence of Declan starting to constantly check his phone, they had gotten the last dregs of help they were going to get from him.

"I'm going to order from that Chinese place in town that you said was good, Declan. We're starving. You want some?" offered Luke. "You can ask Denise if she wants to come over for some too."

Sophie fished around in a bag and drew out a bottle of wine that she waved enticingly at him.

"No, no, I better not." He smiled. "I actually have to head into Cromuck myself. Work thing. I'll grab something to eat in there. Give Denise a buzz if you want but she probably won't bother. She'll be stuck into shitty TV for the night now I'd say."

"Ok, well thanks for helping today," said Sophie.

"Yeah, thanks Deccie." Luke gave him a brotherly hug. "Look, we'll catch up in the morning."

"Not too early," warned Declan.

"Not too early."

Sophie poured the wine while Luke called the Chinese takeaway. The baby crawled the empty floor of the living room until Sophie heated up the dinner she had brought for him and put him in his high chair. His eyes darted around the strange house and she had to keep beckoning his attention towards the spoon. Luke looked at his son being fed and wished he had thought to order their own food earlier.

Meanwhile, in Cromuck, Declan parked round the back of a second-hand car dealer's yard two streets away from Cliona's apartment. He briskly trotted in and out of the lively swarm of pedestrians heading for pubs and bars. He shadily covered his face with his collar while he waited outside her building for her to buzz him in.

Eventually, Sophie's Special Chow Mein and Luke's Kung Po Pork arrived and, although it wasn't nearly as nice as a takeaway they might have got if they were still in Dublin, by the end of the evening it was almost all gone and the bottle of wine was most definitely all gone. A little later the baby was asleep in his newly assembled cot. By the end of their night, in a mixture of relief and celebration, the first bottle of wine had been followed by the best part of another, and they went to bed on fresh sheets in their new room, listening out for any noises from baby Elliott. Twelve miles up the road, by the end of his night, Declan had discovered there was an unwelcome pregnancy he had to deal with.

CHAPTER FIVE

The blue Honda Civic clipped ninety-five kilometres an hour on the stretch of road leading up to the house where Noel Quirke lived. About fifty metres from the house, he suddenly dropped his speed and rolled up his window so the throb of the car stereo wouldn't spook his mother. He couldn't resist pulling a little skid in the driveway to spit some dirt up at his father's shitty old Ford Fiesta, which was parked so carelessly that Noel couldn't position his own car neatly beside it. The Fiesta was white and speckled with a month's worth of old mud. Noel often wondered why a man who was too lazy to wash his car decided to own a white one.

He leaned back to get his jacket out of the back seat. His own car was pristine inside and out. The only thing left in the back after taking out his jacket was a multipack of Red Bull sitting on the floor. The front yard was disgusting with all the junk scattered around. *It looked like a knacker's yard,* he thought. An old gas oven blocked half of the path at the side of the house. There was an old go-kart he had owned as a child lying on its back and missing two of its wheels, an ancient kettle and various bits of broken plastic and unwanted metal. Closer to the road was a small scruffy lawn. Only half of it had been cut a fortnight ago so it looked as if the other half was a stepped grassy platform whose borders were getting higher with weeds. In front of that was a half-rotted wooden fence, painted once, twenty years ago, the year before Noel was born.

When he went inside, his parents were as he expected them to be. His mother was in the kitchen smoking a cigarette and reading a magazine. His father was slouched on the sitting room couch watching something to do with sharks on TV and drinking a can of Heineken.

"You'd better not have blocked me in with that thing," his father grumbled without looking away from the screen.

"Why?" Noel asked in his dull nasal tone. "Are you going out somewhere?"

"He isn't going anywhere," his mother barked from the kitchen.

"I might be going out," retorted his father.

"Count the cans," said his mother.

His father gawped at the four empties down by his feet like they were dumb, friendly puppies and grunted.

"I won't be blocking you in for long anyway," said Noel. "I'm going back out in a few minutes."

Noel tramped down the hall to his room. The house was an old, decrepit bungalow and the same wallpaper hung on the walls now as had done a decade ago. Apart from his sister's room, his was the only one whose decor had changed, and that was just through the sporadic replacement of motorsport posters. Once or twice, he had wondered why his mother wasn't bothered by the unkempt state of the house, why she didn't care about having old drab curtains or worn carpets but, as he was never in other people's houses to make a comparison, he didn't dwell on it for too long. He also had no idea of how much it cost to make a house look nice, so he presumed it must be out of the reach of his father's income.

His father worked occasionally as a builder's labourer. The local builder who employed him for as long as Noel could remember wasn't particularly busy most of the time and didn't seem to care that Noel's father didn't bother showing up when the mood struck him. He suspected there was a large element of cash in hand and likely some welfare fraud going on. Since Noel had started working and paying for his keep, his father tended to go to work less. He also seemed to care even less about what Noel did. He had never been a particularly strict father, and any time he scolded or gave Noel a wallop as a child it seemed to be out of a random and weary sense of duty.

Nowadays the only thing that ever riled him about Noel was the car.

The car had gotten up his nose ever since Noel had bought it eighteen months ago. His father would approach it from the side as if it was a dangerous, sleeping animal he didn't want to wake. He knew there was a wrongness and a menace about it but he wasn't sure how that was manifested. He would creep up to examine the tax, insurance and CRVT discs only to find they were always up to date, in stark contrast to his own. Noel's mother didn't drive and any thoughts she might have of the car were rooted in complete incomprehension. If pressed for an opinion on it she would have ventured that it was 'A Car', but she wouldn't even be stating that fact with much certainty.

They were kind of useless as parents but Noel knew they could have been a lot worse. They fed him, they clothed him, they sent him to school. He had a few good memories of birthdays and Christmases. He had a sister, Jean, who was fifteen now, but they didn't seem to be any more involved with her life than they were with his. She spent most of her time at her friend's house up the road, where she usually had her dinner and did her homework. Sometimes she came home. Back when he was at school there hadn't been any friend up the road for him.

Noel got out of his clothes and went to the bathroom for a shower. After letting the shower run for a while, he realised it wasn't going to get any hotter, so he just splashed the cold water under his arms, around his crotch and feet and let it run onto his hair just enough to wet it through, just until he felt the chill of it in his skull. He dried himself quickly with a musty smelling towel and sprayed himself with deodorant until the room went hazy. Some futile time was spent trying to style his hair in the mirror. He wasn't good-looking. He knew that and didn't try to fool himself that it was any different, afflicted with a small chin and a nose that could have been crafted by a glass blower with hiccups. His skin was a strange sort of pasty texture that didn't want to welcome stubble or suntan, but was haunted by a ghostly rash that would appear often and without reason, leaving behind a trail of small pink spots. His hair was dark and greasy most of the time. It rarely saw shampoo because he had yet to find one whose use didn't result in a snowstorm of dandruff. He wasn't fat, he had that going for him at least, but he was also without muscle and stood a measly five foot six. At school there had been some people less clever than him, but if they were good-looking or athletic then they were helped along or encouraged. There were some who were more disadvantaged; there were situations in certain homes from which you could just sense the horror coming off the kids in waves. There were bruises and bloodshot eyes and absenteeism that just couldn't be hidden, but most of these kids were eventually helped in one way or another. Noel just went unnoticed. He wasn't neglected enough to be of concern to the teachers and he possessed no charm or looks or latent talents for any of them to take an interest in nurturing him.

He put on a fresh T-shirt, tracksuit bottoms and a clean black hoodie. Surprisingly enough, if he left his clothes in the laundry basket they always got washed. His mother seemed to be happy enough to do laundry. In fact, he often saw her held in dumb reverie by the washing machine as it churned round and round, or else sitting outside smoking as she stared at the clothes drying on the line. But to receive this service he always had to put the dirty clothes in the basket in the utility room. She wouldn't go looking for them, and he had to go and collect the clean ones himself or else they would sit, unfolded, in that room indefinitely.

He went back down the hall and peeked into the sitting room where his mother had joined his father to watch a gameshow on TV.

"Did you want dinner?" his mother asked, as if leading up to a punchline.

"Is there dinner?"

"No. We ate it earlier. We never know when you're going to be here so I didn't make you any."

"It doesn't matter," he said.

His father was asleep.

"I guess he's not going out then," Noel said.

"He might go out," said his mother snippily.

"Right."

Noel swirled his keyring on his finger and departed. There was a pile of green and brown organic material on the ground near the front door underneath a broken drainpipe. The warm weather seemed to have dried it up from the slimy mush it usually was. He kicked it absentmindedly and found that the inside of it hadn't quite dried up. With a disgusted face, he wiped his trainer on the generous grass of the lawn. At least he had worn his black ones instead of his new white Nikes.

This time, when he got into his car, he wasn't bothered about disturbing his mother. He revved the engine hard and spun out the gate without looking whether there were any other cars coming. Foot slammed down, he sped up their road, yanking the steering wheel hard at the end of it to launch the Civic to the left and up another narrow country route. He stayed on this one for about three miles, passing through a couple of small crossroads where he sometimes liked to spin doughnuts. These were ok but there were other places he preferred. There was a good crossroads up near the Gaelic football pitches, and also a junction near the Twisted Tree that was better.

In no time he was off the country roads and hitting the main road towards Cromuck. He was well over the speed limit but not speeding completely crazily. No sense in attracting too much attention this early in the night. Past the industrial estate on the edge of town where he worked. He remembered back in school, only once having a meeting with the career guidance teacher. He told this disinterested man in his drab V-necked jumper that he wanted to be a mechanic. Maybe there had been other meetings and he couldn't remember them or maybe there hadn't. If there were then he would have said the same thing at them. He couldn't recall being given any guidance one way or another. He finished school two years ago and actually passed most of his exams. No high marks in anything but he did better than anyone would have expected, if there had been anyone who cared enough to pay attention. As soon as he had his results, he went round all the garages in the area hunting for an apprenticeship. Most just shook their heads at him. Some let him leave his name and number but none ever called. After a few months of getting under his parent's feet at home he started to worry that his father might start to show an unwelcome interest in what he should be doing with his time, so he told the man in the jobseeker's department that he would actually interview for something that wasn't a mechanic's apprenticeship. The first job he went for he got. It was in a warehouse and he didn't really do an interview as such. He just filled out an application form, gave his clothes and shoe size and started the next day.

It wasn't the worst job in the world, although he had no real frame of reference. The other employees didn't really bother talking to him except for giving instructions until he got the hang of things or the odd bit of small talk that he wasn't able to respond to very well. He didn't share interests with any of them, usually ate his lunch on his own, went for his infrequent cigarette breaks on his own and they rarely bothered him with invitations to after work drinks. He did get sent on a forklift driver's course so he could operate one when it was required, and that alone was enough to make him thankful for the job, apart from the fact that it allowed him to afford his car and the massive cost of an insurance policy for someone of his age.

Noel dropped his speed as he entered the town, passing lines of houses with neat front gardens, each one expressing its misguided individuality through the diverse designs of its front porch. He turned his stereo up and his window down, causing an old couple out walking to aim sour expressions towards him. There weren't that many cars on the street but, as he drove slowly into the heart of the town, the pedestrian traffic got heavier. Young couples and groups of friends all dressed up to go to the many pubs and bars, some of which already throbbed with music that competed with the decibel level of his own. Whenever he stopped at traffic lights, he drummed his fingers on the side of the car door, keeping his head straight forward, affecting a disdain for the social hum of the streets. He saw a few heads that he knew, or at least recognised, but he didn't give any waves or nods and he didn't receive any. There was that bastard, Garda Maguire, from Kilcross, who had abused him earlier. That wasn't the first time he had hassled him for no reason and threatened to take the car off him. He had even done it when he wasn't in uniform. Noel was always careful to keep things above board with his tax and insurance and he never had as much as a broken bulb for as long as it took to replace one. He had never been caught in the act of dangerous driving, although people had reported him and he was sure the people in his locality knew he was the cause of the late-night engine roars, tyre squealing and the black tracks of rubber left in circles at crossroads and junctions. Couldn't prove it though, could they? Maguire was acting sneaky out and about without his uniform, like he didn't want to be seen. Noel roared his engine just as he passed him and caused his exhaust to bang angrily. Then he cruised out towards the edge of town to the big Maxol service station.

The Maxol gleamed with blue and yellow signage and hard, white light filled the forecourt. He pulled in. It was busy tonight. The shop was large and the immense glass front made it seem like you were looking into a massive circuit board with the geometric shapes of all the brightly lit displays. There was a seating area inside but nobody was sitting in it. Everybody here was parked together a short distance away from the pumps, sitting in their cars in twos, threes and fours, music pounding, young men and girls hopping in and out but the drivers staying behind their wheels like they were sitting on thrones that they didn't want to abdicate.

Noel parked a discrete distance away from them and turned his stereo down low. Sneaking down his passenger window, he could better hear the thrum of activity. It was important not to look any of them directly in the eye or spend too long staring over at them. He took a can of Red Bull from the multipack in the back and carefully pulled back the ring-pull. One long slug of the sweet, sticky liquid before taking out his cigarettes. Smoking inside the car was against his usual rules but he was far too self-conscious to get out in front of everyone. Also, the worst possible thing that could happen would be if he got out of the car to smoke and the shop assistant announced over the forecourt tannoy for him to refrain from smoking near the pumps, even though he wasn't that close to them. He could imagine everyone turning to look and laugh and sneer at him.

They weren't all in the same group, he figured as he watched from behind the wheel, holding his cigarette out the window and blowing the smoke away from the nice clean upholstery. There were two pairs of cars set apart from the large central crowd with maybe four or five lads in each of those splinter groups. The best possible thing that could happen, the best ever, would be if one of them came over to him, especially if they drove over and casually said, "Nice alloys," or "Good paint job," or "I used to have one of those," and followed it up with, "You wanna park up over here with us?" But it hadn't ever happened in all the times he had come here. They must see him, he knew they must, but nobody acknowledged him in any way, good or bad.

A girl from the big group headed over towards the shop. She had long, straight, dark hair and was probably around as tall as he was. He'd seen her so many times before. She was wearing a bottle-green bomber jacket and a short denim skirt with no tights. Her skin was pale and he could see red marks on the back of her thighs, like a series of crimson birthmarks or a rash that flared up with the warm weather. It made his heart ache to see it, this imperfection. It wouldn't bother him, he wouldn't mind it, he wouldn't even mention it, if he could only be with her. Or maybe he would mention it, if she wanted to talk about it, that is. Then he would listen, he would be the one she could share her insecurities with.

They usually went into the shop in pairsbut she had gone in on her own. He stubbed out his cigarette. He could go in too. Now could be his chance. She'd have to notice him, they'd be the only two in the shop apart from the cashier. Surely she'd say something to him, or … or he could say something to her. What could he say? What would he buy? He'd have to buy something, he could talk about that. It wouldn't matter what, something for the car maybe, just something to start a chat. His hand pulled slowly on the car door handle. He could offer to buy her something too, isn't that what people did?

Too late. She swaggered back towards the automatic doors and they slid open for her. She was chewing gum, her eyes lit up beautifully by her smile. She opened up her jacket and spread it wide to reveal something stolen inside, a glossy red packet. One of the lads in the cars hollered her name in a sing-song voice, Aimee. She winked. Noel started the car. He knew her name now, he had a name to put to his useless, pointless longing while she shoplifted stuff to impress other lads. He crept as silently as the Civic would allow up to the exit of the service station and drove away.

At the first crossroads back in Kilcross, he performed doughnuts with a fury. He found an album in his glove compartment he had hardly ever listened to before and which sounded like hammers thrashing against steel. Both front windows were down and the air whirled through as he circled round and round. He had been smoking in the car since he left the service station, not caring about the smell anymore, lighting cigarette after cigarette. Now, in the draught that swirled from passenger window to driver's window, each cigarette was lasting about thirty seconds and sending a swarm of small sparks into his face.

The screech of the tyres pierced through the music and, as he expected, the lights of a nearby house came on. What he didn't expect was when the lights of the car in the driveway glowed like the vengeful eyes of a vicious guard dog. He spun out of his loop and accelerated away before those headlights had the chance to chase up the road after him.

At the next crossroads it seemed to him that he was making an even greater noise, because it was hemmed in by overhanging trees, creating a little bowl for him to spin around in. It was less than a minute before he became aware of a dog barking from what seemed like a distance, but he knew from past experience was in the farm just beside the crossroads. Then he heard what sounded like a gunshot and he slammed on his brakes. He listened carefully for anything else. The dog was still barking. It could have been an automatic crow-scarer in the fields. It could have been the fire-crack of an exhaust like his one, but he didn't hear a car engine to go along with it. When the outside lights came on at the farmhouse, he didn't take any chances and sped away from there as well.

There was one last spot he liked to tear around before he got on the road to his own home: the junction nearest the Twisted Tree. It wasn't too close to any houses. The nearest ones were where Garda Maguire lived and the Weldon's old place beside that. It was just approaching two in the morning. He turned up the car stereo. It was the third repeat for the album but he didn't really hear it anymore, he was just using it as noise to stop any thoughts forming in his head, any thoughts about what he might be or what his life was or all the things that he didn't have to look forward to. It was there to stop all thoughts apart from *turn the wheel, tyres screeching, smoke in the lungs, roaring engine,* over and over and over until - thud!

He could feel, as if the car were a part of his body, his front left wheel hit something hard. It knocked the car out of its spin and made it bounce up from the tarmac and land back down with a judder. His heart pounded. He yelped as the cigarette he had dropped in his lap burned through his tracksuit bottoms. Noel hopped up off his seat, couldn't see where the cigarette fell. He switched on his interior light quickly, found it nestling down beside the handbrake, and stubbed it out in the ashtray. Noel's next thoughts were of concern for his car. He took a few deep breaths to settle his nerves before he opened the car door and got out. He hadn't thought that the night was as dark as this a few minutes earlier. A cloud must have come by to hide the moon and it was as if the stars had no power to prick through the heavy black blanket of sky. The only lights were those of his car.

He switched on the torch on his phone and examined the wheel. All buckled alloy and torn rubber. What had he hit? The blurry circle of weak LED light revealed a massive rock, the size of a large suitcase, planted in the middle of the road. That didn't make sense. How had he circled around it so many times without hitting it? It couldn't have just appeared out of nowhere. As if to mock his confusion, a strange laugh, almost animalistic in nature, came from behind him. Noel spun around frantically, waving his feeble light around. He wanted to shout out but couldn't find the power in his throat to use his voice. A small dark shape ran, hunched, through the beam of his headlights. Shit! He lurched back. It must be an animal. Skin bristling, he stole back to the car, trying to watch all around him, moving the phone around as if the light was a forcefield no one could enter. *If there was a dog or a fox then it surely wouldn't come into the light*, he thought. It would be as afraid of him. But surely an animal couldn't have moved a rock that size onto the road and there was no way that he had been spinning around here in circles for the last twenty minutes without hitting it if it had already been there. The physical contradiction of the situation was making him lightheaded. He gauged the car's position in relation to where the rock sat soundly on the road. He had driven past it before he'd started spinning. But that was impossible. It was too big. The rock must have just appeared. Its dirty grey face seemed to defy him to make sense of its presence. He trembled back to the Civic and stood there, leaning his back against the passenger side, wondering if changing the wheel was going to be enough to make the car mobile again. A bang like that implied that there was more damage done to the undercarriage.

Noel rested there for a moment, just to calm himself, just to get his nerves back together before he had to face the ordeal of sorting this out. First, a cigarette. They were in the side pouch of the driver's door. Just as he moved to get them, something grabbed him around the ankles from underneath the car and yanked his legs from under him. He fell and hit the road hard, face first. His skin tore along the rough surface and grit gathered in his eye. A horrible fear flooded his veins, froze his limbs and stopped him from moving. He was aware of his feet being bound and, when he heard more laughter, he knew in his young heart that the only thing left to wish for was for death to come quickly before the worst of the pain.

Chapter Six

Luke had a headache that was the child of wine and sleeplessness. *If he stayed in bed*, he thought *it would probably disappear*, but a nagging sense of having things to do was disturbing his lie-in no matter how tight he shut his eyes and what way he curled up under the sheets. He became aware of a soft voice that further foiled his attempts at slumber.

"Morning … morning, it's a lovely morning."

Sophie's voice. He opened his eyes very slightly but he didn't see Sophie. Instead, he saw a large yellow moth sitting on Sophie's pillow, its wings like ancient yellow parchment. His mouth craved water.

"Morning, sleepy, time to get up."

He stared at the moth and into its big black eyes, wondering how it was able to speak with his wife's voice when he couldn't see its mouth moving or even if it had a mouth. Then the curtains opened and brought the morning light fully into the room. The moth flew away and his eyes focussed on Sophie's figure beside the window.

"Why am I so tired?" he asked, finally relinquishing his last hope of more sleep. "Did Elliott keep us up last night?" He could taste his own breath and it wasn't pleasant. "How much wine did we drink?"

"Well, you drank more than a bottle," Sophie scolded jokingly. "But it was the joyriding that kept us all awake. Poor Elliot couldn't settle at all."

Luke remembered then the noise of a roaring engine and music that had gone on into the early hours.

"Oh yes. I know that little bastard's name. Noel something. He was speeding around here yesterday as well. I'll get Declan to sort him out. How come you're not tired?"

"I am," she replied, and Luke noticed the redness of her eyes. "But I couldn't sleep on. I didn't sleep right at all, even after all the noise stopped. Do you remember hearing screaming last night as well?"

"Umm, I don't think so. I can't remember."

"No, I think you had dropped off at that stage. I said it to you when I heard it but you just mumbled and snored."

"I'll get Declan on the case, don't worry." Luke pulled on yesterday's clothes which were sitting in a pile on the floor. "Anyway, I'll just have a coffee and toast and we'll get stuck into unpacking again."

"I'll tell you what," said Sophie. "I'll start unpacking and sorting things out here if you go to the shops for us. We have nothing in the house apart from coffee and bread, so you can have that breakfast you want, but then we need a proper shop. I made a list while I couldn't sleep."

Luke decided to take the car rather than the van to the shops. He reckoned he'd be happy if he never had to drive the van on these roads again, particularly with the flaky head he had this morning. He would, however, have to drive it tomorrow to return it to the rental company on the way to work, and he was planning to take the bus back home in the evening. It would be a good test to see how feasible public transport was for his commute, just so he'd know for any future times he might want to have a drink after work or didn't have the car available for whatever reason. They would have to buy a second car, there was no way around that. Sophie and Elliott couldn't be left without transport out here while he was at work. The plan was to let the financial dust of the move settle before shopping for cars. He had been prowling the car sales websites for the last month and he knew what was available in their budget. He just hadn't quite decided yet whether to go for something small and zippy for himself that would be cheaper on fuel, tax and insurance or to get a bigger, more comfortable family vehicle for Sophie and use the old Renault for his commute. His last look at their bank balance was steering him towards the first, cheaper option.

He piled a bundle of empty shopping bags on the passenger seat but they caught the corner of his eyeline, so he threw them into the backseat, took a sip of water and tried to blink the tiredness out of his eyes. Finally, he turned on the engine and pulled out of the driveway. When he got to the junction at the end of his road he stopped, looked left and right for traffic, then rubbed his tired eyes hard, like a cartoon character disbelieving what he was seeing. The first thing he noticed was the blue Honda Civic facing the wrong way on the road. It took him a moment to register that it wasn't moving and, despite the secretive tint of the windows, he was fairly sure nobody was in the car, at least nobody sitting upright. The other thing causing him confusion was the amount of crows on the road as he approached. Most had scattered as he got close but a few bravely or greedily alighted back down to pick at things in various places. The road was marked with the black residue of tyre marks, the evidence of the noise that had kept his small family awake last night, but there were also red marks that seemed to follow the tyre tracks, a scarlet trail intermingled with the black, crossing it over in places and congealing in small piles here and there. It was these small piles attracting the crows.

He pulled the Renault in off the road, near the strange tree bedecked with pieces of cloth, and approached the scavengers. The ragged cloth whispered on the branches behind him. He waved, stamped his foot, and the birds sullenly dispersed. It appeared to be tiny bits of some sort of roadkill they had been picking at, but he couldn't see any fur in those small piles that might give him a clue as to what unfortunate animal it might have been. The red trails that intertwined the tyre marks glistened. They were definitely tracks of blood. His nostrils filled with a ripe smell that got caught in his chest. He wondered if that boy racer was so sick in the head that he would have tied an animal to the back of his car for his noisy extravaganza of doughnuts. The thought made him wince. A poor, defenceless animal ripped to shreds in a manic spinning circle. There was no fur though, just blood. Surely there would be clumps of fur sticking in the mess if that was the case. No fur, but there were some strands of black hair.

He went round to the back of the Civic to see if there was a rope or chains attached to the towbar. No, nothing like that. He tried the driver's door and found it unlocked. There was a smell of cigarette smoke inside, a crushed can of Red Bull and some more in the back that were full, but nothing else. The keys were still in the ignition. A breeze blew, rustling the leafy ditches.

Luke walked up and down the road, kicking at the long grass at the verge, looking for something that might make sense of what had happened here. The sight of all the blood on the ground in its horrible pattern was not good for his hungover nerves. His hands twitched uncomfortably as he took his phone from his pocket and rang Declan's number. After what seemed like ages his friend answered, greeting him with a voice both sleepy and impatient.

"Luke. What do you want?"

"Declan. I'm up past the end of our road and there's something odd. You know that blue Honda Civic, the boy racer, Noel. His car is here abandoned. The wheel is all busted up, the keys are left in it and, Declan …"

"What? What is it?"

"Declan, there's blood on the road. Tyres tracks and lots of blood, like he was making spinning circles with blood or something, and bits of flesh, I think. It's disgusting. It's like he was killing animals or something, I don't know."

"That little shit! Luke, stay right where you are. Don't you touch anything. I'll be there in five minutes."

"Thanks, Deccie, thanks." Luke could hear the relief in his own voice and his breathing started to calm from the crescendo it had reached talking to Declan. He walked towards his car, then decided he didn't want to sit in it. The fresh air was clearing his head and the drama of the scene had made his mind and body too restless to sit.

He leaned into the car and switched on his hazard lights on the off-chance of approaching traffic. Traces of blood appeared to have made it back as far as the ugly roots of the tree. Just his luck to be the person to discover this mess. He went back to the Civic and turned its hazard lights on as well. Then he remembered Declan's warning about not touching anything. Stupid. He turned them off and went to see if he still had that traffic warning triangle in the boot of his car. It was in the corner of the boot, shoved over behind Elliott's folded pushchair. As he placed it in front of the abandoned car, he heard singing, and he knew who was coming before she appeared, cycling casually up the road in bright purple and green sports gear with a broad smile on her face. The bicycle girl's grin got wider in the brief second that she recognised Luke, then evaporated in an expression of bewilderment at the rest of the vista before her.

"That's Noel Quirke's car," she said. "Was there an accident?"

"I don't know," said Luke.

"Is that blood? What's going on? Why is there blood on the road? Whose blood is it?"

"Now, listen, it's ok. Sorry, I never got your name yesterday. You remember me, don't you? Luke. My friend Declan, the Garda, he's on the way up to sort all this out, so it's ok."

Her feet pressed imperceptibly on the pedals so her bicycle moved in tiny increments, but it was moving backwards. He tried to explain further.

"I was just driving up here to go to the shops and I came across the car and the blood and the, well, there were a load of crows picking at bits of something. It's just as well I was here or you would have come across it yourself and—"

"Why does that matter?"

"Well, I guess it wouldn't have been nice for you to find. It's a gruesome sight."

"Because I'm a girl, is that it?"

He couldn't tell from her voice if she was annoyed or not, she seemed to have quickly gotten over any fright she may have had and her tone was back to its usual playful nonchalance.

"No, not that. I'm sure you're very capable of dealing with something like this, it's just … actually I'm surprised nobody has driven this way already this morning. I heard him driving around here last night. Kept us all awake."

"No, you're right. I'm glad that it wasn't me to find it. Can I tell you something, Luke?"

"Of course. You haven't told me your name yet though."

"This isn't the first weird thing I've encountered on these roads. Recently when I've been out training, I've felt like there's something eerie around. I wonder if this is connected to it. If I have my headphones in and there's a quiet part in the songs, then sometimes I think I can hear voices in the ditches or from in the fields or even laughter sometimes, but if I stop to check there's never anyone there. It happens more when I go out later in the evening. I go out later on Tuesdays and Thursdays but I'm thinking of not doing that anymore, especially now the evenings are getting darker. Do you think that might be something to do with this? Where is Noel?"

"I don't know. He was gone when I got here."

Her eyes traced the patterns of blood to the base of the tree.

"My granny used to say that old tree was like a door that shouldn't be here. She'd bless herself whenever she passed. Grannies believe all sorts of things, don't they? Here comes your friend now. I can hear his car."

Luke turned to look down the road. "Look," he said to the girl. "Do you want to head off? There's no point in you getting dragged into this just because you happened to cycle by at this particular time. I'll probably have to make statements and all that kind of stuff. You should get going."

"Will that not be fleeing the scene of a crime?"

"Ha, sure, we don't even know what crime there was. No, don't worry, I'll say you were just passing by."

"Ok, Luke, thanks for that. I do have to be getting on with my training."

She pressed leisurely on the pedals and rode off just as Declan parked his car in front of Luke's. His face was flushed and irritated. He wasn't wearing his uniform but he had his notebook in his hand as he got out.

"Where's she going?" he asked abruptly.

"She just passed by this second," said Luke. "You hardly want to drag her into it?"

"Well, she should at least have stayed to let me know that. Ah fuck it, let her go. I couldn't be listening to her this morning anyway."

"Are you ok, Declan? You don't look great."

"Long night."

"Did you hear all this racket last night? Sophie thinks she heard screaming as well. This blood, have you ever seen anything like this before?"

Declan wandered round the scene. Occasional shakes of his head could have been born of incredulity or just made to wake himself up. He opened the door of the Civic and examined the interior. He supported himself against the car and started making notes. "Anything about the scene changed since you got here?"

"Eh, no. I don't think so, Declan," Luke replied cautiously.

"You haven't disturbed anything?"

"Nope."

"Right. Well, in that case, I'm going to do you a big favour and pretend that I found it instead of you. This is just a day's work for me but it'll be a big hassle for you and if you can't add anything to what I can see here myself then there's no point in dragging you into it any more than your friend on her bicycle."

"But I don't mind," he murmured against premonitions of interminable questions in the Garda station. "I want to do whatever the right thing is."

Declan walked over to his friend and Luke could see how tired his eyes were.

"I know you do." Declan put his hand on Luke's shoulder. "But let me decide what the right thing is. Honestly, it's just easier for me if I found it myself. Less paperwork."

"What do you think happened? From first impressions?"

"I don't know, but I get a sense of something cruel and nasty. Seriously, just disappear. You can make it up to me later by coming out for a pint with me. Now go on, before somebody else shows up."

Chapter Seven

The day after a sleepless night Sophie would always feel hyperactive. Even those who knew her well were always surprised by this. Over the years, dozens of all-nighters had been pulled to meet deadlines in college or work but she would always be itching to start some new project the morning after while everyone around her collapsed in a heap. Even after all-night parties she was energised. This morning was no different. If she kept working at the rate she was going, then she would have all their belongings unpacked and sorted by lunchtime.

Sophie would always feel lighter at these times, as if there had been too much sleep inside her, weighing her down, and it needed to be purged from her body to give her a boost of energy. She wouldn't eat on mornings like this either, barely drink, maybe some tea or coffee to further increase her intensity. She glanced at the mirror in the bathroom as she tumbled the contents out of a bag: soaps, gels, shampoos. Her normally pale, placid eyes had turned as manic as dark wasps trapped in a fire pit. This was happening a lot in her first year of motherhood too, when sleepless nights were dished out with generosity by young Elliott. She often did hours on the laptop after a night punctuated by teething cries.

Her son didn't seem to have inherited this trait of hers. After his disturbed sleep last night, he now dozed away in his cot, despite the fact Sophie was playing experimental classical music in the kitchen loud enough for her to hear it in all the rooms she was speeding around. An occasional suck of his lip was his only note to the world outside his slumber. Elliott was like Luke in that way, his default mode was laid-back. That was why she had sent her husband off to the shops, to be out of the way of her whirlwind of activity.

She knew, of course, that she would crash. She would crash in the early evening and she would just come to a halt, lie down on whichever was closest; couch, bed, or floor, and slumber contentedly until the following day. The doorbell rang and, as it was the first time she had ever heard it, it took two more rings before she realised it wasn't part of the song she was listening to. She scooted out to the door and opened it to find Denise Maguire standing there with her three-year-old son beside her.

"Welcome to Kilcross," announced Denise. It seemed like she should have handed Sophie some sort of gift to go along with that statement but there was none.

"Hi. Thanks, Denise. It's good to be finally moving in. Would you like to come in for a cup of coffee?"

A strange expression crossed Denise's face, a sort of confused irritation that clustered around her neatly made-up eyebrows.

"Oh," said Sophie, still brimming with unpacking energy. "I suppose that must be weird for you, being invited in, what with you growing up in this house? I hope it isn't. We really love the house. You're welcome to visit anytime, of course. We should get to know each other better, and the boys, as they get older, will hopefully become friends."

"Yes, for sure. I still see it as Dad's house," said Denise. "But we should definitely get to know each other better. That's why I'm here actually, to invite you over to my place this afternoon. I would have just rung but I don't have your number."

"Oh, Declan would have it," Sophie interjected and saw that frown appear again at his name.

"It's kind of a tradition I have with my friends. We each take a turn to host on a Sunday afternoon every fortnight. We all get together for lunch and a few glasses of wine. Most of us have young kids but we rope in a babysitter or two to come along and mind them while we all catch up on things. No husbands allowed. Strictly for the girls."

"That sounds like fun," answered Sophie unsurely. "We have a load of stuff to do here but I'm sure I could head over for a little while and leave Elliott with Luke. He's still a bit young for me to feel comfortable leaving him with someone he doesn't know."

"He's good with the baby, isn't he, Luke? You can tell. Declan isn't very good with Willy."

Sophie glanced down at the boy but he was more interested in something up his own nose than his mother's conversation.

"Well, it was a surprise to us when Declan became a father, alright," she said with good humour.

"Not as much of a surprise as it was to us," said Denise flatly. "So, it'll be two o'clock. Bring a bottle but we'll have plenty of food. What is that awful music? Is that on the radio? What station is playing that?"

"No, I put that on."

"That's right, I remember now. You're into weird stuff, aren't you." Denise took her son's hand away from his nasal exploration and marshalled him away. "See you at two!"

***

When Luke came back from the shop bearing bags of random and ill-considered groceries, he was very encouraging of Sophie going round to Denise's get-together. Apparently, Declan was twisting his arm to go for a pint later on so it was only fair that she should get to socialize in the afternoon. When she asked him where he had run into Declan for them to be arranging pints, he said he'd met him at the shop, but she found it hard to envision Declan doing a Sunday morning grocery run. She had an uneasy feeling about the way Luke was acting. He was coming across as shifty and furtive, and if there was one thing about Luke it was that he was no good at being secretive. This better not be the start of some new strand of their life influenced by Declan where Luke would be cajoled into doing things that would exclude her. She remembered in the early days of their relationship that, as they got more serious, Declan's behaviour started to get more impulsive, as if trying to show his friend there was a boisterous and fun place by his side that Sophie couldn't offer. However, the things that Sophie could offer were always going to win out in the end. Declan eventually seemed to realise his best option for keeping close to his friend was to be close to her too, so he took on the role of a feckless but caring rogue when in her company. Against the odds they did actually become solid friends in their own way. What she definitely did not want now, though, was to be granted the friendship of Denise as some sort of dubious consolation prize while the two men created their own little camaraderie in the countryside.

Apart from being a bit secretive, Luke had also appeared distracted. It was like there was something he really wanted to tell her but as he was just on the cusp of revealing it, he would remember some reason that he shouldn't. Quickly enough she got sick of this, grabbed a bottle of Pinot Grigio which had predictably made its way into his shopping trolley—and not on its own either—and headed next door.

She wasn't planning on having more than two glasses. Sophie had been caught out before by these sleep-deprived bursts of energy and discovered that when wine was applied to them in excess, it resulted in a volatile spew of chat that might attach itself to any innocent subject and turn on it with paranoia and spite, until the wine expelled itself from her mouth with similar force. Two glasses, that would be her limit. She didn't need to introduce ratty drunk Sophie to her new neighbours just yet.

It was nearly half two when she strolled over. There was only one car outside the house so she was surprised to be introduced to four of Denise's friends and then shown the playroom, which contained a scurry of small children being minded by two teenage girls, cousins of one of the friends.

"I persuaded my husband to be the taxi driver for a few of us," said one of the women.

"And I'm stuck with being a designated driver," said another.

"Lucky you, able to walk over," added a third.

Sophie's first impression was that they all seemed quite alike. They were younger than her by four or five years, but all had children older than Elliott. In their smiles she sensed hardness and mistrust in varying degrees. The most extreme version was the one Denise sported.

"Well, thanks very much for letting me join your traditional Sunday drinks," she said to one named Moira.

"Huh?" replied Moira. "This is only about the third time we've done this in the last two years, I'd say. I thought it was a welcome party for you. Still, any excuse to get out for a few drinks and a chat."

Sophie sipped slowly at her wine and chatted briefly to a couple of the women, trying to find a common interest among this new bunch of people into whose company she found herself clunkily inserted but, beyond the subject of motherhood, she was finding very little.

She extracted herself from the conversation to go to the bathroom. She had been in Denise and Declan's house before and could remember her way around. This time too, her design sensibilities reacted against the place. The décor put her in mind of a spa hotel. It was intended to be calm, soft and serene but it made her feel like her sleep-deprived crash was going to come earlier than expected. There were lots of paintings and ornaments around the house but they all got swallowed up in a yellowy blandness.

As soon as she got into the bathroom, she splashed her face with water, then sat down on the toilet. The bathroom was as pale and colourless as the rest of the house but hiding down to her right was an incongruous occupant. There was a small glass table tucked between the toilet and the bath and abandoned on it was a black, heavily dented metal bucket daubed with red painted writing. She read the words Zamioculcas Zamiifolia 'Raven' at the same time as admiring the black-leaved plant that it held. Its thin stems spread upwards and held its dark, waxy leaves with a sinister elegance that enhanced the trashy style of its container. Everything else in the house spoke to Sophie with a muted conformity apart from this plant with its sly, creepy tendrils and the junkyard goth of its container. When she stepped out of the bathroom, she saw Denise checking in on the kids in the playroom and was compelled to comment.

"I love the black plant you have in there. It's very unusual, it could really stand out if it was put in the right place."

"What?" Denise shuffled past her and stuck her nose in the door. "Oh that? Ha, ha. Declan got me that for our anniversary this year. It's disgusting. I put it in there beside the toilet to let him know what I think of it. I hope it dies, I haven't even watered it yet, but if you like it then you're more than welcome to take it."

"Ah no, I couldn't. It was a gift," Sophie replied apprehensively, unsure if this was a line of conversation that she was best to avoid for as long as possible. She didn't fancy either the role of defending Declan or supporting Denise in her denunciation of his many flaws.

"I'd hardly even call it a gift. He forgot all about our anniversary until the second he walked in the door that evening, then he turned on his heel and went to the nearest place he could get a present, any present, he didn't even care whether I'd like the horrible thing."

"So, where did he get it?" Sophie asked with genuine interest.

"There's a woman nearby who grows plants and flowers, but it's not like a regular garden nursery. She grows all these dark, freaky looking things. Roisin's Gothic Garden, she calls it. That's probably one of the less spooky ones, to tell you the truth. He just went up there and grabbed something because that took the least effort possible. Although, come to think of it, maybe it's actually a fitting comment on our marriage."

"I'm … I'm sure it's not like that at all …"

"She's not even a real gardener," said Denise. "She used to be a teacher before she lost it. Weird woman."

Sophie took a last appreciative glance at the plant in its position of ignominy.

"Well, I really like it."

"Yeah, you're into strange sort of things, aren't you? You might get on with her, come to think of it. Roisin Kelly. She was a Mitchell before she got married. Witchy Mitchell we used to call her."

By the time Sophie had poured a second glass of wine for herself everyone had gathered in the kitchen. Denise was asking one of her friends, a slightly plump woman named Sinead, how she was getting on with her jogging. She was the one who was driving and not drinking.

Sophie had spoken to her earlier and found her the most pleasant and interesting of the bunch. She had a warmth and an awareness about her that seemed to be lacking in the others.

"I stopped doing it," said Sinead glumly.

"Aw no," said Denise. "Well, you might get back to it in the future. It just takes willpower, that's all. You just have to have the determination to get up off the couch and away from the TV snacking."

"It's not my willpower," retorted Sinead with a sharpness that made everyone flinch. "I have willpower. I don't snack in front of the TV that much. I just don't want to run on the roads anymore, that's all. I'm thinking of joining a gym instead, if someone else would go along with me. I don't fancy doing it on my own."

"I might like to join," chanced Sophie, who thought that the pace that Sinead might set would be relaxed enough for her. She also got the feeling that here was someone she would enjoy being around and who didn't involve herself with the kind of low-level nastiness that Denise tried to foster among her friends. "Is it a good gym? Or, if you'd like, I could jog on the roads with you and keep you company. It sounds like it might be nicer running in the countryside rather than the stuffiness of a gym."

"I'm not jogging on the roads again!"

Sophie put down her glass, taken aback by Sinead's tone.

"Why don't you want to jog on the roads anymore?" asked Moira.

"It's just, well, by the time Andrew gets home from work and we have dinner and then I wait for an hour after dinner so I don't get a stitch running, well it's getting dark by then and—"

"Are you afraid of the dark, Sinead?" laughed Denise, drawing chuckles from the others.

"To tell you the truth, I only went out once and I only jogged for about five minutes before I ran back home. Yes, maybe I am scared of the dark. I heard something. I'm scared of seeing something out there too, that's for sure, and now with the stories about what happened to Mr. McGrath ..."

"What did you hear out there, Sinead?" Sophie asked.

"I really did want to go jogging. I was looking forward to it. I had my reflector top on and my iPod that Andrew bought for me to listen to. The kids were waving out the window at me as I was doing my stretches and I was thinking: I'll be doing it for them as well as me, getting fit, so I have more energy for them. It wasn't that late when I set out but it was getting darker. The young Fitzpatrick boy drove by in his tractor and gave me a wave. I remember he had his headlights on. I decided not to put on the iPod when I started off, especially for that first time, so I could get used to running on the roads and in case that Quirke boy came flying round a corner and ran me over. I had bought some good trainers so it wouldn't be too hard on my joints. I'd never worn footwear so comfortable before, they were lovely. I was all set. But as I got down the road a bit, I started to feel nervous for some reason."

Denise yanked the cork from another bottle of white and Sinead brought her hand to her throat. Sophie spluttered on her wine, to everyone's mirth.

"Nervous?" sneered Denise. "Of doing some exercise?"

"No. It was like, you know the feeling you get when you chance crossing a street when a car is too close, or when a small dog starts yapping at you as you pass by it, that nervous feeling in your ankles, like they're going to get clipped by the car or bitten by the dog. When I got to that bit of road just down from my house, you know where I mean, where there's lots of trees overshadowing it like a tunnel. It was a lot darker there but I noticed something up ahead on the side of the road. At first, I thought it was a sack or something that had fallen off a tractor. It was about that size. But when I got a bit closer, I knew it was an animal. It was a dead badger but there was something odd about it. It wasn't lying dead on the ground like it had been hit by a car. It was sitting upright, very straight. It must have been propped up somehow. There was a mound of blood and flies where one of its eyes should have been and there was blood across its belly. I knew it was dead but its mouth was wide open and it was staring at me coming down the road with its one eye and I heard this horrible sounding laugh. It was like it was coming from the dead badger's open mouth. I ran. I just turned around and ran all the way home. I took off so fast I strained my hamstring but I didn't even notice that until later. When I ran it was like I could feel a breath on my neck and I thought I heard a panting sound, but I didn't turn around. I didn't turn around until I could shut my gate behind me and when I did turn around there was nothing there. There was nothing there, but Sophie ..."

"Yes?"

"I'm sorry but I won't go out on those roads again in the evening time. I'd very much like you to join me going to the gym when my leg feels better but I won't ever be going back out on those roads."

Chapter Eight

Conor Gallagher sat on an old wooden chair in his kitchen and ate his dinner. The chair had been painted a long time ago in a duck egg blue but not much of that colour remained. He remembered his father painting it when he was a child and he remembered over the years, as it started to wear and flake away, his mother saying that they must repaint it.

"I'll put it on the list," his father used to say light-heartedly, then he would turn around to Conor and say something like, "That chair is just fine, it's not the paint that holds it together."

What his father was likely trying to say to him was that appearances didn't matter and it was the essence of things that counted. What Conor took from it was not to bother wasting time on things you didn't think were important.

His dinner was a microwave ready meal, a chicken and broccoli bake. Conor didn't believe cooking was important enough to waste his time on. He hadn't eaten a home-cooked meal in the two years since his mother died. Similarly, the old two storey farmhouse was mostly unswept and dusty since he didn't think it important to dust, apart from in his studio where dust might be detrimental to the equipment. He wasn't lazy. He worked hard on the small cattle farm he had managed alone since his father passed away. That had been a year before his mother's death. Conor had no firm attachment to farming, it wasn't ingrained in his sense of self, but he did it because it was the only way he knew to earn an income. Now, in his mid-thirties, he wasn't going to learn many more employable skills and he wasn't much interested in doing so anyway.

What was important to Conor was music. Music was pretty much the only thing that meant anything to him now his parents were gone. He had a few friends and he had his few pints most evenings and he liked a smoke but they didn't move his soul or make him feel warm and excited inside quite like music did. When he was younger, he knew his parents loved him because they allowed him to spend as much time as he needed with his music, as long as he did his work on the farm with his father and did his fair share around the house. They never pressured him to do anything educational or pestered him about his stale social life. They understood that music was everything to him. He knew they understood by the way they referred to it as 'his music' and how they never viewed his obsession as weird like people did in school or like the few girls he dated did.

Conor didn't play an instrument. He didn't write music. He had no talent in performing. He was a connoisseur. There never was a day he didn't listen to it obsessively and he read everything he could find on the subject: music magazines, newspaper articles, biographies. When he was younger, he had thought he might like to become a music journalist. He wrote some reviews of gigs he went to, channelling the arch tone of the magazines that he loved. He sent them to *Hotpress* magazine, he sent them to the *Evening Herald*, he sent them to the local newspaper too but he didn't get any response from anyone so eventually he stopped writing them.

In the last few years, he had started his own podcast, *The Essential Album Hour*. The programme was split in two. First a deep insight into an obscure classic album from his collection, then a whistle-stop tour through those artists it influenced and whom it was influenced by. Conor didn't care much for copyright rules. He knew he wasn't supposed to broadcast songs on his podcast, even though he didn't play them in their entirety, but the way he rationalised it was that he was encouraging others to buy music that they may never otherwise have heard of. He'd garnered a small but dedicated listenership, so he didn't fear coming to the attention of any lawyers and, if by some magic he did manage to make it big, then he was ready to revel in any notoriety that a lawsuit might bring him. He often got into rows with his audience online about this, especially the few international outliers that had somehow picked up his show. Maybe it was his obstreperous and vitriolic attitude to these people that made him popular with his listenership. A rock music messiah, he never admitted to being wrong or even allowed an opinion contrary to his own. He wasn't afraid to insult anyone and he carried these insults over to his podcast recordings, calling out the failings of his detractors in between glorifying the sombre guitar doom of Come's *Eleven Eleven* and the schizophrenic melodies of Whipping Boy's *Submarine.*

Conor had met a lot of his Irish listeners personally. They often arranged to meet up at the gigs they went to in Dublin, particularly the ones who lived down the country like him. All men, all obsessive about music, all outsiders within their local community or workplace. This was the skin they felt comfortable in. They would never change their vintage black band T-Shirts for the corporate shirt and tie or the local sports jersey, no matter what.

Unless it was a night Conor was going to a gig in the city, he generally strolled up to O'Shea's pub in Kilcross. He had a seat at the bar that he had made his own and, despite the future shock he sometimes got from beholding the ancient alcoholics that occupied other designated seats, he knew unconsciously that it was good for him. It was healthy to see other people most evenings and not rot in the isolation of his bachelorhood, particularly since his parents were gone. It was good to talk to others, even if he bored them with his chatter about music and culture they had never heard of and they frustrated him with their ignorance. It was good to be around others, particularly since he had been hearing things outside the house at night, the strange noises, the laughter that may or may not be the peculiar sounds of nocturnal wildlife. Particularly since seeing what he thought—no, what he knew he saw last week. Fuck the police. He knew what he saw.

Tonight, he checked the group chat for his podcast before getting ready to go out. In amongst the usual critiques and arguments about bands with his listeners there had been a few apprehensive comments recently, a few shy little mentions of things from his rural-dwelling compadres. They worried him, these comments. It was as if there was a dark, sour turn in the atmosphere in the Irish countryside. There had been break-ins and vandalism that seemed more mindless and animalistic than was normal. Livestock had been spooked. There was an edge in the night air that unnerved people. Some of his online friends had seen things and heard things that they didn't really understand; things like he had seen, like what he heard at night. An American contributor called them a bunch of retarded potato-eating pussies, but Conor couldn't concentrate enough to retaliate to the insult with the venom it deserved. Not too cold tonight, his black denim jacket would be fine; a couple of pre-rolled joints into the breast pocket. He made extra sure all his windows were locked and all the doors too, left the kitchen light on for his return. He tapped the photo of his parents that hung in the hallway, the one he had taken of them himself at his cousin's wedding in Malta. They had both smiled giddily for most of that trip; they looked younger than they actually were and wide-eyed with the excitement of foreign travel.

"Bye Mam, bye Dad."

Outside, he hopped on his quad bike. Conor didn't stroll up to the pub anymore even though it was little more than a mile away. He had started taking the bike. He didn't like to walk the roads anymore.

Chapter Nine

Luke didn't know why Declan was being such an awkward pain in the arse. Luke had offered to drive them both to the pub and back. He was worried about the length of his first commute the following morning, especially when he had the added hassle of having to return the rental van and he didn't want to suffer it with tiredness or a hangover.

O'Shea's was only a few miles away from the house. He was happy to accept the responsibility of driving to ensure he wouldn't have more than one drink and they'd leave at a reasonable time, but when he rang Declan he was weird about it. First, Declan wanted to take them in his own car but then stuttered that he might be delayed so he'd meet Luke at O'Shea's instead. Luke said he'd wait until Declan was ready, there was no point in them both bringing their cars.

Then Declan tried to convince him to get Sophie to drop them up and collect them later so they could both have a few pints but her earlier glasses of wine had knocked that suggestion right on the head. She was dozing happily on the couch with the pretence of watching a TV movie ever since he had put Elliott to bed, and he had a feeling he would get home later to find her in the same position. The only thing that could wake her when she was that tired was Elliott's cry. It was as if they were connected by an aural umbilical cord ever since the actual one had been cut and even his lightest squeal would tug on it and stir her.

Tonight, though, Elliott seemed as exhausted as his mother. The move was tiring them all.

Declan kept talking in circles and changing his mind about the logistics of getting them both to the pub so Luke finally just said that he'd meet him there at eight and drove himself. Sometimes there was no point in trying to wrap much logic around what Declan wanted to do.

Luke was already getting used to driving these roads, becoming familiar with all dips and humps that variated the unkempt ditches. He slowed down near the Twisted Tree to check out the spot where he had found the car that morning. The car was gone, but he could still just about see the sinister red and black marks on the road in the failing light. It had been quite a disturbing discovery. He had a feeling something horrible had happened, but he didn't want to let his imagination go too far down any sickening possibilities, so the subject just simmered in his mind until he got to O'Shea's then during the ten minutes he was left to wait in the car park before Declan arrived.

"Did you find the boy?" Luke asked as soon as Declan got out of his car.

"What boy?"

"The boy racer boy, of course. Noel whatever-his-name-is?"

"Oh, no, we didn't," replied Declan. "We went round to his house but he wasn't there. Dunno where he is."

"Well, are they out looking for him?" asked Luke, surprised at how blasé his friend seemed on the subject.

"Is who out looking for him?"

"The Gardaí. You. Your colleagues."

"But no one has reported him missing. His parents weren't concerned about him."

"But the car?" cried Luke.

"I got the car towed away. It'll cost him to get it back," said Declan with a hint of smugness.

"But the blood? Did you get it tested? Whose is it? What is it?"

"Get it tested?" repeated Declan incredulously. "What do you think this is, CSI Kilcross? There hasn't been any crime committed. It was probably just roadkill or something that crawled away. Who knows?"

Luke didn't know what to say.

"What?" said Declan.

"Roadkill that crawled away?" said Luke, his voice cracking.

"Ok, yes, of course. The serious crimes division is right on it. We'll be sending the evidence off to get tested straight away, don't worry. Oh no, hold on, it's Sunday today. The crime lab doesn't open on a Sunday." He smirked. "Come on, let's go inside. I'm thirsty."

Luke shook his head and followed his friend. "I don't know. I just don't know."

Everyone called it the O'Shea's, though no one named O'Shea had owned it for over forty years and the letters over the door spelled The Kilcross Inn. It was a modest enough establishment, divided into three parts: the lounge, the bar, and a shop that was little more than a counter, a fridge and a row of old, wooden shelves. Luke had been there before with Declan but it seemed different tonight, being there as a local: smaller, drab.

After Declan's son had been born and Luke and Sophie came to visit with gifts, they had all gone to O'Shea's but they sat in the lounge area that night with its brighter lighting and soft seats. This time Declan led him round to the other entrance and through the tiny shop into the bar.

Here there were only two tables in front of a spartan wooden bench that ran the length of one wall, some small wooden stools pushed underneath them and a line of tall, ageless stools along the bar. Sat upon these were three men. Two of them were in their early sixties with brothers' heads, sipping pints of Guinness and hiding large bellies beneath heavy jumpers. The third man was much older, skinnier, and wore a fusty suit of long-forgotten fashion which hung loose on his meagre frame. The suit smelled of tobacco and farts, and the collar was dotted with stains from the spittle that slipped through the many gaps of missing teeth in his mouth. A young man barely in his twenties stood behind the bar, texting on his phone until Declan asked him to pull two pints of stout.

Luke noticed a shabby old accordion, a fiddle and a bodhran hanging high on hooks behind the bar. "Do they ever get played?" he asked.

"You never know, old Johnny might ask for the accordion later on," Declan said, nodding towards the old man.

Luke watched the old man with trembling hands struggle to pour a drop of water from a jug into his beloved glass of whiskey.

"Seriously?"

"Oh yes, he's a different animal by ten o'clock at night."

The pints were placed in front of them and Declan stuck his hand in his pocket. "And give us change for the cigarette machine please, Ollie. C'mon Luke, we'll sit out in the smoking area."

"I thought you had given up?"

"Ah, I just have one with a drink sometimes, or whenever I'm stressed."

"When are you ever stressed?"

"You'd be surprised," said Declan, pushing open the narrow mahogany door that led out to a semi-sheltered yard. Here a small wonky table with a few ashtrays was placed among some empty beer kegs that had cushions tied on to them as seats. He pulled the cellophane from his cigarette packet with his teeth then took a long swig of his pint before lighting one. He waved the pack at Luke.

"Jesus no, you know I gave them up when Sophie got pregnant with Elliott."

"Ah go on, she won't smell it off you, she's conked out didn't you say?"

"It wouldn't matter if she didn't smell it off me tonight," said Luke. "If I have one then I'd probably be back smoking full-time tomorrow."

"It's just one with a pint. Sure, you said you're only going to have one pint with me so you may as well have a smoke."

Luke took a sip of his Guinness and held out his hand. "Go on then."

Declan handed him the pack and the lighter and took a long draw from his own cigarette.

"I'm in kind of a spot of bother I think, Luke."

Luke was holding his cigarette with the same love and care he held his own son's hand but Declan's statement took him out of his tobacco-induced reverie. "What do you mean? You know, if I can do anything for you I always will."

"I know," said Declan, "and you can't. There's this girl I've been messing around with. She's just told me she's pregnant."

"Ah Declan. What the fuck? I thought you had grown up a little bit at least. You have a family now."

"Listen Luke, me and Denise, it's not like what you have with Sophie. I just kind of fell into my marriage without choosing it. Things just happen sometimes, you know."

"And what about this other girl?"

"Well, she might be a bit of a problem. I'm not sure what way she's going to turn. I don't know how much trouble she's going to cause for me. She's said a couple of things that I didn't really like."

"What do you mean? Does she want to keep the baby?"

"She hasn't decided yet. But she's dropped some hints about having something over me."

"And does she have something over you?" Luke was regretting smoking the cigarette already. He pictured all of the willpower he had used to give them up drifting into the ether with each bellow of smoke he exhaled. A long-banished helplessness had returned, mocking him that he wouldn't stub it out until it was finished and that he'd soon be going back to the pack for more. A familiar feeling was coming over him with the nicotine in his blood, the drink in front of him and Declan's cheeky voice telling him of a situation that he'd pushed too far.

"She's a bit wild, this girl, but she's cool. I met her through her brother, you see. He does some dealing around town and I would usually get coke from him for free. It was just a casual sort of arrangement. I'm not doing anything really wrong. If I notice something that might affect him, I might mention it, and if I was on duty, I'd turn a blind eye to him. He's not a bad guy or anything, he's small time, just deals coke and pills for weekenders. Not a problem."

Luke's stomach felt giddy. "You're still doing drugs?"

Another door into the smoking area opened, this one led from the lounge, and a woman in her sixties with narrow, crinkled eyes walked in with her cigarette already lit. "Howaya, Declan," she squawked.

"Hiya Margaret. Nice night."

A pudgy older man came out to join her with a smile, nodded at Luke, and said hello to Declan. The couple were about to sit down with them until they read the turn of Declan's shoulder and stayed standing together, leaving the friends to their table. Declan leaned in close to Luke and spoke in a whisper. "Why do you sound so surprised? Sure, you took a pill with me on your birthday last year."

"That wasn't last year, Declan, that was three years ago. It's a very rare occasion that I'd take anything now."

"Well, I wouldn't be doing it every weekend, just now and again if I'm seeing Cliona."

"That's her name?"

"That's her name. Look, Denise was never really my type. We have nothing in common. The only good thing about her was that she had a fit body and, since we had the kid, I don't get any of that from her, so what am I supposed to do?"

Luke shook his head silently.

"Anyway, there's two problems. If she tells Denise then I'll be kicked out and I'll have nowhere to live. I can get over that, shit happens, you know. The bigger problem is if she starts spouting that I have an involvement with her brother. There's a possibility I might lose my job if that got out."

"I would have thought it would be a certainty rather than a possibility. But why would she do that?"

"She may have hinted at it when I hinted that if she didn't get rid of the pregnancy I'd have nothing to do with her or the baby."

"Wow, Declan. You're real sweet, aren't you? But would that not get her brother in trouble too?"

"Maybe yes, maybe no. It's well-known that he's a dealer, he just hasn't ever been caught. It's not as well-known what I get up to and if it was then I might find it hard to talk my way out of it."

"So, what are you going to do?" asked Luke.

The smoking area contracted with the expectation of an answer. The woman with the narrow eyes and her companion had finished their cigarettes but were still standing there with their ears aimed studiously at the two friends. Declan shifted his eyes without turning his head.

"Come on, we'll go back inside," he said. "I need another pint."

When they went back into the bar a few more men had come in. Luke asked the barman to put on a pint for Declan, who nodded towards one of the newcomers, a small lean man with dark ruffled hair wearing a black denim jacket over a T-Shirt emblazoned with 'The Fall' in capital letters. He was perhaps five years older than they were.

"I'll introduce you to Conor," said Declan. "You'll get on with him. He likes music."

"Everyone likes music," said Luke with mild annoyance.

"Nah, I could take it or leave it myself. You know what I mean though, he likes the same kind of music as you. The kind that makes you think you know better than everyone else. Conor, how are you?"

Conor's eyes seemed lively and had been nipping around the room, resting for brief seconds here and there, until they engaged with Declan's greeting. "Well, Declan. Has there been anything further about that thing I reported last week?"

"Conor, this is my good friend Luke Sheridan. He's just moved in next door to me. He's into his music as well. I think you'd have a lot in common."

Luke offered his hand and Conor shook it briskly with his eyes still fixed on Declan.

"It's just that I haven't heard anything back since I reported it to you. I rang the station and they said you'd get back to me."

"Why don't you tell Luke about your podcast, Conor?"

Conor drank from the pint of lager in front of him.

"Is it a music podcast?" asked Luke politely. "What kind of stuff are you into?"

"Oh, too many to name. A flavour I guess would be … do you know Godspeed You Black Emperor? Spiritualised, of course. Not forgetting these guys"—he opened his jacket wide to show off his T-Shirt—"I worship at the altar of Mark E. Smith."

"Great," said Luke. "I like all of those. Classic stuff. I guess I'm more inclined towards experimental music though, ambient, atmospheric."

Conor pulled a face like he had tasted something sour. "Yeah, not really for me, you know. Too pretentious, that stuff. I have my own little studio back in the house where I record the show."

"And you can make a living from that?"

For a brief second Luke envisioned a life playing records in his own languorous time, relaxing at home, giving up the commute that he hadn't even started yet but was suspecting he wasn't going to enjoy.

"Conor's a farmer, Luke," Declan said with a spike of meanness in his tone. "He lives about a mile away from here on the way towards our houses."

"No, I don't make money from the podcast, not yet, I'm gaining a small listenership. It's my passion though. I give it most of my spare time."

"When you're not in here," said Declan.

"Your wife and family must be understanding," said Luke.

Conor spluttered into his pint. "Wife? No, I wouldn't have much time for any of that, I'm too busy with the farm and the music for any wife or family." He fixed those busy eyes on Declan again. "Declan, have you even bothered to check out that thing I reported? I can't stop thinking about it. That was the night before Brendan McGrath was killed, you know?"

"What's this?" Luke asked. "Is it confidential police business or can you tell me?"

Conor glanced furtively between the two men and then motioned to the barman for another drink. "Last week, the night before they killed poor Brendan McGrath, I was on my way down here when I saw someone that, well, it still gives me chills to think about him. Did you see my quad parked outside?"

Luke shook his head.

"Right, well, anyway, I have always walked down here to O'Shea's. It's not far. As Declan said, you head towards his place and take the right before you get to the Twisted Tree. I enjoy the stroll. I can plan my podcasts in my head without any distractions. As well as that, I don't believe in drink-driving, unlike a lot of people around the area, some who should know better." He glared at Declan. "Well, I won't walk on those roads anymore, not until the Guards find that fella I saw. I don't care about the legality of it. I drive the quad here and then go home again on it, nice and slowly and carefully, but if I run into him again then I want to be able to speed away as fast as I can."

"Who was he?" asked Luke.

The barman placed a pint of lager in front of Conor and, while he rooted in his pocket for money, Declan stood behind him and made the motion of smoking a big joint. Conor caught him out of the side of his eye. "Yes, yes, if it's not you as a lawman I'm talking to then I admit I often like to have a little relaxing smoke on my walk, but on that night, I had hardly anything. I know what I saw."

"But do you really know what you saw?" said Declan.

"I know it was trouble." He directed his words to Luke now. "You know the Twisted Tree, don't you? You must do."

"The rag tree?"

"Yeah, the Twisted Tree it's called around here. I don't understand how people still believe in it but there's an undercurrent still in this country of old Catholic superstitions, relics and faith healers and all that shit."

"What do you believe in, Conor?" sneered Declan.

"I don't believe in much but I've started to get scared of the things I don't believe in. I've been hearing things outside the house as well, if you want to know. I've reported that too but nobody has come out to me."

"Don't mind him," said Luke. "What was it that you saw?"

There was a plaintiveness to Conor's voice set on deep foundations. It was rooted in the solitude of being an only child and of never having particularly close friends, but since his parents had died it often took on an even lonelier timbre, one that made Luke think of the empty mutterings that accompanied handshakes at funerals. It even managed to shut Declan up for a minute.

"I was approaching the turn onto this road from mine. I was about a hundred yards away from it when I heard someone laughing in the distance. It wasn't a nice laugh. It sounded nasty and mean but also like it was in pain. When I reached the turn, I could hear it was coming from the direction of the Twisted Tree. I stopped and before going up the other way to the pub I thought I should try and see what's going on. I don't usually give a fuck what other people get up to, they can hang around or do whatever they want as long as they don't bother me, but there was something about this laugh that sounded so … unearthly, I guess, that I had to look. I walked down towards the tree. There was no sight of either the sun or the moon, just a flat, calm light, no shadows. The laughter turned into a moan. Then I saw it. At first, I thought it was a child sitting on the little stone wall around the tree. It was the height of a young boy, maybe twelve or so, but its head was far too big for its body. Its head—it may have been a mask, the size of it— but no, a mask couldn't have moved like that." Conor took a sip of his pint and gazed into it as if he was reading memories in the golden liquid.

"I didn't want to get too close, you understand, so I can't swear for sure what it was. If I had to draw it for you, I'd find it hard. It seemed like something that wasn't real. All I can do is say what it appeared like to me. The skin looked waxy and there was growth on it, a dirty, scrawny growth of hair. I could make out a pair of eyes opening and closing like it was drunk. It had a bottle in its hand. I'm not sure what it was wearing, dark clothes, undefined;

wouldn't be able to describe them. I was sort of stunned I guess, you know, like as if you come face to face with a creature that you've never expected to see in real life and it's hard to take it in."

"Maybe it was an animal?" ventured Luke.

"Are you a bit thick or something?" said Conor. "An animal? Holding a bottle? Swaying around like it's drunk? I don't know where it was from but he was trouble, that's for sure. It, him, whatever. I stopped going towards him and started to walk backwards real slowly so I could keep an eye on him. He hadn't seen me yet. Then I noticed some movement in the ditch behind him, someone coming out of it. The first person or thing or whatever the fuck it was, fell off the wall and the bottle smashed and I heard laughter coming from the other one, more cackling, nasty laughter. I turned around and ran and when I got home I rang the Garda station in Cromuck and I got onto Declan."

"We didn't find anyone, Conor," said Declan. "There was no one there."

"You didn't even go out there, I bet."

Declan drained his pint and stuck his face in close to Conor's. "Don't you fucking tell me what I did or didn't do. I'm telling you that there was nobody like that there. I'm telling you that you must have been stoned and you're talking nonsense."

"But you found the broken glass though. You must have, if you checked. I saw it the next day, kicked into the grass. Looked like a smashed wine bottle to me."

"That was from someone else. I know who's been leaving their shit there and I've sorted that out. There's nothing else out there to concern anyone. I don't need you creating nonsense work for me."

Declan pulled Luke over to him to speak privately and turned his back to Conor.

"Luke, I have to go. I have something to sort out in town. Cliona business. I need you to do me a favour. Don't go home straight away."

"What do you mean? Why?"

"I told Denise I'd be out with you until late, so if she sees your car pulling into your house, she'll wonder why I'm not back too. She'll be watching out. She doesn't trust me."

"No shit. So what am I supposed to do? Sit here on my own not drinking?"

"Ah, you can have a few pints and still drive home. It's grand. I guarantee you there won't be any checkpoints around here tonight. Have a chat with Conor about music or something, steer him away from that other shit and you'll have a good conversation. You just have to stay away till about eleven. She'll have gone to sleep by then and nothing wakes her."

Conor piped up, a boxer stunned by a blow to the head who had just sprung up from the canvas. "You can't just brush me off like that. I know what I saw. What are you doing with my report? They could have been the ones who got Brendan McGrath. They weren't from around here, that's for sure. It might have been masks on them. You have to take that seriously, masked men spotted the night before a man was killed."

"You're right, Conor! I'll get on the case straight away. I'll head out right now and start investigating. You stay here and have a drink with Luke and don't bore him too much. See you both later."

CHAPTER TEN

There was a large black slug on the floor of Elliott's bedroom. It was about a metre in from the doorway and its greasy trail shone when the sunlight hit the bare wooden floor. Sophie only noticed it when she turned around from opening the curtains, and then she felt revulsed at the thought that, but for the sake of a slightly different footstep, she might have stood on it in her bare feet. She looked over at Elliott, standing up in his cot and bouncing on his toes with excitement at the presence of his mother. She pointed at the slug and wrinkled her nose, saying, "Eughh, disgusting."

"Eughh," the baby echoed and started laughing.

She bent down to scrutinize the slug. Where had it squirmed in from? Had it been making its way up the stairs all night to get to them or did it slither through from the meagre attic space? It was longer than she thought a slug should be and its upper tentacles, pointed determinedly forward, seemed short for the size of its body. Then it moved. Its body had appeared so longbecause it was stretching obscenely towards her child's cot. The thing contracted slackly then began to lengthen once more.

"Eughh," she repeated and Elliott mimicked her again, delighted with this new sound.

Salt would sort it out. She stepped around the slug, planning its demise, but instead of going to the kitchen for salt she went into the bathroom and grabbed a handful of toilet paper. This would be quicker. She picked up the slug in the paper, taking care not to hold it too tight in case she felt it squirming between her fingers, and threw it out the window.

"Come on, little man," she said, wrapping her son up in her arms. "Let's make some brekkie."

Downstairs on the kitchen table lay Luke's used coffee cup with a quarter of its contents sitting cold at the bottom and a plate with the crumby evidence of eaten toast. Sophie had been in bed asleep when he got in from the pub last night and only stirred when he got into bed and gave her a kiss. She half-woke again at seven in the morning when he got up to his alarm, kissed her cheek again and headed off, sighing with tiredness and confusion. A strong smell of alcohol and cigarette smoke emanated from him and she wasn't particularly happy about either. She hoped the cigarette smell at least had just been from his clothes and not from his intake of them. They had worked hard together to give them up. The presence of both odours had conjured up an image of a smiling, sneering Declan in her sleepy mind. Then she had drifted into a dream where Luke had been younger, like when they had first met, and she was standing right beside him talking to him but either he couldn't hear her or he was ignoring her. It didn't take much interpretation. This would not be a good way to start their lives here, with a sneaky Declan influence trying to drag her husband into trouble.

But picturing him at work, struggling with a hangover, she felt a pang of isolation. Elliott slapped his hands down on his high chair and the feeling dissipated, but she was still impelled to send him a text: 'How was your first commute?'

She took two bowls, filled hers with cereal and Elliott's with rusk, and chopped a banana into both of them.

The text came back from Luke: 'horrible xxx'. Sophie could discern his misery crystallized in those sad little lowercase letters. He missed her. He was still all hers.

The sun was shining and green, hilly fields were framed by the kitchen window. This was a good place to be. It was good for Elliott and it would be good for them. She had grown up in a rural area very like this, about two hours' drive west, and she knew all the good points of living there and the sense of calm it could bring. But she also knew how awkward it could be. Growing up, she remembered always being reliant on her parents for lifts to go anywhere; a sense of disconnect with what was happening out in the world. She had two sisters close in age that tempered any chance of boredom, but they may as well have been the last children on earth outside of school term. She fed Elliott a spoonful of his breakfast. They'd have to make more children, that was for sure. For a long time, Sophie had imagined they might end up living in the city, in some modern apartment block with well-kept communal gardens, and in that situation, she could envision just the one child, but city prices and the opportunity of this house had turned their heads quite quickly and, if she was to live in the countryside, then she wanted a small bundle of kids to enjoy it with.

Since the plan to move out here had been hatched, she had researched and forecast what her practical life might be like. Optimistically, she had imagined scores of remote workers like her, happy in their space, getting together occasionally in small-town cafés, chatting about how they didn't really miss the hectic pace of Dublin, the crowds, the smog. Having read an article forecasting that self-driving electric cars would eventually come to the rescue of the worn-down commuters like Luke was cursed to become, she played a game with him trying to work out how many more car purchases they would make until it would be a little electric, web-connected, pod type vehicle within which they could work, watch TV or sleep on their way to wherever they needed to be. It had to happen in her lifetime. Look how much had changed in the world since she was a kid.

Coffee drank, Sophie spent a while playing on the floor with Elliott. He seemed more interested in his building blocks than in her company so she daydreamed about ideas for the interior of the house. They had ages to do it, she wasn't in any rush to start painting or furniture shopping, but now they were physically in the house she could enjoy planning the style of the place with a long-term budget. She wandered round with a measuring tape and her phone, holding pictures of colour samples up against walls until lunchtime.

After eating, Elliott went for a nap and she took herself outside to get some fresh air and turn her imagination to the back garden. Brambles had taken over one corner of the garden and were beginning to fruit. She picked a few of the dark berries and popped them straight into her mouth, relishing their softness, amazed at how sweet they were. The heavy plants spread deep and wide and the creeping stalks had smothered parts of a flower bed in which some shy flowers were barely surviving. They had better get on top of the garden as a priority over the inside of the house while the weather was still good and the area hadn't succumbed completely to weeds and neglect. Anyway, that would be more enjoyable than painting walls and hanging blinds. That was another reason why they had moved out here, to spend more life outside. She would buy gloves and garden tools before anything else.

But there might be some already here, the unpainted concrete shed beckoned her. Maybe it contained a trove of tools and gardening equipment. The bolt on the door slid across agreeably to give her access. Inside, the air was grainy and dusty. Sophie dug out a set of shears hanging on a nail among the cobwebs on the wall and snipped at some thorny tendrils which were crawling through the long grass of the lawn. Nettles lightly stung her hands but she kept going. Thorns pricked her unprotected fingers when she pulled the brambles away but she didn't mind. A bee flew up from some clover, annoyed at her intrusion, so she stood up to allow it to find a different place to gather its nectar. She heard a song in the still air. For a second, she thought it was a radio playing, until she realised the voice was flat and tuneless and unaccompanied by music. It was coming from out on the road. She scooted round the side of the house. A young woman, not long out of her teens, was perched outside her gate on a bicycle. When the girl saw Sophie approaching, she stopped singing and removed her earphones.

"Hiya," said the girl.

"Hello there," said Sophie. "Nice day for a cycle."

The girl beheld the sky and shrugged as if she wasn't sure. "Is Luke there?"

"Luke? No, my husband is at work. How do you know him?"

"Ah, of course," said the girl. "At the museum, I suppose."

"Excuse me?" Sophie's eyebrows furrowed. "What do you want with Luke?"

"Oh, I was just cycling by and I thought I'd say hi. It doesn't matter. I'll drop by another time." She put the earphones back in and cycled off casually.

"What's your name?" Sophie called after her but the girl didn't hear. Sophie walked back to the house, the rusty shears still in her hands. She put them down carelessly on the floor of the hall before checking on Elliott. He was just starting to stir. She had an odd feeling, a feeling that she couldn't quite place. Everything was quiet, as if the land beyond the house stretched on forever, friendless and silent. The words in her mind were just dumb noises that nobody wanted to hear.

She thought of calling over to Denise and asking her if she knew this rosy-cheeked young cyclist that had disturbed her. Not that she thought there was anything suspicious about the fact she somehow knew Luke. If there had been then she wouldn't have brazenly turned up at the gate asking for him, but she was perturbed by the girl's manner, the fact she hadn't introduced herself, and she found it odd that Luke wouldn't have mentioned that he had met someone local. Unless he met her at the pub last night. She didn't seem the type to be bothered with somewhere like O'Shea's.

No, she didn't really want to talk about any of this with Denise. Thinking of Denise, however, reminded her of the strange, gothic plant she had liked when she was there yesterday. She was intrigued by the mind behind it and remembered how Denise had said she might get along with her. Denise had given her directions to where the woman lived but those directions had mostly consisted of taking turns at odd place names or going past houses of people whom Sophie didn't know. Instead, she searched online for nurseries or florists in Kilcross and uncovered a basic and amateurish website for *Roisin's Gothic Garden*. It was indeed run by a woman called Roisin Kelly and, despite the poor quality of the website, it at least had her sat nav coordinates. It was less than three miles away. She put Elliott and his changing bag into the car and followed the directions for the few minutes of small winding roads that it took her to get there.

Chapter Eleven

Roisin's Gothic Garden was at the top of a steep hill on a bend. Sophie's engine cut out when she hesitated on the incline, admiring the entrance. It was a large, cast-iron archway smothered by a tangle of rose bushes and brambles. A dark shrub with harsh spikes wove its thin branches through it like strangling fingers. Two large, stone pots with gargoyle faces stood at either side of the opening, each overflowing with curling ferns. Sophie restarted the car and manoeuvred through the entrance to park beside a small cottage with a ramshackle extension to its rear. She took Elliott's little stroller out of the car boot and popped him into it, his eyes widening at the myriad of growth that enclosed the site. Shrubs and trees jostled for space. A congregation of beech trees were so lush they might have just reached down their branches and picked up armfuls of leaves. Sophie recognised silvery willow like whispering ghosts and a line of tall, thin ash trees that put her in mind of starving people queuing for food. A clump of black-stemmed bamboo shaded the entrance to a large greenhouse, at which, she now noticed, a woman watched her from its door.

"Can I help you?" The woman wore a black T-Shirt and heavy gardening gloves. A black headband kept dark curls of hair out of her eyes. Sophie guessed her to be in her late forties.

"Are you Roisin?" said Sophie, pushing the stroller towards the greenhouse. "My name is Sophie Sheridan. I've just moved to the area. I'm only around five minutes' drive that way"—she waved vaguely behind her—"I saw one of your plants in Denise Maguire's house yesterday."

"Who?"

"Denise Maguire. Married to Declan Maguire, the Garda. It was him who bought it for her."

"Oh, Denise Weldon," said Roisin. "Yes, I actually remember him coming round to buy that. Rude and in a rush, that's our Garda Maguire. Wasn't it a Zamioculcas … sorry, a Raven plant in a bashed-up bucket? God knows why he bought it for her. She doesn't like things like that. She likes pretty things."

"I think he forgot it was their anniversary and needed a gift in a hurry."

"Ha!"

"And you're right I'm afraid, she didn't like it. I thought it was very interesting though. She actually offered to give it away to me. That's why I came round here, to see what other sort of plants you had."

"Did you take it?"

"No, it felt wrong, with it being a present from Declan."

"I wish you had, I'd rather someone who wanted it had it. Jesus, he's a fool, that man," said Roisin. Sophie's demeanour betrayed a brief discomfort. "Oh sorry, I hope he's not a friend of yours."

"He is actually, well originally a friend of my husband," said Sophie. "They go back years, but you're right. He is a bit of a fool."

Roisin leaned in to Elliott and made a face at him. He had been staring at her warily during the conversation and the change in her serious expression to one with her tongue sticking out sent him into giggles.

"I knew her father better than I know Denise," said Roisin. "Willy was a sour, opinionated old man. He spoiled her rotten and she developed a mean streak way before she hit her teens, if I remember her right."

"It's the Weldon's old house we bought, actually. We didn't get to know him, I'm afraid but I'm starting to notice that mean streak in her."

"Well, it was hard for them, losing her mother before she was sixteen. I don't blame him for turning the way he did. I had a lot of time for him actually, despite his manner. He was very much into gardening." Roisin removed her gloves and tucked them into her belt. "He used to call round sometimes to see what I was growing and to complain about everyone else in the parish. It was amazing in the end that anyone showed up at his funeral. He could be very entertaining in his bitterness though; he could find fault with anything. Apart from Denise of course."

"We were at his funeral," said Sophie.

"They seem right for each other, in a horrible sort of way. What Declan reminds me of is the most troublesome boy in the class, misbehaving for no reason apart from pure devilment. Then someone like that joins the Gardaí and gets a modicum of power." She shook her head. "You shouldn't give power or responsibility to someone like that."

"You sound more like a teacher than a gardener," Sophie winked.

"Ha," laughed Roisin. "Has someone been talking about me? I suppose the good thing about him being with Denise is that if they're with each other it spares other people from them."

"I wouldn't count on that."

"So, can I get you something to drink, Sophie? Tea, coffee? I was just about to put the kettle on."

"Coffee would be nice. Just black."

"Won't be a second. Sorry, it's just the instant crap."

Roisin nipped in to the cottage and Sophie took the opportunity to lift Elliott out for a cuddle and a nappy inspection that turned out to be all clear. Roisin returned with two mugs.

"I was out in the garden this morning," said Sophie as she returned Elliott to his seat and away from the risk of hot drinks. "It's starting to get overrun by weeds and brambles but we'll get to it."

"You have that little fellow to concentrate on tending to as your first priority. Maybe Willy's ghost will come back to give you a hand in the garden."

Sophie smiled. "Do you have kids?"

"No, my husband and I never got round to it. We spent a lot of time around them, of course. We both taught in Cromuck Secondary School. That's where we met. I taught Biology and he taught Accounting."

"And does he run this place with you now?"

"No," said Roisin. "He's dead. Come on into the greenhouse and you can have a look at what we have."

Sophie followed the woman into the greenhouse, carefully parking Elliott's stroller at the narrow entrance.

The first thing she noticed were hanging baskets suspended from the rafters. They contained mixtures of black grasses and dark flowers that hinted of poisonous fragrances. The baskets themselves were woven of an earthy brown fabric held together by black metal mesh, but the ropes from which they hung caught her eye most of all. They were thick brown cords which encircled the bottom of the baskets and gathered above them in a knot that recalled a hangman's noose.

"I'm sorry," said Sophie, "about your husband. Was it recent?"

Roisin began putting compost in a foot long container that was shaped exactly like a coffin. Sophie could see more of them on the benches with lurid veiny ivy spilling over the sides, surrounding a dark iris that sprouted from where the head might be if a corpse sat up in them.

"Five years ago. Is that recent?"

"I guess …"

"It feels like it is, but in another way, it feels like I've been doing this Gothic Garden business forever, and I only started it after he died. I couldn't go back to teaching after it happened. I started doing this because I love plants and I like the dark side of things. To tell you the truth I don't really need to earn much money. Gavin's life insurance paid off the mortgage. I don't spend much, I don't do much. I just like to do this."

"Well, it's probably just as well you don't need the money." Sophie tried to lighten the tone. "I had a look at your website to find your address. I'm surprised you manage to get any custom at all through that."

"Ha!" Roisin laughed. "My nephew set that up for me. He knows a bit about that sort of thing but he's not very creative. I think he did it just to keep on side with me so I'll remember him in my will."

"Well, I don't want to do anyone out of their inheritance, but I would love to have a go at doing something for you. I'm a freelance graphic designer, I could design a basic website for you, at neighbour's rates."

"Why? You don't know me."

"I just like what you're doing. I like to work on things that are interesting. That's more important than money."

"You obviously care enough about money to be able to buy a house. Or else your husband does. That's not easy these days, even out here in the sticks."

"We just about scraped it. We'd rather have time than money though. Especially with this little man." She beamed down at Elliott. "Hopefully Luke's commute won't become too awful though. We're worried about that. He's still working in Dublin but who can afford to buy in Dublin?"

"Sure. Ok then," said Roisin. "Come round again tomorrow and tell me what ideas you have and what kind of money neighbour's rates means. I'll make you up a special basket as a welcome present."

"So how do you manage to attract customers?" said Sophie. "You must have a good few. I'm sure you're not growing this amount of stuff to let it rot in its pots."

"No. I have a lot of regular customers. Not many new ones in the last while though. I had some good publicity back when I was starting off. A goth couple I knew got me to do the flowers for their wedding. I guess they were only having a church wedding for their parents' sake. I went all out with the displays, because it was my first big job. I wanted to make a statement, Black Calla Lilies, Black Hollyhock, Black Velvet Petunias."

"Lot of black."

"Oh yes. The priest didn't like it though, funny considering his choice of clothes. He called them the devil's flowers and refused to perform the ceremony with them in the church. We had to take them all out and transfer them to the hotel for the reception. Then the following week he announced in his sermon that he wouldn't allow my arrangements at any wedding, funeral or christening in the parish. A local journalist got wind of it and wrote an article. The national radio stations jumped on it as their quirky story of the week and suddenly I had an influx of interest from all over the country. Biker funerals, alternative weddings, some private parties that I won't describe to you over coffee."

"And that keeps you going?"

"A lot of customers have stayed loyal but I haven't had any more priests giving me publicity from the pulpit. So, if you can design something that could help then I'll happily change that website. I know I said I'm not in need of a lot but I do want to be able to keep the business viable. This is the only thing that keeps me going since Gavin died, and there's no way in hell I'm going back to teaching."

"Why would you not go back to teaching?"

Roisin went over to a blue glass pot with a skull and crossbones etched on it above the word 'Poison' and, in brackets underneath, 'Black Pansy'. A bunch of stunning black silky-petalled flowers sprouted from the soil within. She poured a murky liquid from a large clear bottle into it.

"It was the school, I guess, as much as teaching. When I went back after Gavin died, I began to see the worst in everything. I noticed cruelness and bullying among the children that I hadn't been aware of before. I heard snide comments out of their mouths that I must have been oblivious to in the past. Maybe it was me, I wasn't sleeping right still and everything in that school was reminding me of Gavin's death. He died there, you see."

"He died in the school?"

"Yes. It was winter time, after the school day had finished. I was giving grinds to some of the students and the school allowed me to use my classroom after hours. There was no point in Gavin driving home then having to come back in for me, so he would usually correct papers in his own classroom to make use of the time. It was cold, a real old building. It was especially cold in the part of the school where his classroom was situated, but he kept a portable heater in the cupboard and if he was staying after class, he would bring it out beside his desk. You know those Superser ones with the gas cylinder?"

Sophie nodded and put down her coffee cup. She felt like she was listening to a ghost story beside a midnight campfire rather than in an afternoon greenhouse.

"He looked like Bob Cratchit there," Roisin continued. "Shivering beside his little heater with a stack of papers beside him and his coat buttoned up. It didn't always work properly though, that heater, it was an old one and Gavin wasn't very good with things like that. He was brilliant at organising our bank accounts and getting the best deals on the utility bills but he wouldn't have been able to change a tyre and I don't think he was even sure how to go about replacing a lightbulb. He just didn't have a head for practical stuff at all. So, I believe that when the heater wasn't lighting, he got down in front of it and just kept clicking away at the switch to ignite it. The switch wasn't working but gas must have been releasing out all the time. I know that if his mind was preoccupied with his work, he wouldn't even have been aware of the smell. Apparently one of his students had been messing around with a lighter earlier in class and Gavin had confiscated it. He must have taken it out of the drawer and leaned down to see if he could get in to where the spark should ignite. The flame was set very high."

Elliott cooed, like he had met an imaginary friend. Sophie turned to see his fingers raised in wonder and she stepped out of the greenhouse.

"Do you know what annoyed me?" said Roisin, following her. "They kept saying afterwards that he mustn't have suffered that much. They said that because the injuries to his face were so bad, he likely passed out from the shock before he died. But I knew they were just lying to me. He wasn't even in his classroom when he was found. His shirt was wet with water as well as blood so he must have run to the toilets and doused himself with water before running back out into the hall. The school secretary found him collapsed against a wall. Myself and the few others staying back late came running when we heard her screaming. I could see his face and I could see his fingers and it looked like he had been trying to tear away at the burning pain of his face. I took nine months of compassionate leave and then I thought I could go back. I thought I could go back to the same school. I thought it was what Gavin would have wanted but I just kept seeing him around every corner, slumped against every wall with his face burned away."

She took off her gardening gloves and brushed a stray curl of hair from her eyes.

"I'm a barrel of laughs, aren't I? I'm bet you're glad you and your son came round to visit me. Well, Sophie, if you still want to come round tomorrow then eleven is a good time."

"I'll … I'll still come round," said Sophie.

Elliott watched a wasp fly over towards his nose. Roisin stepped over and steered it away from the child.

Chapter Twelve

On the way home from Roisin's Gothic Garden, Sophie chatted away to Elliott. She often chatted to him about other people and social mores that were way beyond his monosyllabic concepts, but she figured the language might seep into him and when he learned how to speak, he might attain a huge vocabulary very quickly. Also, it gave her a real sense of having him as a companion. She was sharing herself with him in a way that was deeper than just the words she said. She spoke to him now about the new person they had met. Roisin had certainly left an impression with her tragic story and her greenhouse of grief. Even in the daylight there had been an unnerving sense of doom about the place, almost as if it was growing with the sinister artistry imbued in each floral display. She was sometimes too empathetic for her own good. There was a sadness in that woman that Sophie would more likely get entangled in than help Roisin rise out of.

One of the reasons Luke was such a good match for her was because he had none of that sort of darkness about him. He had an airiness that some might have mistaken for being shallow but which buoyed her and left her feeling secure. With Roisin, she could already feel she was attracted to her tragedy as if it was a physical thing, an actual object that she could hold and examine and be fascinated by. She explained all this to her son. Elliott just gurgled his best attempt at saying 'Mama'.

Then Sophie spotted something on their side of the road that she hadn't noticed on the outbound trip. She pulled the car over. She found the very idea of fly-tipping hateful and disgusting. She couldn't fathom the selfishness and ignorance that would lead somebody to take their waste and throw it on the side of the road where it would become someone else's or nature's problem. The sneakiness of it repulsed her as much as anything. There were three white plastic bags, bulging with rubbish, lying in the grass verge. One had split open and old food packaging spewed out from it. There seemed to be crumpled paper in amongst the rubbish too, maybe letters, maybe letters with names and addresses.

"Right," she said to her son. "I'm going to investigate this crime and bring the perpetrators to justice."

She got out of the car and noticed there was broken glass near her front tyre. There were smashed wine bottles in among the bags and the debris had infested the side of the road.

"Ah shit."

She was only two minutes' drive from home. She reckoned that even if she had a puncture, she'd likely make it back, and she could worry about it in the driveway rather than on the side of the road. First, though, she wanted to examine the discarded rubbish. She found a small branch in the ditch and poked at the scattered papers on the ground. They were mostly takeaway wrappers, stained with ketchup. She poked through the bag that was split open and saw more paper, junk mail. She figured some mail shots might be personalised from people signing up to things. There might be an address. One of the scraps looked promising with a neat square of text. She tried to pull it towards her with her branch but only managed to flip it over.

"Shit."

It was demeaning to be prodding at someone's dumped rubbish, but they deserved to be reported. She stepped off the road into the grass, risking messing up her shoes. Then a roll of movement in the undergrowth froze her. She had switched off the engine but left the car window open so she could hear Elliott. She looked back at the car tyre resting on sparkles of dark green glass. She prodded at one of the flyers in the bag with her stick, trying to drag it out towards her. That movement again. Was that a groan?

She craned her neck to see over the ditch. Perhaps livestock in the field had made the noise. No. It was empty apart from some distant sheep, too far away to be heard. Elliott whimpered.

"I'll be finished in a minute, little man."

There was another groaning sound as she spoke and her nostrils were filled with a disgusting smell that cut through the stench from the rubbish bags, a smell like shit and vomit. The grass moved. Elliott started to bawl, a persistent and panicky cry that grasped at her heart. Sophie dropped her stick and backed away towards her car, feeling nauseous and confused. She kept her eyes on the part of the ditch where she had seen the grass stir. A thick growth of long nettles beside it started to shake. The back of her leg touched the car and she spun round. There was a long shard of glass sticking out of the tyre. Surely that hadn't been there before. It nearly looked like it had been stabbed into the rubber, right in one of the threads. She scurried round to the driver's door and got in. Elliott wouldn't stop crying.

"It's ok, Elliott, it's ok, we're going home now."

As she drove away, the car drifted towards the left on its deflating tyre, but she kept going. Something stopped her from looking in the rear-view mirror, even to check on her son, until she had pulled up to their gate and had to get out and open it. Breathing heavily, she braved a view back down the road, but the spot where she had been stopped was too far back to be seen. She parked up. She cursed at the shredded tyre but her dismay at that was way below her concern for her son. She took Elliott into her arms, went inside and kissed his sobbing face until he calmed down.

It was half past four. She texted Luke to see when he thought he'd be home. She found a number to call at the local council to report fly-tipping, got an answering machine, and left a message describing the road she had seen it on and her name and number. Luke replied to say he was hoping to get a bus at half past five but when and where exactly that would deposit him, he couldn't say for sure. She made mashed vegetables for Elliott and pasta with chicken for herself, leaving enough for Luke to heat up later. By the time Luke rang her at seven o'clock she could barely remember the sick and frightened feeling that had come over her earlier.

CHAPTER THIRTEEN

Luke was going to buy another car. He was going to buy a nice small car, easy on diesel and fast and he was going to transfer his whole music collection to digital format and have it all in the car so he could immerse himself in whatever album fluttered into his memory and be happily insulated from bad weather or traffic outside. He was going to buy it on his next day off, this Saturday, no delay, and he didn't care how much it cost, as long as it didn't cost more than five grand, that is. He reckoned he could get what he wanted for about five grand judging by the car seller's websites he was scrolling through while squashed, standing in the aisle of the bus between heavy-coated commuters. Maybe six grand. Definitely no more than seven. Luke was never getting this bus again, that was for sure. The bus was horrible.

When he first got on, he was dismayed that all the seats were taken. He had a book ready to hand, already taken out of his bag, to sit back and delve into for the slow, lumbering journey, but he had nowhere to sit. He couldn't figure out how it was full already, he had thought this was the first stop.

An older man got on behind him with resignation on his face and a small sports bag on his back. The bright casual bag contrasted with his drab business suit.

"Is it always this full?" Luke asked him, feigning good humour.

"Sometimes it's worse," said the man glumly.

Worse? Luke surveyed the trail of people standing behind him and forcing him further and tighter down the vehicle. How could it be worse? Where would they put them?

He was extremely tired and, although the headache that had plagued him throughout the morning had faded, he feared that the stuffiness of this bus was going to bring it roaring back. He had gotten up on time that morning, despite only getting to bed around half twelve and with the nervous guilt of having driven home from O'Shea's with four pints of Guinness in his belly and half a pack of cigarettes in his lungs. The journey up in the van had been hellish. The first part, on his country roads, had gone by in a blur. It made him shudder to realise that he couldn't remember it. Then he hit the main roads, and he met the traffic. He had expected that he would have gotten to the van rental depot before it even opened and been waiting outside it, listening to the morning news, but every road he turned onto from before the outskirts of the city was rammed with traffic. It was gone half past nine before he dropped the van back. His worries about the scratches on the side of the van from Saturday made no impression on the flat, bored expression of the young man he handed the keys back to. Luke asked him if they wanted to inspect for damage so he wouldn't get any credit card surprises later but the man just said, "Vans get bumps and dents, I wouldn't worry about it."

Getting from the rental depot to the museum took another fifteen minutes of walking to a bus stop, then a plodding bus ride, then more walking, so he was full of apologies and excuses when he finally bustled into work close to eleven. He was glad that Sophie had texted him to ask about his commute. It made him feel closer to her and Elliott and when he pictured them it was against a background of the lush green surroundings of their peaceful new house. That would be worth the extra travel every day. He didn't have the most productive work day, being tired and listless and a little hungover, and he earned a few raised eyebrows when he left before five to try and get the homeward bus he was planning on. He had spent a lot of his day checking out the options for his return commute but he couldn't dispel the feeling that there was some sort of code to public transport information that he just didn't seem to be able to crack.

The journey out of Dublin was as uncomfortable as it was meandering, but when the bus finally got past the outskirts of the city it had deposited enough people that there was a seat for Luke to squash into and attempt to read. When they stopped in the first large town after Dublin, he went up to talk to the driver as some passengers disembarked. He popped into the seat behind him and tapped him on the shoulder. The driver, hugely overweight, strained to turn around and signalled for Luke to come round in front of him. With the fat of his neck now huddling comfortably on the cushion of his chest, the man spoke. "What can I do for you, young man?"

"I'm just wondering where is the best place for me to get off. Which way do you go after Cromuck?"

"Which way do you want to go?"

"Do you know the village of Kilcross?"

"I do."

"Do you go near there?"

"I can drop you at O'Shea's pub," said the driver with a tone that suggested that if he had the choice he'd be getting off at O'Shea's with Luke.

"That's great. What time will we be there at, more or less?"

"Half seven, on the button. Now that we're out of the city it's plain sailing."

"Ok, great."

Luke was almost starting to warm to the idea of bus travel as represented by this corpulent font of knowledge. Maybe if he could just get into a set routine then it might be an option for him. Now that there were seats available the bus was quite comfortable. Imagine the amount of reading he could get through on his weekly commute if he didn't have to keep his eyes fixed on the road. Or if he was tired, he could have little bus naps.

"And tell me," he said, "does this bus pass O'Shea's in the morning time as well? I was on the website but it was hard to figure out the routes."

"Which bus?" said the driver cryptically.

"This bus," said Luke.

"Well, it does sometimes, if it's doing the 139A route or sometimes the 139C, but that only goes once a week, usually on Thursdays. The thing to watch out for, though, is if it's the 139A then it can take over two hours to get to Dublin because it meanders through a lot of places for little pick-ups."

"Over two hours!" said Luke.

"Unless it's the 139 Express."

"Oh, and how long does that take?"

The driver waved off the last of the passengers for that stop and slowly pulled away.

"Depends on the time of day, but if it's rush hour it would usually be an hour and a half or thereabouts, as long as there's no major delays."

"Oh right. That's not too bad I suppose."

"Of course, the Express doesn't go past O'Shea's," said the driver.

"Right," said Luke, and he slunk back dispiritedly to his seat. He rang Sophie.

"Hi baby," he said when she answered.

"Hey. How are you getting on? I thought you'd be back by now."

"This public transport lark is not going to be an option for me, I think. I can't work it out for a start."

Sophie laughed at the frustration in her husband's voice.

"It's not funny, Sophie. I'm going out this Saturday to get us a second car. Driving is the only way to get to work from out there and I don't like leaving you and Elliott without any transport from one end of the week to the other."

"Yes, I know. Well, we thought we'd have to do that, didn't we? Just I thought we were going to try and wait a bit until money wasn't quite as tight."

"I know, I know, that was the plan, but I didn't realise how bad the commute was going to be. It's bad enough in a car but it's impossible any other way. This bus will drop me at O'Shea's at half seven and you'll have to pick me up from there."

"Oh," said Sophie glumly.

"Oh?"

"I can't pick you up from there."

"Why not?" said Luke. His mind quickly jogged back over the night before and that morning leaving the house. "Are you annoyed with me about something?" A sliver of guilt passed through him, whispering reasons that she might be annoyed. Its voice was Declan's voice and it reeked of cigarettes and irresponsibility.

"No. Should I be annoyed about something? You had a visitor today, by the way. Some young woman on a bike. Who's she, I wonder?"

"A blonde girl?" said Luke. "I met her the other day."

"What's her name? She seemed to know a lot about you."

"I don't know her name. Every time I meet her, she disappears before telling me her name."

"Every time?" said Sophie. "How many times have you met her?"

"I mean, just twice. Sophie, don't be silly. I have a headache and I'm exhausted. I stayed out longer than I had planned last night. I'm paying for it now. Please come and pick me up. Pretty please. I just want to snuggle up with you and Elliott on the couch."

"Aw, poor little Luke had too many pints with his friend last night. I'd love to pick you up but I can't. The car has a puncture. We were out visiting this woman … it's a long story, but there was glass on the road and the tyre is wrecked. I haven't had a chance to try and change it. I was hoping you'd do it when you got home. Come on, you do the manly thing and change the tyre and I'll forgive you for having your affair with your silly bicycle girl."

Luke sighed. "Ok, ok. I'll try and get some other way home from O'Shea's. Maybe Declan will come and get me. I suppose it's not too much of a walk otherwise."

"That's the spirit. We'll be waiting here with open arms."

"Bye, bye." Luke hung up and slumped back into his seat. He closed his eyes and hung just on the cusp of sleep with the soft thrum of the bus's engine lulling him towards slumber and the drivetime conversation on the driver's radio dragging him out of it until finally a voice broke through both sounds over the bus's PA system. "O'Shea's pub. Wakey, wakey, buddy, it's your stop for O'Shea's."

He roused himself, blinking idiotically at the few people left on the bus, and walked down the aisle.

"Thanks very much," he mumbled to the driver.

"See you again," smiled the driver and he waved a pudgy hand.

Luke stood outside O'Shea's and took a deep breath. The road to his house twisted into the distance like an endless grey snake. He contemplated the walk and both his legs and back ached with pre-emptive exhaustion. Time to see if Declan would come to the rescue. He sauntered round the corner of the pub, phone raised to his ear. A chunky, red quad bike shared the car park with a navy Toyota Corolla that had been tucked into the corner like it didn't want to be bothered.

"Hey, what's the story?" Declan answered.

"Not much. Just a bit stranded. Do you fancy collecting me from O'Shea's?"

"O'Shea's …"

"Yeah, the car has a flat so Sophie can't do it. Are you still at work?"

"No."

"So, you're at home?"

"No."

"So?"

Declan sounded like there were a myriad of things taking his attention away from this conversation.

"Yeah, should be able to. I'll give you a call back in a few minutes, ok Luke?"

The call went dead and Luke walked over to the door that led into the bar via the shop, pushed it open and wallowed for a second in the comforting, dusky air of the pub. No better place to wait.

CHAPTER FOURTEEN

Roisin Kelly checked on the lasagne in the oven and decided to give it ten minutes more than the suggested half hour cooking time. These ready meals were always telling lies. She piled some lettuce on a plate, chopped some tomatoes and sprinkled oil and balsamic vinegar over them. Dessert would come from her land. She took another bowl and went outside.

Over her back door a high wattage bulb flickered behind a metal grill like an angry firefly in a cage. She walked away from its erratic illumination and past her greenhouse. The area to the rear of the greenhouse was small but crowded. There wasn't a whole lot of lawn left to grow up between all the statues and fountains she had collected there. There were gargoyles and large foreboding dogs of chipped and weathered stone. It was a surprise that birds came down to the bird baths and feeders in amongst them—the fearsome stone lion and the creepy goblins—but the garden was always filled with their chirping and songs. There were three benches which she had the choice of to sit on and read or think or drink. The one she liked best was the cast iron bench that sat furthest away from the house in the shade of a sad, twisted willow. Also beside that bench was the cluster of raspberry bushes which she was heading for now. She didn't cut back the garden too much, instead letting it grow full and wild, but she was careful to keep control over the raspberry bushes, so their eager shoots wouldn't take over. She switched on the torch tucked under her arm so as to be able to identify the ripe berries. The soft red fruit pulled easily from the bush and soon filled her bowl. This was one of the first plants she had planted in the garden back when she and Gavin had first moved here. He had been majorly impressed with the return from the bushes for so little work and compared it to the cost of buying raspberries from the shop. *The savings they made were as delicious to him as the fruit itself*, she thought. It wasn't that Gavin was mean or particularly tight with money, but he derived an intellectual pleasure from such achievements. Other fruit bushes were dotted around the garden but none were so abundant as the raspberries and she had always preferred the slight tang and richness of their taste than that of the blackcurrants, blueberries and redcurrants.

Roisin strolled back through the lawn, noting its length playing at her ankles, and promised herself she would cut it before it got too thick. Back in the kitchen she left the raspberries to soak in water while she dished out her dinner.

Most evenings were like this for Roisin since she had settled into life without her husband. She would work in the garden and greenhouse until early evening, prepare an uncomplicated dinner accompanied by a glass of wine, and spend the evening either reading or watching a movie before going to bed early. She rose early in the day so that she would be tired enough to sleep before midnight. She didn't change her routine for weekends except to fit in grocery shopping on a Sunday afternoon.

The movies Roisin watched and the books she read were predominantly of the horror genre. When Gavin died, she had expected her taste in this would have changed, that she would no longer have the stomach for the shocks and gore she had always loved since her teens but, if anything, she found herself drawn more towards the milieu. She could still remember the thrill of wandering into the horror section of her local video store in her early teens and being transfixed by the trashy glory of the covers that all declared that she was too young to watch them. Her parents were avid readers and she would search among their bookshelves for anything that seemed forbidden or terrifying. Occasionally she found old, slightly damp collections of short stories with garish cover art that had survived the page-thumbings of a string of family members before meeting her excited mind. She remembered curling up in her bed with an illicit reading light and finding the fear more perverse for the fact that she had chosen to inflict it on herself.

As she grew older her tastes were reflected in her clothes, the music she listened to and the friends she spent time with. It was maybe her lack of squeamishness that allowed her to excel at biology in school then university. Her personality was more open than gloomy, however, and everyone who knew her thought she was making a great choice by then opting for teacher's college. Even there she made no secret of her obsession with the macabre, so much so that by the time she was doing her teaching placement her pupils plumped straight for the nickname that would best befit her maiden name: Witchy Mitchell.

With his fusty, beige accountant's style, Gavin struck an almost comical contrast by her side but she knew the fierce depths of his devotion to her.

Roisin chased the last forkful of her lasagne around the plate before deciding not to eat it. When they started to live together Gavin would force himself to watch the occasional horror movie or television series with her, but it was really just a hobby for her to enjoy alone. She liked to step back from the day job of teaching Biology to unruly teenagers by losing herself in the scariest stories she could find. Gavin liked to unwind from teaching accountancy to bored kids by watching and reading the scariest economic forecasts he could find. So, when he was gone, she had lost her companion in her life but not in her interests.

She was sure that watching zombies with their faces rotting off or gruesome spectres with the bones exposed through their ghostly skin would upset her too much after seeing the horrible aftermath of Gavin's death but, after all the family mourners had left her alone and the visitors had stopped calling to pay their condolences, she found herself itching to watch something that would scare her out of feeling so sad. She needed something that might give her nightmares strong enough to dislodge the recurring one where her late husband screamed in agony as he clawed at his burning face and which left her feeling empty and isolated and burned out inside when she woke.

A glass of wine and bowl of raspberries accompanied her to the sitting room. The perusal of tonight's nasty viewing choices was distracted by the memory of her visitor from earlier in the day, Sophie Sheridan.

Roisin didn't get many visitors. Since Willy Weldon had died, she didn't have any company that she might call regular. Now here was this Sophie woman and her cute little boy. It would be funny if this bright, appealing woman came to replace the gruff, critical Weldon as a new companion.

It wasn't that Roisin craved company but she knew deep down that it was necessary if she wanted to keep going. If she thought of the future—and she usually tried not to—then she knew that times may come when she would neglect her gardening and her plants would die in their pots, food and drink wouldn't interest her or she would forget to eat. Movies and books wouldn't hold her interest then. She wasn't sure if that scenario was inevitable but, to have any chance of avoiding it, she knew she needed somebody checking in on her. At the heart of things, she couldn't see this life she was living lasting for many more years but if there were distractions from the sadness and the loneliness, if there were distractions to stop her dwelling on her nightmares, then she would just keep on going. At the moment, with the Halloween season just over the horizon, she was excited by her work. She gave up on choosing a movie and started to think of what sort of basket she could make for Sophie as promised. Those 'hanging' baskets with their nooses had taken up the last few days so she fancied doing something different. She took a sip of her wine and ate the last raspberry from her bowl. The deep redness. She would make one of her old 'bloodbaths'. She would start on it now. Why not? She could work whenever she wanted, she could do whatever she liked whenever suited her. Roisin went out to her greenhouse, topping up her glass on the way.

CHAPTER FIFTEEN

Luke loved the heavy smell of stale alcohol and wood and the dim, windowless light that never worried what it was like outside. He could stay in a pub like this forever. As he suspected, Conor was sitting at the bar on the same stool he had occupied the night before but Luke didn't really care who else was in the pub. He just wanted a nice pint of Guinness. He raised his eyes in greeting to the young barman, Ollie, who indicated questioningly to the black tap. Luke nodded. There was a warmth in being acknowledged, of settling into a predictable and cosy place.

"And whatever Conor is having," he said.

Conor turned around. His clump of dark hair was sticking up in tufts that accentuated his surprise at seeing Luke.

"Well, man. How are you? What has you in here again?"

"I'm just back from work," said Luke. "Bloody public transport is an absolute nightmare from Dublin."

"Would you not drive?"

"I would normally, but I had to leave a rental van back and now our car has a puncture and Declan isn't in a hurry to give me a lift back."

A pint of Guinness and a pint of Carlsberg landed on the bar and both men swept back nearly half of each with their first gulp.

"I'll give you a lift," said Conor. His eyes were like watery red shells that hadn't slept a whole lot since Luke had last seen him.

"You will?"

"Course I will. Sure, you're a neighbour now, aren't you? We'll just have a few more pints and then I'll take you back."

"Oh, great, thanks. Well, if Declan gets back to me soon then he can drop me home but if not then … I'm fairly tired and Sophie will be … well, I suppose one or two more wouldn't hurt."

"You see," said Conor. "I need to talk to you about something anyway. I need to talk to someone. This stuff has been going around in my mind. I got the fear last night on the way home again, fairly badly. I keep expecting to see those, well, I dunno what to call them, those things waiting for me on the roads. Or what would be even worse is if I don't see them and they're waiting for me somewhere. I couldn't sleep last night thinking I heard people outside the house. I couldn't keep my mind on work today at all. I packed it in around lunchtime and came up here. I thought if I had a few pints early in the day and maybe a bit of a smoke then I could head home before dark and I'd get some sleep."

"It'll be dark in a little while, Conor."

He smiled. "Yes, but you'll be with me on the way back. I'll be ok if I'm not on my own. I've been sitting here just thinking about them. And trying to remember exactly what they looked like and I've been doing some research. Online." He held up his phone and waggled it around. "I've been trying to figure out what they were."

Luke finished the rest of his stout and asked Ollie to put on two more pints. The feel of the cold, smooth liquid going down his throat and into his chest had balanced him. Time was slowly morphing into something that didn't concern him anymore.

"So, what was this research that you did?"

"The more I've been dwelling on it the more I think there's something otherworldly about what I saw."

"Otherworldly? So, you do believe in that kind of stuff?"

"Not normally. I never would have imagined that I'd start believing in anything supernatural, but I guess I've never had to give any consideration to it before. I live a simple enough life, Luke, I always have. I have the farm, I love music, I spend a lot of time listening to it, doing the podcast, going to gigs. I like a pint and I like a bit of weed. I have a few friends who are into the same things as me, other men from rural areas. They've noticed some things that they can't explain too, sinister things. Look, I've always felt that I know what I know and that's enough to know. I'm on solid ground with that. Since last week though, I've had this horrible feeling that there's something all around us that we haven't been properly aware of. It feels like it's always been there but we haven't been able to see it before. It makes me feel stupid and it makes me feel frightened."

"Conor, man, they were just, I don't know, just troublemakers. Who knows? They could have been from a criminal gang using these country roads to get rid of something. Thugs wearing masks. You hear that they head down places like this where they know they won't be seen. I've read stories in the papers about farmers in remote areas stumbling across people up to all kinds of stuff."

"They weren't criminals, Luke, or a gang or anything like that. They weren't the right size. They moved weirdly. The more I think about it, I don't think they were wearing masks. I think their faces were wrong. They weren't men. I've been seeing them in my dreams. I can't sleep at night for thinking about them. They weren't human."

"Ah Conor, come on. What were they then?"

Conor stood up off his seat. He picked up his pint and indicated to Luke to follow him. Luke sighed, resigned to the fact he was going to be smoking again, and followed Conor out the door. The smoking area was empty. In the last drops of daylight, it seemed miserable and untidy. There was a gate made of corrugated iron that led out to the car park at the back. The bottom of it had been forced up to leave a small gap underneath and there were bits of broken glass around it. They sat down at the little table, its old wooden surface marked with scratches and burns. Conor handed Luke a cigarette and lit them both. He spoke quietly.

"You work in a museum, yes?"

"Yeah," said Luke suspiciously.

"What did you have to study for that. History, yeah?"

"Among other things."

"What about folklore? Old wives' tales, legends, that kind of stuff?"

"I did a module on folklore when I was in college. I'm not sure how much of it I remember. There's a lot of things I did in college that I can't now remember."

"The way I understand it all of those stories have a root in reality."

Conor stubbed his cigarette out in the ashtray and from the top pocket of his denim jacket he produced a short pre-rolled joint. He lit it, took two deep inhalations and offered it to Luke.

"I really shouldn't," said Luke as he accepted the joint.

"You'll need it. You might need to loosen your mind a little to hear what I think."

Luke took a drag, feeling the hot burn in his throat.

"There are loads of old myths about supernatural creatures in the countryside that cause harm to people," Conor continued. "The cluarichaun, an fear darrig. They must be based on something. All stories are based on something. I mean, people believe in leaving offerings at that tree up the road to cure people, why is that any stranger than there being dangerous entities around?"

"There are dangerous *people* around," replied Luke through an exhalation of smoke. "There always has been. Myths are based on rational fears. But you're talking about what? Monsters? You're not telling me that's what you think you saw?"

"I dunno but they weren't normal. Their faces. The size of them. I mean, their bodies were smaller than adults, but their faces looked wrinkled and old. And then there's the drinking."

"Hardly uncommon among criminals, or anyone else for that matter."

"Do you see the gate over there? Last night someone broke the frame of it and twisted up the metal. There were old, half-empty liqueur bottles just inside the gate. They were gone off, real old horrible liqueurs, Advocaat and Benedictine, shit like that. Nobody in their right mind would drink them. They managed to reach under that to grab them and pull them out. The gap is only a few inches. And how did they know it was there? It was like they sniffed them out. Those things I saw could have done that; I can just imagine them doing that. Look at what I've found online. It's like there used to be these alcoholic half-humans, half something else, something evil. They went around attacking people, attacking livestock, destroying property. They were vicious."

Conor took out a bundle of paper from where it was tucked inside his jacket. The pages were covered in a scrawl of notes and snippets of sentences. He had made little sketches on there too, vague faces with beady eyes and unruly beards. "Read these," he said. "I've done the leg work. I just need you to write it up for me as a report that I can present to them. They'll listen to you."

"Present it to who?" asked Luke. Words were underlined like 'rattish', 'slouching', 'leering'.

"To the Gardaí. You have credibility. Read over it. I'll get us another drink."

Luke's phone interrupted them. Sophie's name appeared on the screen.

"Another? I should really be thinking about going home, Conor."

"One more, while you look through my research. Sure, a bird never flew on one wing."

"But this'll be my third wing. And you've already had a load of wings." The phone stopped ringing and he giggled to himself at the image he'd put in his head of Conor as a large feathered bird with a multitude of wings. Conor shook his head at him.

"One more won't hurt, Luke. Then I'll drop you home."

Conor headed towards the bar like he was being pulled towards it on strings. Luke wobbled on his chair. He put the papers aside and rang Sophie back.

"Hi," she answered at the first ring. "How are you getting on? Is Declan dropping you home?"

His words were lead weights on his tongue and his jaw muscles ached as he spoke.

"No, sorry Soph, I'll be home soon. I'm just in O'Shea's. Conor Gallagher is going to drop me home on his quad."

"Who? Listen to me, Denise is here. She's looking for Declan. He never came home last night and he's not answering his phone. I thought you two were together last night. Was he not with you when you came home?"

"He … well he was with me for a while but then he had to go. Denise is there now?"

"Yes, she's worried about him."

In the background Luke could hear Denise's voice, a streak of anger in it, asking what he knew. He dropped his voice to an exaggerated whisper, as if she could overhear him through the phone.

"He's ok, she has nothing to worry about. Well, she has got something to worry about but I can't talk about it. It's, well, it's Deccie being Deccie." He could almost see Sophie's lips tighten as she held in an expletive.

"Right," she said firmly. "So where did you see him last?"

"Ah Sophie. I guess, just tell her he was still in the pub when I left. I don't know what to say that isn't going to either worry her or get him in trouble."

Her voice dropped to a whispery hiss. "For fuck's sake, Luke. Just come on home, will you?"

She hung up. He drank what remained of his Guinness and rifled through Conor's papers. He scanned them unthinkingly, the occasional phrase landing in his mind, 'violent pranks', 'solitary creature'. Conor returned and placed a fresh pint in front of him.

"So, what do you think? It makes sense, doesn't it?"

"What? No, no, sorry, Conor, none of it makes sense. These are just fairy stories, myths. But even by their logic it doesn't make sense. You saw two of them together, didn't you? Here you have a note that they're solitary creatures."

"Yeah, I know that, but what if they weren't solitary anymore? What if they got together in gangs because they felt threatened by population growth or something? They see people everywhere and cars everywhere and they don't like it. They're coming out of the shadows. They're starting to turn on us."

Conor lit another cigarette and offered one to Luke but he waved it away.

"When do you think you'll have the report ready?"

"Ah Conor, can we talk about something else? You saw people wearing masks, hanging around, drinking and causing trouble. You did the right thing to report them. The Guards aren't going to listen when you start spouting this other shite."

"You don't believe me. You think I'm just some thick, stoner farmer."

Conor lit his cigarette and slammed the lighter on the table. However mad this stuff sounded, Luke didn't want to upset him. This was his best chance of a lift home by the looks of things.

"No, no, come here now, how about I talk to Declan? I don't need to go through all this or write up a report. If he checks up on it then it won't matter if it's criminal gangs or, or whatever you think it is. The result will be the same, won't it?"

Conor grumbled out a breath of smoke.

"Is that ok?" said Luke.

"Fine."

"I'm sorry. I'm just exhausted after work and the move this weekend. I enjoy having a pint with you but you're not doing yourself any favours dwelling on whatever gave you a fright last week."

"No, you're right, you're right," Conor stood up as if he were in a sudden rush and knocked back his pint in one go. "Come on then, we'll get you home."

Chapter Sixteen

Inside Roisin Kelly's greenhouse, the space was losing the memories of the day's warmth, but the overcrowding of plants created a fragrant stuffiness. Apart from a small workbench, every conceivable space burst with green leaves, tendrils or flowers. In the corner where she kept stacks of pots and containers of various shapes and sizes, Roisin located a long, narrow white tub with a curved lip that resembled a miniature porcelain bath. She went outside and took some small pots of mini heathers from where they sat on a small, sheltered bench. They were a silvery colour and she arranged three of them in the container, spreading out the foliage. It had been a while since she'd created one of these 'bloodbath' displays. The silvery heather represented the water and her next step was to choose her reds. Some miniature roses were in bloom, their neat heads like sacs of plasma in a hospital. She set these gently in between the heathers as the main body of the display. Now she needed to add more effect, to create a sense of blood in the water. Outside, beside one of the benches, the wooden one whose corners were starting to rot away, there was a vibrant red rose bush whose petals would add to the impression she wanted and she also thought of the bird-cherry tree behind it whose fruits had started to come in. If she picked some of them, they would look like dark droplets of blood scattered around the heathers.

She took her secateurs from her work bench and hung the handle from her belt. She would prune a few of the rose heads rather than just pull their leaves. The red of the raspberries entered her mind. Best to take a few that were not quite ripe, firm enough to keep their shape and bright red shade if preserved with glycerine. She went back into the kitchen to bring a bowl for the berries. Maybe she'd pick some more to eat as well. While there she grabbed the wine bottle. She had a feeling that she might spend most of the evening in the greenhouse with her plants.

In the garden, the night clouds had parted to allow the moon to share some of its weak light. Roisin went first to the rose bush and carefully removed two heads with her secateurs, hearing the neat, satisfying snip as the sharp blades cut through the stems at a good clean angle. A leaf glided towards the ground. She followed its gentle flight and a movement beneath it startled her. It was a small frog. It hopped once more and then, aware of her towering presence, it sat still in the moist grass. Gently, she hunkered down close, careful not to frighten it off. She remembered the specimens that caused emotions ranging from mirth to upset in teaching college. They had stopped dissecting frogs by the time she had started working in Cromuck. She was happy about that. Roisin squinted at the small amphibian and admired the beauty of its dark glossy skin. Its eyes were thoughtful and deep. She stepped over towards the bird-cherry tree and was relieved to see the frog hop back into the undergrowth. She was always glad to meet a frog in her garden. There weren't as many around anymore. She picked off seven hard, purplish berries from the bird-cherry tree and put them into the bowl with the rose heads, then went over to the raspberry bushes. There was something odd about the raspberry bushes. She tucked the bowl in the crook of her arm so she could turn on her torch and shone the light across the bushes. She lifted the leaves and foraged beneath them. All the berries were gone. All of the ripe ones; all of the ones that had been so overripe they were almost black; all of the ones that had just started to blush. They were all gone from the bushes. She checked the ground to see if some freak wind had blown them off while she had been inside but there were none in the grass and she knew logically that nothing like that could have happened, the night was so still. Had something eaten them? Were there birds awake and hungry still? Birds being so quiet as to be unheard? There wasn't even as much as the usual hooting of an owl on the air. She walked backwards, confused and disappointed.

Back in the greenhouse, Roisin poured herself more wine and stared outside as she drank, trying to figure out what could have possibly happened to her raspberries. There had been so many of them earlier. She would have to examine the bush again in the morning, in the light. She returned to her 'bloodbath' planter and arranged the rose petals and bird cherries on it. With a sharp knife from her bench, she engraved the word 'bloodbath' in slasher movie style on the container. She rooted out a small jar of red paint from a box filled with paints and dyes and brushes and sponged it into the letters. Next a name card from her supply, blank apart from the website name in the bottom corner and a black border of thorny roses. She wrote Sophie's name on it, fixed it to a small wooden spike, and stuck it in the planter. There was a sheltered display rack just outside the greenhouse where she put her finished pieces and she brought the planter out and put it with the other orders she had finished that day.

Standing back to admire her display rack, slightly misty-headed from the wine, Roisin thought she might do just one more piece before turning in for the night, and maybe she'd have another slow glass of wine while she was doing it. She stood there in the still night and tried to think up something new to create.

She leaned against one of the large water butts, kept near the greenhouse so rainwater was always to hand for her plants. The black grasses were in abundance at the moment, they would need to be used. She stared up at the moon, asking it for inspiration, then she looked down to see whether its reflection was trapped in the water of the container. She could just make out its faint shimmer. If it had been a full moon then it would show itself more clearly in there; full moon, werewolves, lurking. Their eyes in the bushes. Yellow eyes, like yellow berries. She had Yellow Pyracantha hedging in the garden, also in its fruiting season. Its yellow berries with their black point could represent wolves' eyes in the black grasses. What if she prepared a lot of them for Halloween, in the right containers, and get Sophie to make them prominent on the website as a special offer, or approach one of the grocery chains. They stocked flowers for Valentine's Day, why not plants for Halloween? Excited, she went back inside the greenhouse to get her secateurs. She would cut some Pyracantha tonight, just to see it placed against the black grass, to try out the design. But the secateurs were not where she remembered leaving them. She searched around the ground in case they had fallen but they weren't there. Indeed, the work bench was clearer than it should have been. The knife was missing too, the sharp knife that she had used to scratch out the letters on the bloodbath. Where was her wine? The glass was gone. And the bottle was missing.

Roisin moved backwards towards the door of the greenhouse, starting to worry but not yet sure what to worry about. She knew something was very wrong, the realisation dropped like a stone in a pond. Was something wrong with her mind? Had she misplaced all these things: the wine, the knife, the secateurs? What about the raspberries, vanished from the bush?

If it wasn't her mind playing tricks then the alternative might be worse. She halted and searched around her workbenches again frantically, under empty pots, behind half bags of compost.

If it wasn't her mind playing tricks then was there an explanation to hope for that wasn't so bad? Stray animals, kids playing an innocent prank maybe? Old students on a dare? She couldn't find any of the missing items so she dashed outside to see if she had left them out there absentmindedly while absorbed by the moon's revelations. She whirled around, shining the torch over the gravelly ground. It was just occurring to her that the next step was to go inside and lock her door when a dart of pain stung the calf of her leg. It was like a vinegar-soaked nail had been driven into her. Her hand went down instinctively and felt a wetness. Hopping on one leg, she shone her torch onto a tear in her leggings and blood on her hand. Then a sharp hard wallop to her other leg, along the back of her ankle, brought her to the ground with a yell. She grabbed her Achilles tendon and squeezed against the pain then squirmed around, bringing her ankle before her. It was totally drenched in blood. She swung the torch about. Sophie's bloodbath was on her display rack. The reds of the rose petals. The darker shade of the bird cherries. Which colour was closer to the blood on her hands and streaming over her legs? Something awful was happening and she didn't want to think about it. Her mind latched onto those shades of red instead. It was hard to compare colour in the dark but she tried. At the same time, part of her knew she had to get up, so she crawled on her knees over towards the water butt closest to her. She reached up to the rim and pulled herself upright. Her eyes locked onto the water. She could see the reflection of the moon very clearly in there now. There it was, still and silent, like an apparition, like the visions of her dead husband that her mind conjured sometimes, not the nightmarish ones where he screamed in agony and blindness but the ones that appeared to her unexpectedly at the end of her hall or waiting at the end of her driveway, staring sadly at her. Then, beside the moon's reflection, appeared a set of mean yellow eyes, and something grabbed her head and pushed it down into the water. The water forced its way up her nostrils and hurt her head until she felt a hand pinch the flesh of her arm. Her eyes bulged in terror as the pinched skin was snipped off. Her head was pulled back out of the water and she screamed inward as she gasped for breath. Then her head was pushed back down and this time she closed her eyes in the water. She closed her eyes and she saw Gavin and she knew that those times that he appeared to her, silent and sad, were not because he was sad for himself, but because he looked upon her and he loved her and he knew that she was going to have a death that was far worse than his. The pinch of flesh was bigger this time and it was below her ribs and when it was snipped off, she understood where her secateurs were. Again, she was pulled from the water. Through the ringing in her ears and her own screaming she heard the sound of glass being smashed and laughter. Her head went under again. A searing pain sliced the side of her stomach. Fingers pulled at the skin and entered inside her and moved around as if they were rummaging around for something.

She passed out before her heart gave up.

Chapter Seventeen

It was dark now. They stood outside under the meagre illumination of the car park floodlight, beside the large red Suzuki 700 King Quad while Conor finished his cigarette. The many angles and bevels of the machine, with its black trim and solid form, put Luke in mind of a vehicle from *Star Wars*. He ran his hand over the smooth plastic panels.

"It's nice," he said. "Do you have a spare helmet?"

"For what?"

"Ah," said Luke. "I see. No helmets. Where do I sit?"

Conor hopped onto the seat and patted the black metal rack behind it.

"Right, do I stretch my legs around you? You're a skinny lad but it looks kind of awkward."

"No, you sit with your back to me, facing behind, and hold on tight to the rack here."

Luke clambered on to the bike and nestled his back against Conor's bony shoulder blades.

"You don't have to press up that close against me," said Conor. "Save that for your wife."

Conor started the machine and Luke's stomach lurched as they accelerated out of the car park. He was reminded of the time in college when Declan bought himself a moped after a summer of work that he was curiously vague about describing. Many times, they had zipped off to some pub or other, spoilt with the options this new transport allowed them. Many times, they slowly met the ground under the weight of the bike, their drunken balance either gone or fighting against each other's. The moped only lasted about a month until, one day, driving on his own, Declan managed to walk away from a crash in a remote part of the Dublin mountains. He was relatively unhurt but the bike was beyond saving. He left it where it lay, in a ditch beside the tree that had buckled its steering column and, as far as they knew, it was still there, corroding away under a decade of weeds and grass.

Conor, after the initial burst of speed, seemed to sense Luke's tension or else he was just relaxed from the joints and pints and drove calmly and slowly. Luke gazed up at the clear night sky and lost his thoughts for a few moments in the distant stars until the quad came to a halt. Over the purring of the engine, he heard Conor curse.

"What?" he said dreamily.

"Look there. At the Twisted Tree. Where I saw them before."

Luke twisted his body round awkwardly. He could just about see something up ahead in the dim light that the clouds allowed from the moon: a figure sitting on top of the small stone wall that jutted out of the ground. It held an odd disposition, its body loose like a scarecrow's, the shoulders slumped forward.

"Is that one of them?" he hissed.

"No, it's bigger than they were. There's something strange about whoever that is. I don't think it's a living person, it looks like a dummy or something. But there's something familiar about it. Hold on. I'm going to drive up closer."

Luke gripped the bars on the quad tightly and was suddenly aware of the heavy, fast beat of his heart. He tried to twist his body around to get a proper view as they trundled towards the figure. He could just about hear Conor's voice in the light wind that had picked up.

"I know him, I know him," Conor said. They slowed almost to a stop. "It's Brendan McGrath! Fuck, it's Brendan McGrath's body!"

Luke turned himself around on the quad and tried in the dimness to make out the features of the figure sitting down low on the stone marker. Its face was pale but bespeckled, like it was covered in white powder and dirt. Then its hand started to rise up and Conor yelled out before speeding away on the quad, almost spilling his passenger.

They parked on the side of the road about a mile past the Twisted Tree, not very far now from Luke's house. If Conor kept driving the way he did when fleeing from the figure he was going to have them both in the ditch.

"He waved. He fucking waved at us but he's dead."

"Are you sure it was him?" said Luke to Conor. "We've had some drink. We've had a smoke. It's dark."

Luke got off the back of the quad and come round to face his driver while he talked to him. He hoped he was far enough away that whatever they had seen couldn't chase them, though what that was he really didn't have a clue. Conor stayed on the quad with his hands on the wheel and his foot on the pedal, ready to go if he saw anything coming up the road behind them.

"It was him. It was definitely him. I was as close to him as I am to you. Jesus, I don't know what to think. Are they robbing the graves now? I thought he was just a corpse until he moved his arm. There looked to be no life in him until he moved."

"Look," said Luke. "I think we should get off the roads, get some rest. It'll all seem clearer in the morning. Ring the Guards and let them know what you saw."

"What *we* saw."

"Yeah, yeah, what we saw. Just, I didn't really get a proper look at it. I have to go to work tomorrow but I'll call you at some stage to see how things are."

Conor took his hands from the wheel and lit a cigarette, muttering to himself, "Never listen, they never listen to me."

Luke climbed back on the quad and pointed in the direction of his house. "Come on, Conor, it's been a long night, just drop me home. We don't want to be out here if there actually is anyone strange around."

Conor started the engine and drove cautiously down the road, still smoking his cigarette. Luke felt his head spinning slightly, as if he was already aiming it towards his pillow. Just before they got to his house the quad slowed almost to a stop. Conor took a last drag of his cigarette, threw it on the road and called out to his passenger. "Hold tight."

"Ah no," wailed Luke as Conor crouched forward over the handlebars and zoomed off past the house.

Luke recognised a helplessness that was all too common for him. It was the same one he felt when Declan used to drag him from bar to bar if they were on a session. The same helplessness he felt when Declan would slip a pill into his hand and give him a wink and a slug of water to wash it down. The same helplessness he felt when he was given different projects or roles at work. The same that he used to feel when Sophie arranged their holidays for them or anything that involved more planning than going down to the pub. The same helplessness that he felt throughout Sophie's pregnancy.

He had learned over the years that being led in these directions, whether by Declan or Sophie or his managers at work, invariably ended in somewhere he actually wanted to be, but he had a feeling Conor wasn't about to do the same for him now.

The quad halted in front of the graveyard he had visited to find Declan on the day he moved in. There were only two flat pieces of land within the visible landscape: the graveyard and the GAA pitch that neighboured it.

All around those landmarks were small hills and slopes. They formed a natural viewing area around the pitch. Behind the graveyard, on an incline, were dotted the foreboding old headstones of an older graveyard, leaning forward towards the newer plots as if in judgement of their descendants. The cemetery gate was open. Vines of ivy festooned the walls and a few long tendrils grew round the gate post, hanging in the air like curling fingers beckoning them inside.

"Come on, Conor," said Luke. "Leave it. Let's go home."

"I have to see. I have to get proof. They won't believe me otherwise. I need you with me, they'll believe you before me. And it's safer with both of us together."

"I don't think it's safe no matter how many of us there is." Luke scanned the area hoping he might see another local around, maybe someone locking up the GAA dressing rooms after a late training session or the priest on a night-time reverie from the nearby church. The longer they were out, the more worry was rising in his bones. "If there are people here, the kind of people who would dig up a body, then they might have weapons. We should head away. It's ok, I can ring the Gardaí tomorrow if you want. As you said, they'll listen to me."

"Weapons," mused Conor. "I have my father's old shotgun back in the house. I'm going to start carrying it from now on. I'm not going out again without it."

"Yeah," said Luke. "We shouldn't be out here unarmed. Let's just go."

"Too late for that now, though," said Conor and he steered the quad through the gate of the graveyard and drove up the path between the headstones. The gravestones in the old, higher part were predominantly stone Celtic crosses, but down in the new section they were mostly neat marble squares in various shades of white, black, and grey. Countless Virgin Marys stood in prayer, attached to the headstones in her different forms. The small, coloured stones spread on the ground within their kerbed boundaries glinted under the moon. The pair drove up to a fresh plot with a mound of earth still raised on the ground.

"This is McGrath's," said Conor as they dismounted.

The headstone was a pale, grey marble bearing the names of Brendan McGrath's parents above his own and, at the bottom, the date of his demise. Around it the two men could see a broken wine bottle and some scraps of dark fabric.

"His suit," said Conor. "They must have torn some of his suit."

"Look at the grave," said Luke. "It's not open. If there was a body taken from there then why would they fill it back in?"

"Who knows? But they did. The earth should have sunken back down more than that by now. That grave has been dug out, trust me."

"I don't know, Conor, maybe there were kids out drinking here. Isn't that what you did when you were young in the countryside, drinking cans in graveyards? Maybe they disturbed the ground."

"And what about the body?" shouted Conor, spittle dotting Luke's face. Luke didn't like the wave of aggression that had come over him.

"Come on, Conor. You're not sure what you saw."

"Get on the quad!"

"Ok, yes, it's time to go home."

"Get on the fucking quad. I'll show you. We're going back and you'd better look properly this time."

Luke sighed. He wondered if he should just walk home and let Conor ride around the roads on his own, hunting for dead bodies, but the thought of walking for ages in the dark seemed like another nightmare and, after the string of nightmares today that had been his commute, then work, then the bus journey home and now this, he couldn't allow himself to enter into another one. He just wanted this ordeal to be over and to get home.

"One look, Conor, please then leave me to my home. Pull up at a distance and if we see a body, we'll ring the police tonight and you can talk to them and you can leave me home. If there's a body there then they'll have to believe you. You won't need me."

Conor grunted his assent.

They drove out of the cemetery and back past Luke's house and crept cautiously round the corner before the Twisted Tree came into sight. They stared down the road into the darkness.

"We can't see from here," said Conor, and he drove further towards the tree.

"Wait," said Luke. "Let me face the right way."

He turned around and positioned himself awkwardly behind Conor, resting one hand on his shoulder. "Go slow."

The headlights of the quad picked out the low stone wall.

"I don't see anything there," said Luke.

They drove right up to it. Luke could sense the edginess in his companion, he was concerned by the latent twitch in the hands on the handlebars and the tension that caused the shoulders in front of him to rise. If something or someone jumped out of the ditch right now then Conor would speed off without a thought and Luke would be bucked off the back of the machine. It was this worry that made him get off the quad.

"What are you doing?" said Conor.

"Just having a closer look. Do you have a torch?"

"There's one in that hatch back there."

Luke unclipped a pair of latches and part of the bodywork lifted to reveal a compartment. He took a chunky black rubber torch out. There were tools in with it and he took a spanner as well. He noticed that Conor's hands hadn't left the handlebars even to point out where the compartment was.

"I thought you didn't have any weapons," said Luke.

"You won't do much damage with that," said Conor.

"It's better than nothing."

"Maybe. There's a long screwdriver in there. Hand it to me, will you?"

Luke rummaged around then passed him the tool, almost a foot long and with a wicked flat head. He wished he had taken that instead of the small blunt spanner. He shone the torch around the ground. The grass didn't grow within the low wall's enclosure and any weeds present cowered close to the stonework. There were tracks in the soft earth. They were the shape of a small foot but indistinct around the edges. There were no patterns or lines from the sole of a shoe. Behind the stone wall, the grass appeared flattened down. Luke stepped cautiously over towards it. Here, vigorous limbed plants topped with small clusters of white flowers grew thickly. They looked as if they had been disturbed.

"What can you see?" Conor strained to keep his voice low. "Is the body there?"

Luke waved his hand back dismissively. He tried to think of the name of the plant. He knew what it was called. He pushed aside the fern-like leaves. Cow's Parsley, that was it. The stalks were hollow. He put his foot onto one extremely large plant in front of him and broke it down, causing a loud snap, and then from down in the ditch came a deep, humanlike groan. Luke careered backwards to get out of there, hopping backwards across the wall.

"What the fuck?" Conor cursed.

The quad took off just before Luke managed to reach it and he fell back onto the road instead. A dark shape rose out of the ditch and came towards him, stumbling forward angrily and erratically. Luke scampered backwards on the road, using his elbows so he could keep hold of the spanner and the torch, which sent wild beams of light all around with his frantic movement. Then, for a second, the figure was lit up and he could see it was almost ready to leap on top of him. He caught a brief glimpse of hard skin and sickly yellow eyes. A mouth with raging teeth opened in front of his face before the creature was sent flying out of his view by the impact of the returned quad. There was a roar of pain and a screech of tyres. He shone the torch to see Conor standing up on the quad, swinging the long screwdriver in front of him. Luke got to his feet and lurched over to his companion. Conor stabbed at the empty air in front of him like a terrified child fighting a waking nightmare. Luke raised his palms for fear the weapon would be turned on him.

"Conor, Conor, Conor. Come on, let's go now. Sit down. Drive."

Conor beheld Luke with shock in his eyes, his mouth moving soundlessly. Something was moving in the darkness, down near the roots of the tree, but whether it was disappearing or getting ready to attack, they weren't going to stay to find out. Luke leapt onto the back of the quad and yelled, "Go!"

Conor put the machine into motion, skidding hard as they tore away. Under the roars of engine and fear, they got back to Luke's house and got off the quad, both of them shaking. Luke put his arm on Conor's shoulder.

"Did you get a proper look at it?"

Conor nodded and winced, as if burdened with bad news.

"What was it?"

The answer curdled like vomit in his throat but he couldn't spit it out.

"It must have been a dog," Luke answered for him.

"It wasn't a fucking dog, man."

"Whatever it was, it was vicious. Did you see how it went for me?"

The porch light came on and Sophie opened the door. She judged the state of the two men and frowned at the vehicle that had brought them. "I don't even want to ask," she said.

"Sophie, this is Conor. Conor, this is my wife, Sophie. Conor dropped me home from O'Shea's but we had a … we saw a … there was a thing and it attacked us after we were searching the graveyard and Conor managed to hit it with the quad before it got me."

"Wow," said Sophie slowly. "What are you talking about? You two are so out of it. Look at the eyes on both of you. I know you've had a shitty day but come on, do you know how late it is?"

Luke glanced dumbly down at his phone and the last bit of battery life in it told him that it was almost midnight.

"I kept you some food, I'll heat it up," she said. "I don't know if you're inviting your friend in for a cup of tea or coffee but if you are then you'd better stay as quiet as he is because Elliott is asleep. And don't forget you still have to change the tyre on the car so you'll be able to go to work in the morning, if you are going to work in the morning, that is."

She went back inside, leaving the door open for them. There was an inflection Sophie used when Luke got into idiotic scrapes. Not anger or disappointment; rather that she was pointing out his foolishness for his own sake. Luke always reacted to it with gratitude, as if she had pointed out a pile of dogshit he was about to step into or, more often, had already stepped into. As he was starting to lose the threefold effect of alcohol, joints and adrenaline, he looked at Conor with his eyes still wide and wondered how much of the night's facts he was going to be revising in his mind the next morning.

"Is she annoyed with you?" asked Conor. "She seems very calm."

"Yeah, she's very calm alright. I think I should have a chat with Sophie before we say anything to the Guards."

"Yeah, well, I need you to back me up. They won't believe me on my own. What's this about your tyre?"

Luke pointed towards his car and the shredded tyre sitting low on the passenger side.

"Do you have a spare?" asked Conor.

Luke nodded.

"I'll help you change it. It's the least I can do after what we've gone through tonight. Are you really going to work in the morning? We've had a hell of a scare. I'm still not right."

"Yeah," said Luke. "I will have to go in. Thanks for this. I'll go inside and make us a coffee. Or do you want tea? Or a drink?"

"I'll make it," Sophie called from where she had appeared back at the door. "Thanks for helping my husband with the tyre, Conor. Now, no more pub on work nights if this is the state you're going to end up in. Unless I get to come as well, ok?"

"Trust me, Sophie," said Luke. "You would not have wanted to be with us tonight."

Chapter Eighteen

That man Conor Gallagher was on Sophie's mind the next morning. He had a strange way about him. He carried himself with a relaxed stoner ease but underneath that an agitation kept rising that made his wiry frame seem almost aggressive. It was good of him to help change the tyre and, as he did that, he moved calmly and expertly, stopping for a while only to drink the coffee Sophie brought him. But when he had finished, he seemed antsy, like he didn't know if he wanted to stay or go, and he had a fearful look about him. This wasn't some great insight on her part, he actually told them that he was afraid to make the short journey back to his farm.

Conor made them promise to wait up until he texted to say he had arrived home safely. If they hadn't received a text from him after fifteen minutes, they were to ring him, and if he didn't answer they should call the Gardaí. Luke didn't even manage to stay awake for fifteen minutes. After Conor left it was like he was walloped around the head with tiredness. He went for a piss, stumbled out of his clothes, didn't bother to brush his teeth, and collapsed into bed. He muttered something about not being sure what had gone on that night and fell asleep. Sophie sat up on the side of the bed and grudgingly watched his phone for Conor's message. She nudged him awake to ask what time he wanted the alarm set for and when he didn't answer coherently, she set it for six-thirty am, the same time as the previous morning. She was weighing up the worry she had seen in Conor's face against his state of inebriation and trying to decide whether or not she would actually call the

Gardaí when, two minutes after the promised fifteen, Luke's phone received the text: 'Home now'.

Luke had always been good at getting up for work after a night out but she was still impressed by the fact he did so this morning. During breakfast that feeling turned to concern about whether he would have been in a proper state to be driving that early. She texted him to make sure he got in safely and received one back that said: 'Yes thanks, very tired, weird shit last night, talk later.'

Tonight, she would make it her mission to ensure he got an early night. If he was going to have to get up each morning for that commute then he would need to get into a proper routine. And what exactly was this 'weird shit' they had gotten up to or encountered? Might be an idea to ask Roisin about this Conor character when she visited her.

Elliott was in good form that morning. He was intrigued by every little thing they did from the moment he woke up, so when she wheeled his pushchair out the gate and onto the road, he was ready to hop out of it with excitement. Sophie was more nervous than excited and wasn't completely sure about the wisdom of walking with the pushchair on these country roads with no footpaths and their sinister blind turns. She would just have to keep a good ear out for traffic noises. If she heard anything, she would get right up on the grass verge for safety.

She reckoned it would be a solid half hour's walk to Roisin's place but it would be good for her to be active. She spent too much work time sitting in front of a screen so, if the countryside was right at her doorstep, then she was determined to get the benefit of it. When they got a second car she might drive to other, more pedestrian-friendly places for a walk but, until then, she should see what it was like on her own road.

She glanced towards Denise's house and pondered whether or not to call in and see if Declan had shown up, but before she could ponder it for too long, she had already strolled past their gate. It was a shame she felt no warmth towards Denise or even her child. Maybe it would come in time, especially if young Willy and Elliott ended up as playmates in the future, but at the moment she was veering towards outright dislike of both of them, with Denise's righteous sneering and Willy's spoilt expression, borne from the worst of each side of his parentage.

She put Declan's family out of her mind as promptly as she could. This, she suspected, was something she was going to have to learn to do over the coming years if they were to have them as neighbours. She talked to Elliott instead. She told him about the trees they passed, surprising herself by being able to identify most of them. She told him about the old Ogham alphabet and of Irish legends and folk beliefs about trees she half remembered from school, like about hazel being a tree of knowledge whose branches were used for divining and that rowan was said to have the power to stop the dead from rising. She told him about designs she had done in the past based on Irish mythology, which led her to talk about the ideas she had written down for Roisin's website.

Talking to Elliott like this, she found, helped her to see her ideas actualised and, you never know, it might all seep into his forming mind and he might become a designer or an artist. Luke often talked to him in a similar way about music and classic albums, trying to wedge in some lost masterpieces between his nursery rhymes. So, maybe he might become a music critic instead or an art historian or maybe just a weird little child with funny interests. She wondered at what age she might have to start tempering the things she talked to him about. She supposed she should always be censoring herself a little bit, even now in his pre-language state, but at the moment it was nice to just talk away to him about whatever she wanted.

They came up towards the spot where she had gotten the puncture yesterday, that creepy old tree. The split bags of rubbish were still there. Some of their contents had scattered out to encroach on the road. She didn't really want to go rooting around in them again. She felt a bit exposed without the car. It was the buzzing noise that made her decide to cross to the other side of the road away from them. A few unseasonable wasps dipped in and out of the bags and hovered over the soiled food wrappers that had sprung loose. They flew as if they were carrying weights, slow and unsteady. She knew a September wasp could be a mean wasp, so she pulled down the cover of the pushchair, much to Elliott's annoyance, and hurried past.

It was just before eleven when Sophie walked through the arch of Roisin's driveway, its tangly thorniness even more impressive close up. She was pleased with the pace she had made and only two cars had passed her on the journey. One had been going a little bit fast for her sense of safety, but she heard it in plenty of time to move up off the road. The other had politely slowed, giving her space and a friendly wave. If she took a walk like this and back most days then it would be great for clearing her mind as well as keeping fit. So long as the weather stayed dry, she would try.

She approached the greenhouse but couldn't see any movement inside. The display rack outside it was laden with planters. Was that her own name was written on a card sticking out of one?

"Hello," she called out. "Roisin?"

She walked the pushchair round to the back of the greenhouse where a gravel path led to a secluded green area with untamed bushes and trees, creating an eerie secret style garden with benches, statues and bird feeders dotted about.

"This is nice," she said to Elliott. "It's a little spooky though."

The sunlight struggled to break through here and, where it did, it was slashed by the shadows of many branches. Suddenly a pair of crows clattered through the leaves of a tree just beside them, fighting over something that each of their beaks had a claim on. Elliott cried with the fright. One of the crows won the wrestle and backed off with his prize, a nice, red bit of meat. The loser cawed bitterly at him.

Sophie backed out of the garden and tried the house. There was no doorbell. The door was locked and knocking brought nobody to it. She parked Elliott beside the door and walked around the windows, trying to peer in. The curtains were closed on most of them. There was a black hatchback car around the other side of the house. She squinted in the window of the vehicle and saw scattered parking receipts, a half empty water bottle; signs of recent use. It was unlikely that she owned two cars, so Sophie guessed Roisin must be home or at least hadn't walked too far. She returned to the roadside and looked down the opposite way she had come from. The road was straight and narrow here. No point in calling Roisin's name down the road. She doubted her voice could travel any further than she could see.

Elliott might be getting lonely or worried without her. She jogged back to the rear of the house. No, he was sleeping in his chair, tired from being outside in the fresh air. She only noticed then that the porch light above him was turned on. Strange. Now that Elliot was asleep, she didn't want to call out again too loud. The mobile phone reception wasn't great here but she had enough to load the Gothic Garden website and check the contact number. There was no mobile, just a landline number. She dialled it and, after a few rings, stopped listening through her phone and went closer to the house to check if she could hear a ringing inside. Yes, through one of the side windows and its heavy blinds, she could make out the faint ringing of a phone. It rang out, unanswered. She dialled the number again and listened at the window, hoping to hear footsteps of movement from upstairs, but there was none and the phone rang out once more.

Elliott was still asleep. It wasn't cold but she still didn't want to have him outside for too long. The greenhouse didn't look like the most appealing place to wait either. There were garden tools everywhere, empty pots and bags of compost as well as shelves and benches filled with plants, but there was nowhere to sit.

She went over to inspect the display rack. It was indeed her name scrolled on the card, in a white container with the word 'bloodbath' inscribed on it. *It was sort of untidy*, she thought, *not as elegant as most of the other displays.* There was a bed of silvery heather and, strewn over that, a mess of small red berries and other dark pieces that she couldn't identify, some chunky square bits and other stringier parts.

This was annoying. Roisin had obviously forgotten about her invitation or else hadn't bothered to ring her to rearrange it. Inconsiderate. She took her planter with her and pushed Elliott's chair back down the driveway, and started off home. He stirred a little but then nestled into the padding of his chair and slept peacefully as she walked on. She hooked the handle of the 'bloodbath' planter onto the arm of the pushchair and it swung lightly back and forward with the motion of the walk. There was a bit of a smell from it that she figured must be either a compost or a spray of some sort. Whatever it was, it was attracting flies.

When they got close to the Twisted Tree, she slowed down, wary of the wasps still scavenging through the dumped rubbish. Before she could cross the road, a few of them flew over and began buzzing around the planter. She stepped back instinctively and waved at them to try to get them away from the pushchair. One hovered worryingly close to Elliott's face. Sophie tried to shoo them away without angering them too much but they were too attracted to the planter to be deterred and more of them were coming. She pulled her sleeve over her hand so at least there would be some defence against a sting and took the handle of the planter. One of the wasps went into a frenzy and she dropped the whole thing, spilling earth and berries and the other decorative bits onto the road. Quickly, she moved the pushchair into the side of the road, away from the manic insects, and went back to see if it was possible to rescue her gift.

After a few kicks and swipes at the wasps, most of them dispersed, happy enough to go back to the rubbish bags after the annoyance they had caused.

Sophie gathered a handful of the soil spilt from the pot, put it back in and rooted the fallen heathers in it. The other pieces were strewn all across the road. The flowers and the red rose petals were limp and tattered after the fall. She picked them up and laid them across the heather along with any of the berries she could see. She lifted one of the other pieces, one she wasn't able to identify, and was surprised at how wet and soft it was. It left a red stain on the road. She raised it to her nose and recoiled. That same smell from earlier. It was the smell of meat that had turned bad. The taste of her breakfast rose in her throat. She searched the ground for more pieces, not because she wanted to save them but because she had an uncomfortable curiosity about them now.

She found a wet cluster of them together, sniffed anxiously at them then gagged. In among the red bits was a round white sphere, speckled with grit from the road. Her stomach was starting to misbehave but she forced her fingers to turn the object around. It was an eye, red stringy trails hanging from the back of it, blood spread through the iris. She released a deep involuntary breath as if she were a bellows being squeezed.

"What is it made of?" she spoke aloud and the nervous crackle in her voice was the answer to her question. It was real. Sophie knew something awful had happened and she knew she couldn't leave these gruesome scraps on the road. She looked over at Elliott. He was still sleeping. The commotion hadn't woken him. All she could hear in her head was the buzzing of the wasps getting louder as she held her breath against the smell and made herself pick up the eye gently and not dwell on how wet and slippery it felt. She put it into the planter on top of the heather then picked up the small chunks of flesh and the long stringy pieces and laid them in with it. Her hands were shaking and stained with blood. She didn't want to touch the pushchair with them. She didn't want to use them to touch her phone. She didn't even want to wipe them on her clothes but a call had to be made. Was it the right thing to go back to Roisin's place and wait there until the Gardaí arrived? There was no way she could take her baby back to the scene of a crime. It was unnerving they had been there at all. What about when she left Elliott on his own and went around the house; had he been in danger?

Images of Roisin kept flickering in her mind but she didn't know if she should be seeing her as a victim or a danger. If these were really body parts then were they Roisin's, or had Roisin cut them from somebody else?

Finally, she wiped one hand on the front of her jeans and took out her phone. If Luke was here, he would tell her to ring Declan. The call tone sounded so plaintive against her ear, staring into the silence of the roads. Finally, Declan's recorded voice offered a gruff invitation to leave a message.

"Declan, it's Sophie. I've just come from Roisin Kelly's Gothic Garden. Something odd has happened. She wasn't there but there are these, these … maybe I'm being stupid but I think there are body parts. Please call me back."

A strange relief that he hadn't answered flooded Sophie. In that moment, she didn't trust that he would be able to do the right thing. He would do something to cut a corner or make a decision that would cause more problems for her.

She looked up the phone number for the Garda Station in Cromuck. If Declan answered then at least she was now going through the right channels. Her call was picked up after the first ring she was happy to hear an older man's voice. She calmly told him she suspected that a crime had taken place and at the same time she continued walking with Elliott in the direction of her home.

"A crime, you say. You've witnessed a crime?"

"No, not exactly. I've found something weird but I can't be sure if it's what I think it is."

The man asked her to tell him what had happened, to tell him from the start, and she could imagine him writing it down as he hummed encouragement at her words.

"An eye?" he said. "A human eye?"

"I think so," said Sophie. "It seems the right size." Queasily, she regarded the evidence in the planter.

"You stay there, love. Don't go anywhere. I'm going to drive out there right now. My name is Sergeant Harris. Can you take down my mobile number and if anything funny happens before I get there you call me straight away and I'll put the boot down."

"I've left there already," said Sophie. Elliott opened his eyes and yawned as if he knew that their new home was just ahead.

"I'm almost home. I didn't know there was something wrong until—well, I told you I had left, were you not listening? Go back over your notes. I have a baby with me."

"Now, ok miss, ok. No need to be snippy. We're fairly overworked and understaffed up here today so please bear with me. I'm going to drive out to you first to have a look at this, um, plant pot of yours. So, whereabouts do you live?"

Sophie sighed. "Do you know where Garda Declan Hartnett lives?"

***

Half an hour later, while feeding Elliott his bottle, Sophie watched a squad car pull into her driveway. She had time to get some cushions and arrange them in the playpen to sit her son upright and support the bottle as if he were feeding himself before the knock on the door. She wondered why he didn't use the bell. Perhaps he was the type who would mistrust whether a bell would be working, when he knew for sure he had his knuckles and knew they would make a sound.

When she opened the door to him, she reckoned her reasoning was correct. He looked exactly like the sort of man who would always rely on a good, hard, traditional knock.

"Mrs. Sheridan?" he asked.

"Are you Sergeant Harris?"

"That's me," he said in a tone that suggested there was nobody else he could possibly be. Sophie noted how clean and crisp his uniform was compared to the untidiness of the man inside it. His eyebrows were trying to escape from his face in different directions and shaving rash affected the parts of his neck where he hadn't missed the stubble.

"Nice day all the same," he went on. "At least there's been no rain. The puddles do be a nuisance on these roads with the white car. You end up having to get it washed every time you come out this way in the bad weather."

Elliott let out a cry that she interpreted as a dropped bottle and she beckoned the sergeant in as she hurried back along the hallway.

"Please, come in, come in. I just have to check on my son."

She darted to the sitting room and returned the bottle to Elliott's mouth. The sergeant didn't wait in the hallway but followed her into the room and was scrutinizing everything as if he was a property surveyor. "There's the little fella," he said when his inspection settled on Elliott. "How are you?"

"Sorry," said Sophie. "He's a bit out of his routine today. Well, for the last few days, I guess."

Elliott smiled at the man's waggling finger. "So," he said, finally drawing his attention away from the child. "You're the ones who bought Old Weldon's house. You haven't done much with it."

"What?" snapped Sophie. "We only moved in at the weekend. Look, can I show you what I found up at Roisin Kelly's place?"

"Oh yes, please do," Harris said, as if that wasn't the reason he had called round at all but rather a pleasant incidental surprise. "Now you do know about what she does, don't you?" he continued as she led him towards the kitchen. "She's not really a proper gardener the way you and I might know it. She makes up creepy displays, Halloweeny sort of stuff, but they're not real. I could see how someone might get confused."

"Yes, I know what she does. I would say that she's an artist as much as a gardener."

The sergeant contemplated the mess of plants and bloody scraps that Sophie had left on the kitchen table. "Is that what you'd call art?" he asked.

"I don't know what you'd call that," said Sophie. She pointed towards the eye, its pupil gaping at them longingly, as if waiting to be acknowledged. "Is that real? Is that human?"

"I don't know, I don't know," said Harris leaning down to examine it. "It might be an animal's. I'm no vet, or an ophthalmologist for that matter, but I don't like the look of it, or the smell of this stuff. Do you eat your dinner from this table? You'll want to give it a good scrubbing."

"What about the red pieces?" Sophie said, parking her annoyance at his last comment. "Bits of human organs?"

"Hmmm. Well, even if they're from an animal there may have been a crime committed. She's a troubled girl, poor Roisin, ever since she lost her husband."

"Well, that's only to be expected I guess."

"Yes, well, this sort of thing isn't expected. You didn't expect to see it, did you? She wrote you a little card, I see. How well do you know her?"

"Not well. We met for the first time yesterday."

"And do you know your neighbour well? Young Garda Hartnett?"

"We do, actually. Declan and my husband are old friends. That's why we moved here, I suppose. Why do you ask?"

"Oh, just asking. Is he at home, do you know? He's not answering my calls for some reason."

"I know he wasn't there yesterday. Denise was looking for him. But I haven't paid much attention to the comings and goings over there since then."

"Probably not best to get too involved, alright," said the Sergeant.

"What do you mean by that?"

"Don't get me wrong," said Harris. "I'm very fond of Declan, but I also know he can get himself into trouble. He hasn't turned up for work today or yesterday and I can't get in touch with him. I'm not sure what's going on with him at the moment but whatever it is might become a serious problem if he's not careful. Now, I'll go out and check on Roisin Kelly. I'll take this with me."

Harris took the planter, keeping it at arm's length while Sophie opened the front door for him. He placed it carefully on the passenger seat of his car and turned to Sophie.

"Evidence," he winked.

"Well, make sure it doesn't scatter off the seat and go everywhere."

He frowned then placed it on the floor of the car instead.

"Don't you be worrying now. You did the right thing to call us. Don't feel like you're wasting our time or anything."

"I don't feel that," said Sophie.

The sergeant got in his car and started the engine. He rolled down his window and gave an airy salute. "I'll be in touch."

Chapter Nineteen

"Have you rung them yet?"

"No, Conor. I haven't had the chance."

The clock in the museum cafe had a creepy image of a bog-body on its face. Luke noted the time and smiled at Louise behind the counter as she gave him his Americano at staff discount. He must have looked rough. She raised her eyebrows sympathetically at him and put a glass of orange juice on his tray for free. It was ten o'clock.

"Why haven't you rung them? Am I going crazy here? Is there something I'm missing? We were fucking attacked last night. There was a body removed from a grave."

Louise's smile strained at him and he realised how loud the volume of his phone was. He sat down in the corner of the cafe before answering Conor.

"Now, we don't know that for certain, do we? We're not sure if the grave was tampered with and we're not sure if we saw Brendan McGrath's body."

"I am fucking sure. You don't even know what he looks like so you have to take my word that it was him. Anyway, apart from that, you were attacked by that thing. You have to report that. You said you'd report it today."

"And I will. I just need to get it all straight in my head. It's still a bit unclear to me. I mean, what exactly was it that attacked us? If it was an animal like a badger or a fox then they won't want to know about it."

"A fucking badger? Fuck off, Luke!"

"Alright, alright. I'll call Declan as soon as I get off this call."

"Not him," said Conor.

"Why not?"

"He'll just sweep it under the carpet like he always does. C'mon Luke, just call someone who'll take it seriously."

Luke washed down two Paracetamol with the end of his coffee and brought the orange juice with him. He found a dark exhibition room that was closed to the public where he could pretend to be working. The walls were covered in old framed documents from the Irish Civil War. He tried not to think too much about the previous night. His head was too fragile to deal with it yet. He put something soft, melodic and Scandinavian on his iPod, attached his earphones and hoped nobody would bother him. Sporadically he got up on a small step ladder and re-focussed some pin-spots.

That really didn't help his eyes or his head. The soreness of both had ushered him into a chemist before work to get eyedrops as well as the headache tablets. He wished now he had gotten the even more expensive drops instead of the ones that were half price, because these ones didn't seem to be doing a whole lot of good. It said to only use them once every four hours, but he had now used them five times and it wasn't even lunchtime. At first, he wondered whether it would do him any harm but he was starting to believe that he had just bought an expensive and very small bottle of water.

Applying them had become second nature. No need to go to the bathroom and check in the mirror that he was aiming the little bottle directly over his eye before squeezing. Now he was able to whip it out of his pocket and drop them in with the same grace he displayed when delivering a cigarette from its packet to his mouth. That was part of the problem, he guessed, the smoking over the last couple of days had dried out his eyes.

Despite Conor's misgivings, Luke sent Declan a text during lunch.

"Saw some crazy shit on the roads with Conor last night."

"What kind of shit?" came the reply.

"Hard to tell, was a bit stoned. Could have been wild animals. He wants me to report it to the Guards."

"Consider it done. Don't you worry about it."

After lunch, Luke was even more tired so he snuck into a large storeroom in the lower floor of the museum and curled up behind a couple of semi-clad Celtic warriors who were missing some limbs and a smelly model of an ancient Irish elk with water-damaged fur. He was dozing in and out of sleep for maybe half an hour when he thought he heard one of the Celts talking. He stirred and stared into the gloom at the mannequins frozen in their unnatural poses. Then the lights came on and he realised the talker was one of his colleagues, an older, dandruffy man whom Luke found particularly repellent. "Is somebody there?" he was saying.

Luke stood up. "Uh, yeah, Cyril. It's just me. I'm just looking for something down here that I was, um looking for."

"You were looking for it in the dark, were you?" sneered Cyril.

"Yeah, that's right, Cyril. Maybe that's why I couldn't find it," said Luke, striding past him out the door and up the stairs.

He had kept his phone on silent for his sneaky rest and he checked it now to see the time. There were three missed calls from Sophie. He rang her back straight away and went outside the building for some privacy.

Sophie was upset. She told him about what she had found that morning when she visited this Roisin Kelly person. He didn't quite understand exactly what she was getting at when she said there were bits of organs and an eye in a plant display that she brought home. *It was supposed to be like that*, he thought. He was sure she had told him at some point yesterday that this woman made Gothic horror style displays. Then she said that the police had come round and taken it away.

"So, it was a real eye?" he ventured, still feeling sleepy.

"I don't know, that's the point. Neither did the sergeant. It smelled bad, the stuff in the planter. And Roisin can't be found. He just rang me to say she's not up there. They're getting men down to search the property."

Luke's head hurt. He swallowed two more Paracetamol using just his saliva to wash them down.

"Why are you making those noises?" asked Sophie.

"Tablets," he said. "Headache. So do they think that she was chopping up people to use in her plant displays?"

"I don't know. He said it might be from an animal either, or it might be her own eye. Or maybe it's nothing. You know you can get plants that give off a smell like death or like rotting flesh. Oh, I hope it's nothing, I really do, but I had to call the Guards, didn't I?"

Luke remembered the bits of flesh that the crows near Noel Quirke's car had feasted on.

"Was Declan around?"

"No. I tried him first. He didn't answer his phone but I left a voicemail. You must be wrecked after last night. We'll do nothing tonight, just crash on the couch and watch TV."

"The TV isn't connected yet."

"Then we'll read a book," Sophie said. "We'll listen to some music. We won't drink any wine."

"Ok. That'll be nice. I'm exhausted. I'm still not sure exactly what happened last night. I'm going to try and get out early so I don't get stuck in traffic. Love you, Sophie, see you soon."

But Luke didn't get to leave early. Professor Stafford, whom he reported to, asked him to complete a cataloguing job that he had been putting off for ages. He made a smart comment about the ancient weaving needles he had to catalogue not going to be any further out of fashion if he did the job next week instead and the professor, who was usually very easy going, particularly with Luke, admonished him for being late that morning.

"But I had to go to the chemist," Luke protested.

"And I don't want to make any accusations," said Stafford. "But a little birdy told me you may have been sleeping down in the storeroom during work hours."

"That flaky-haired prick!" said Luke.

The professor held up his hand in warning. Luke didn't like this new development. Stafford usually let Luke get on with things whatever way he wanted to and was accommodating towards late mornings or flexible afternoons. That was one of the reasons he had made the decision to move out of the city. So Luke skulked off to finish his work and when he left at a quarter to six he was confronted with the worst traffic he could have imagined. He sat in the Renault, crawling through the city, constantly adjusting the air-conditioning or opening and closing the windows. His temperature was so erratic, he thought he must be coming down with something.

By the time he got to the outskirts of the city he had seen three ambulances barging through the static traffic to get to incidents he heard tell of on the radio drivetime reports. He had blared his horn at two drivers who had bullied themselves ahead of him in merging lanes and more than two had beeped at him for similar transgressions. It was well past seven when he reached the motorway and was able to put his foot down.

The sky was infused with the same ashy colour he was imagining in his lungs. That was it; no more smoking. When he left the motorway to get on the national roads that led to Cromuck, that sky colour was like smoke rising from burning turf, and by the time he got on the local roads towards Kilcross it was as grey as charred logs, but crisper and clearer in this smog-less landscape. He could see the stars clearly and the glowing edges of the moon that smudged the sky. He drove past a house under construction and a site whose ground was just being broken. Quite a few of the houses that had sprung up along these roads were new. It must have seemed even more remote ten years ago. In another ten years he wondered how many more it would have built up. Would the roads have to be improved? Would there be more opportunity for work without having to drive as far as Dublin? He wondered as well about the people closed in behind their doors and what they all did for a living. They couldn't all be farmers or gardeners or Gardaí in the nearest town. How many made this commute like he did?

He passed O'Shea's, driving slowly, and noted very few cars in the car park and no quad bike. He felt guilty he hadn't bothered to call the Gardaí about last night. The conversation earlier with Conor had bothered him as well. There was something off about the man's state of mind. Must be too much smoke. Maybe he'd try to avoid him for a while until he could get his head around things.

Just ahead he could see the Twisted Tree. He didn't fancy slowing down beside it—it creeped him out—but he wanted to see if there was anything unusual, anything that might make sense of the night before. The branches appeared busier and fuller than he remembered. He stared at it for a split second too long while passing, so he wasn't watching the road when he heard a snap like the crack of a whip. He slammed on the brakes instinctively and swerved towards the side, just about halting before his tyres met the soft verge.

He put his hands across the steering wheel and lay his head on them. His pulse throbbed through his temples. His mind recalled a frame of an image that had registered in his sight before he directed his attention to the tree. There had been a line stretched across the road, the height of the top of the car. He tried to make sense of it. It must have been a rope or a wire. Who would have put a rope or a wire across the road? Was it an ambush? He lifted his head up quickly and looked behind him, into the road. There was no sign of anyone around. His next thought was that it was a prank by local kids, bored and irresponsible, and the annoyance almost made him get out and shout at any hidden, sniggering culprits but, as he pulled at the door handle, he felt the oppression of the shade around the vehicle. Anything could be out there. The animal that had jumped out at him last night? They had been drunk and stoned. It had to have been an animal, not one of Conor's stupid theories. He released his grip and tried to think clearly. Maybe it was a farmer guiding cattle into a nearby field. They did that sometimes, didn't they? They moved livestock up the road and tied a string or a wire across to stop them going past their gate. He had seen that before, surely. They must have forgotten to take it down. That was plausible. No need to get out and investigate. That's all it was, some idiot, irresponsible farmer. Who knows, maybe Conor, nervous and stoned, had done it himself. Did he farm cattle?

Luke hadn't turned off his engine all this time and the hum of it was soothing. There was no need to get out. He could just drive home to Sophie and Elliott. Then he saw what was on the side of the road, lit up by his headlights. Perhaps he had already glimpsed it, but because it was so disturbing a thing he hadn't allowed it into his conscious mind. Now, after the panic of the broken wire and his evasive swerve had passed, he could no longer mistake it for anything else.

He recognised her short bob of blonde hair. A smile still split her face, so he thought for a moment that maybe it was a stupid joke, like when people bury themselves up to their necks on the beach. She didn't have the rosiness anymore that usually pinkened her cheeks and when he strained his eyes he saw a pool of blood where her neck rested on the ground. He held the steering wheel tight and pressed his chin against it. Instinct guided his fingers to his phone and down the line of dialled numbers.

"Hey. What's up?"

"Declan, where are you? I … I've found … oh Jesus. It's her head Declan, it's that girl's head, it's been cut off."

"What? Are you with Conor again?"

"No, I'm at the Twisted Tree. On the way home from work. I can see her head. It's been chopped off and it's sitting on the ground. There was a wire stretched across the road. It must have sliced it off."

"Ok, now Luke, come on, pal. Calm down. I'm not far away. I'll check it out but you'd better get the hell out of there. I want you to just keep driving. Just go on home."

"But she's dead, Declan!"

"And that's exactly why you need to get out of there!"

Luke let the phone fall from his hand and when he picked it back up his friend had disconnected. Three deep breaths, still staring at the gruesome vista before him, wishing it would just vanish, just be a figment of his stupid imagination, then he called Sophie.

"Hiya," she said. "Everything ok?"

"Sophie," he paused and swallowed. It was hard to make the words come out. "Did you say that Garda Sergeant left you his number?"

"Yes. Is everything ok, Luke? What's the matter?"

"I've found something horrible, Sophie. What was his number? Will you text it to me?"

He hung up, fixated by the lifeless eyes of the girl's head on the ground. A text message arrived with the phone number. He called Sergeant Harris and explained who he was and where he was and what he was looking at.

"Right," said the sergeant. "I'm still up in Roisin Kelly's place. There's a team of us here so I'm going to come out to you with a couple of men. I want you to stay there, Luke."

"Ok."

"Now, lock your doors."

"Ok."

"Put on your hazard lights and make sure you're pulled in safely off the road but don't drive in too close to the … to the head. I don't want you to disturb the scene."

"Ok."

"And, Luke?"

"Yes?"

"If you see anyone approach you who doesn't arrive with blue flashing lights and in a uniform, get the hell out of there. Understand? Now I'll be there as soon as I can."

Luke lobbed the phone on the seat beside him and slumped back in his seat. Her eyes were open wide. She had such a pleasant expression on her face, as if she was really enjoying a cycle, listening to her music. One earphone was still in her left ear and the other dangled down by her chin. He put on his hazard lights and the orange glow of them warmed her face in intervals of one second. He couldn't bear to look at her any longer. He put the car in reverse, remembering what Sergeant Harris had said about not disturbing the scene, and slowly pulled back towards the Twisted

Tree, where there was more space to stay off the road. As he reversed, her head got lost to the darkness and a lump came to his throat. *They'll be here any second*, he thought, *just stay in the car and wait.* The tree loomed beside him. It definitely had more offerings on its branches than before. He tried to make them out in the moonlight. There was her bicycle helmet hanging by its strap. It was the same one she had been wearing the other times they met. A muddy white sports sock was suspended from a branch beside it. The end of the branch was pushed through the top of the sock but it didn't dangle limp and loose like the other socks on the tree, this one had shape and solidity. It was as if there was still a foot inside it. His head started to spin again. It wasn't mud that discoloured the sock, it was blood.

He scanned the other branches and his hand went up to his mouth. What he had first thought was a glove was not made from fabric at all. It was a human hand, severed at the wrist, tied with straw from its forefinger to hang from a thin, leafless branch.

The noise of approaching vehicles barely registered with him. It must be the bicycle girl's hand. There was another hand on a lower branch, dangling by its thumb. Something didn't make sense about what he was seeing on the tree. The area filled with blue strobing light from the two cars that slowly pulled up behind him. His eyes flitted from one hand to the other. She didn't have two left hands, surely? He opened the door and stepped out of the car, taking in the full view of the tree as the police lights pulsed behind him. A song repeated over and over in his head, a stupid nursery rhyme song:

'Heads, shoulders, knees and toes, knees and toes. Heads, shoulders, knees and toes, knees and toes.'

In among the rags and soiled socks were two more hands, and three more feet, chunks of flesh and bloody organs speared by various branches. He recognised a heart, he recognised a kidney, surprised that he could actually identify them. He didn't know what the other lumps of flesh and offal were.

'And eyes, and ears and mouth and nose.'

"Luke?" called the nice, round country accent that he had heard on the phone.

"That's me," he said. "I'm Luke." He couldn't take his eyes from the tree. He couldn't turn away from it. "I don't know what's going on here."

Chapter Twenty

"Did you know her name?" asked Luke. "I met her a few times and we talked but she never told me her name. She seemed very nice. She seemed to be just happy out cycling, she was harmless. Why would someone do that to her?"

Sergeant Harris sucked in his breath. He found it strange to be in Willy Weldon's kitchen with this young couple and their child talking about these things. There was the old sacred heart light, still on the wall beside the table at which they sat. He wondered if they would get rid of it when they began making the place their own. The woman, Sophie, seemed like the kind who would keep it, thinking it was retro or vintage. Willy Weldon hadn't been religious but his wife was. He had kept it there even though Harris knew he cursed God every day after his wife died just as much as he cursed and denigrated everyone and everything else apart from his daughter, Denise.

"I try not to concern myself anymore with why people do the things that they do. I'm sick of finding out that I'm mistaken about whatever I thought their motive was. Maybe that says something good about me, that I can't comprehend their reasons, but it's probably not good professionally speaking. Sometimes, though, they don't even know themselves why they do it. Anyway, my job only starts when the crime is committed, whatever the reasons behind it. Your job now is to tell me every little detail that you can possibly think of and then try and wipe it all from your mind and get back to rearing this little family of yours. Her name was Mary."

"Mary?"

"Yes, Mary Macklin. Are you seriously telling me you don't know who she is?"

They both shook their heads.

"Mary Macklin, the boxer. She was a national champion a few years back. She's pretty famous around these parts."

"That's why she kept saying she was training," said Luke. "How come she was just cycling around on the roads? Why was she not with a proper trainer or in a gym?"

"She was on a bit of a downhill slope, if you'll pardon the expression. I guess there's not much support in women's sports if you're not winning anymore. She had to do everything for herself recently, no trainer, no sponsorship. We all thought the Cardoza fight was as bad as it could get for her but I guess we were wrong."

"Well, you know everything I know," said Luke. "I only got there shortly before I called you. There was a wire strung across the road and my car snapped it so no other cars must have passed before I got there. She must have been cycling and not seen it. She must have been going fast enough for it to slice her head off."

"Unless they removed her head after she came off the bike," mumbled Harris.

Sophie picked up Elliott and held him against her chest. She wondered whether she should take him out of the room and put him to bed, but he didn't seem at all tired. He was fascinated by Sergeant Harris and his scruffy grey hair. She was conscious of protecting his innocent ears from what was being discussed but Luke seemed to need them both there. He kept reaching out to stroke his son's face or to hold her hand. The words in their conversation were awful but the tone was calm and sombre and quiet.

Perhaps it was alright for Elliott to listen. Perhaps the discussion of what his father had seen wouldn't seep into his precious little consciousness.

"I believe you're friends with Declan Hartnett" said Harris. "Any idea where he might be at the moment? Herself next door says she hasn't heard from him."

"No," said Luke. "Why do you ask? Surely, there's enough manpower without having to chase him down. He has personal stuff going on."

"Oh, we never have enough manpower unfortunately," said Harris. "Somebody said they spotted his car near Roisin Kelly's earlier today. Would you know anything about that?"

"I left him a voicemail before I called you about Roisin," offered Sophie. "I presumed that you'd have caught up with him by now. Luke, have you tried calling him? He might answer you."

"What?" said Luke. "Yeah, I mean no. I tried. He's not answering."

"Ah, he's a shocking man for getting himself in a fix," Harris shook his head. "Mary would have been known to him, you see, and not just for her celebrity. She previously made a complaint about Declan. For, ahem"—he glanced apologetically at Sophie —"for unwanted advances."

Sophie groaned. Declan shook his head. "No. No way. He hated her. I could tell from the way he spoke about her."

"Hated her?" asked Harris.

"Well, no, not, like, he didn't hate her as such, he just didn't have anything nice to say about her."

"It would help me if you knew where he was, Luke. It would help Declan."

"Look, I don't know where he is, but there's a girl."

"There's always a girl," said Sophie.

"There's a girl," continued Luke, after glaring at his wife, "that he's involved with. He said her name was Cliona. I can't remember if he mentioned her surname but I would guess that he's with her."

"I think I know who that is," said the sergeant. "I wish I didn't. I'm tired of making excuses for your friend."

"But he couldn't be involved in what happened to that bicycle girl," blurted out Sophie.

"I'm not saying that. God no, I'm not saying that, but I don't like the fact that this business with Mary and Roisin is going on and we can't find him. There also appears to be some … ahem … male body parts stuck on the tree."

Luke's face turned even paler than it had been. "Do you mean they might have gotten Declan too?"

Chapter Twenty-One

Conor Gallagher sat in his home studio with a CD blasting through his speakers. It was the first Stone Roses album. The riff from "I Wanna Be Adored" had been ticking away in his head all day so he had searched through his albums and breathed a sigh of relief when he laid his hands on the paint-splattered design of the cover.

That was fifty-three minutes ago and, as soon as he heard the tune outside of his own head, a calmness came over him. It was like a valve had been opened and the pressure of having the song inside his head was released.

He didn't pay attention to the rest of the album after that first song finished and when the last song had played out, he didn't bother to put on anything else. He just sat there, holding his father's old shotgun across his knees and rolling shells around in his hand. Now that the album had finished, he thought he could hear low, mean laughter outside in his yard.

CHAPTER TWENTY-TWO

This was a bad place to be. This was a place of frayed nerves and doors slamming and shouts down stairwells and curtains closed to the daylight. Declan wasn't sure what time it was when he woke. The light peeking under the blinds suggested that it was likely around noon. He had a vague awareness of it being Wednesday.

They were on a mattress on the floor in Cliona's brother's apartment, a cheap little one-bedroom place on the third floor of a block of flats in Cromuck. He sat up and dragged his jeans over from where they lay crumpled at the end of the mattress. He pulled a packet of cigarettes and a lighter from the pocket, surprised to find them both still there and even more surprised to find five Benson & Hedges left in the packet. He lit one. It was after his third pull of the cigarette he realised that the ashtray was on the breakfast bar that separated the kitchenette from the living room where they lay.

He flicked the first pile of ash on the floor but then decided he'd need the ashtray eventually to stub out the cigarette so he got up and sat at one of the kitchen stools to finish it. Cliona slept on, undisturbed. The thin blanket only covered half of her back. Her rich copper hair wrapped around her neck like a scarf. It was warm in the apartment. The nicotine made his veins tingle. Her shoulder blade was a thing of beauty to him at that moment, its skin smooth, its shape elegant. It was enticing him to crawl back in under the blanket and kiss it, lie up against it, sleep against it, but he was too fidgety to get back into their makeshift bed. He was antsy and twitchy and wanting.

He put on his jeans and sat back on the stool with his top off, examining his own skin, fascinated at how pale it looked in the drab grey light of the room. His phone was on the breakfast bar, hiding among empty lager bottles plugged into a charger. He had twenty-nine missed calls. He knew that would put the fear in a lot of people in his current condition but he wasn't that type of person. The phone rattled silently with what would become the thirtieth missed call. He learnt two things from the screen of the phone: that the time was indeed just gone midday and it was Luke who was ringing him again. Cliona's brother Tommy came into the kitchen wearing tracksuit bottoms and a black vest.

"Are you still not answering that yoke?" he said.

"Nope," said Declan.

"It's been hopping since you showed up here last night with a big frightened head on you. Why don't you just turn it off?"

The phone pinged with the receipt of a voicemail. Declan stubbed out his cigarette in the ashtray and smiled.

"I like to hear what's going on. See who's looking for me. Listen to my messages."

"I hope no one comes here looking for you," said Tommy. He filled the kettle and switched it on. "I'm making coffee. Do you want some?"

"Is there any beer left?" said Declan.

"Oh, it's like that, is it?" Tommy opened the fridge and placed a bottle of Heineken on the counter. Declan opened it and took a long gulp.

"This place would drive you to it. Jesus, it's so grey and depressing. Is it just full of teenage mothers with screaming brats and drug dealers?"

"Yeah, that's about all that's here alright, and you of course," said Tommy.

Cliona stirred. "What time is it?" she asked through dry lips.

"It's after twelve," answered her brother.

"I feel like shit."

"I dunno why," said Tommy. "You didn't drink much."

She threw a conspiratorial glance towards Declan. "I told you last night, Tommy, I'm not feeling well these days." Then she noticed the beer. "Declan, are you drinking already? How long are you up?"

"Just up. You should just tell him, Cliona. Tell him if you want to."

"Maybe I don't want to."

"Tell me what," said Tommy, sipping his coffee.

"She's pregnant."

"Fuck you, Declan." She grabbed her T-Shirt from beside the mattress and pulled it on while marching out to the bathroom.

"Ah, so that's what all this talk of getting away was last night," said Tommy. "That's why you were planning to run away to London together."

"London? Oh yeah. Did I agree to that?" said Declan, lighting another cigarette.

"Agree to it? It was your idea," said Tommy. "Well, congratulations anyway. It'll change your life I'm sure, fatherhood."

"It hasn't so far."

"Oh yeah, that's right. You already have one. Well maybe this one will." Tommy took a packet of papers from the cupboard over the kettle and started to roll a joint. "It changed me, I'll tell you that much."

Cliona came back from the bathroom, her face still glistening from washing it, her hair pulled back from her face. "How did it change you, Tommy?" she said, snidely.

"Well, I don't just have myself to think about now. I have to put a bit of money aside, for his future, and for maintenance and stuff, you know."

"Men are pricks," she said, stepping into her jeans.

"I'll be sorry to see you go again," said Tommy. "It's better for you over there though. Like you said last night, there's opportunity for you there, you have better friends over there. There's nothing in this town worth staying for. You'll be ok too, Declan. Fuckers like you always make out alright."

"Yeah, sure, why the fuck not," said Declan leaning back precariously on the stool. "When are we going, Cliona? What's keeping us?"

"Whenever you want to, Declan. You said you have to sort out a few things here and then we're gone. You said you know people who would get you a job in security over there. You said we can get a little place and start a new life."

"Fuck, yeah, let's do it. Tommy, gimme another beer."

"Here you go, Declan."

"Good man." Declan flicked off the cap. "What about a little something to wake me up as well, huh Tommy?"

"So, is that what today is going to be, Deccie? You disappeared for ages yesterday evening and spent the whole night getting wasted," sighed Cliona. "I thought we might start making arrangements today with a clear head."

"I'm going to have to ask you for some money for this one, Declan," said Tommy. "You know, if you're leaving your job and all, and leaving the country, then what am I getting out of it apart from a hole in my stash?"

Declan slammed his bottle of beer down on the counter, creating a volcano of foam from its neck. "What's that now, Tommy? You're a fickle fucker, aren't you? Do you think I won't have any sway around here even if I'm in another country? You'll give me whatever the fuck I ask for whenever I ask for it, understand! And here I am about to make you a proud uncle as well."

Tommy cast his eyes downward and swirled the end of his coffee around in his cup. He didn't say anything. He knew this was a hassle he likely wouldn't have to deal with for much longer one way or the other, so he took a small half-full bag of white powder from his pocket and tossed it onto the counter.

"Good lad, Tommy."

"Fuck's sake," said Cliona.

"Don't worry, baby, we'll put things in motion today. I just need to put a pep in my step. Here, Tommy, here's a line for you."

Tommy shook his head.

"Come on, Tommy."

Tommy shrugged and took his offering. "Thanks, Declan."

"Cliona?"

"Ok, fuck it, who cares," she said, tempted by the line that was being cut for her. "Just a small one, ok. Just a little bit won't hurt anyone, I suppose."

Declan put his arm around her waist as she leaned over the counter.

"One thing I have to do is get my passport and a few things from the house," he said. "Ha, ha, oh fuck, she is going to kill me, ha ha."

CHAPTER TWENTY-THREE

Luke didn't go into work in the morning. He was awake early enough to have got there on time if he'd wanted to. He actually got out of bed and went to the bathroom, stared into the mirror and thought of shaving, but when he ran the razor under the tap and rubbed the blades with his thumb to remove some old stubble residue he winced, and a dart of displeasure speared his stomach. He put the razor away in the cabinet beneath the sink and stared back at his face and the dark rings around his eyes. Their unwholesome colour matched the shadow of stubble on his jaw. *He looked gaunt and unkempt but in a handsome enough way to get away with it*, he thought.

When he had finished admiring himself and trudged back to the bedroom to get dressed, he found Sophie sitting up in bed to greet him.

"Don't go in," she said. "You look terrible. You look so tired."

"Alright," he said, needing no further persuasion, and got back into bed.

He shut his eyes but didn't sleep. At nine o'clock he rang the museum to say he wouldn't make it in. He scoured his brain for a believable lie, chose a vomiting bug and was ready to conscript it as an excuse but he realised then that the truth was a perfectly acceptable explanation for his absence today. He told Professor Stafford about the Twisted Tree and its grisly decorations, the police involvement, the missing woman, and the girl's head on the ground staring at him, staring into the glare of his headlights that made her eyes glint and sparkle. He went into great detail about the head and also the girl it belonged to and how she seemed like a friendly, nice, healthy person, the kind of person who made you smile when she approached and again when she cycled away, singing aloud, unselfconsciously. Although he had only met her a couple of times, he was enveloped by a sadness even stronger than the shock of discovering her body. It was a rotten world where that could happen.

By the end of their conversation Professor Stafford was expressing his deep concern for Luke and offered anything he could do to help, whether it was an ear to listen or an elder's advice or simply whatever time he needed to take off work to recover. Luke thanked him for the latter and, when he put his phone on the bedside locker and leaned back against the pillow, he felt a little relief. At least Stafford was back on his side. He reckoned he probably even appeared a little heroic to his boss now.

Sophie kissed him on the forehead and got up to make them all breakfast.

Luke lay there, feeling at peace for about five minutes, until the memories of the last few days crawled back into his thoughts. The discovery of the boy racer's car came back to him. Was that connected to his other gruesome discovery? And where the fuck was Declan? He reached for his phone, rang his friend but it went to voicemail.

"Declan, ring me back. Everyone is wondering where you are. There's something very dangerous out there; whoever or whatever cut that Mary girl to bits and used her to decorate that fucking tree. I need to know that you're alright."

During breakfast with Sophie and Elliott, he couldn't smile even when Elliott tipped his bowl of soggy rusk over his own head. Luke wanted this day to just disappear. He sat down with Elliott on his knee and put on a *Teletubbies* DVD, which made his son coo at the colourful characters and slow repetitive sounds. Luke's eyelids fell like curtains. On their insides played distortions of the child's programme where the slow actions of the characters became increasingly sinister, and they all moved around in a nightmare garden of body parts. The weird noises they made were the sounds of them eating those dismembered limbs.

He spluttered awake. He needed to do something practical with the day to occupy his mind. Anything to keep his mind off what he had seen the night before. He decided to tackle the problem of them having no TV signal. Then at least he would have the distraction of television when the evening came round.

There was a cable coming from a port in the wall but when he plugged it in and searched for channels, he found that he couldn't tune anything in. Luke was reasonably good at fixing things, in a haphazard kind of way. He ventured outside to make sure that the aerial was still on the roof. It was there alright and, from a distance, it looked to be in good nick. The attic space was accessible through a painted wooden panel above the landing of the stairs. He found a step ladder in the shed that would get him up there. The panel was stiff but he managed to force it open and stick his head up into the darkness. He ran his hands around the edge of the opening and a splinter bit into his palm. There was a light switch attached to the outside of the wooden frame. He tried it a few times but nothing happened. He shone the torch of his phone into the space and could see the bulb dangling from its cord in front of him. The bottom of it was black and blown out. He could make out the water tank, an old suitcase and a box of dusty toys, and he could just about see where the cable from the aerial came through the roof and into a splitter box. It was too far away to reach without getting up into the attic and crawling across the joists. All of a sudden he felt exposed and vulnerable with his head sticking up into the space and he was visited by a memory of Mary's decapitated head. He scrambled down the ladder and into the kitchen.

"Are you ok?" asked Sophie.

"We don't have any light bulbs, do we?" he said breathlessly.

"I don't think so."

"It's too hard to work up there with just a torch. I might have a look in the shed."

"You should just rest, Luke."

"No, no. I'd prefer to be doing something, you know, need to keep busy."

So, he bustled out to the shed and spent the next half hour rooting through ancient tins and musty boxes for a light bulb until the gardening tools began to appeal to him instead. His head was getting cloudy and sore from the dust and the dim light. He pulled out the old lawnmower and set it out on the lawn.

He took out anything he could find for garden maintenance and arranged them beside it. There were spades and a rake, bulb planters and rusty shears. Sophie emerged from the back door with Elliott balanced on her hip and Luke's phone in her opposite hand.

"I was thinking of getting stuck into the garden the other day," she said. "Are those things still working?"

"Let's find out," said Luke, and he pulled the cord of the lawnmower. The cord fought against his efforts. "I suppose I should have checked it for petrol first."

He opened the cap and shook his head. He went over to the brush cutter and could see through its clear fuel tank that only a dribble coloured the bottom of it.

"Your phone rang. It was Sergeant Harris. He wants you to go down to the station to fill in a statement."

"Aw no, did I not answer enough questions last night?"

"Apparently not," said Sophie. "There was a call from Declan as well. It went to your voicemail before I could get to it."

Luke lunged for the phone.

"Are you not telling me something, Luke?"

"What? No, of course not."

"When was the last time Declan was in touch with you?"

The beat it took for him to figure out a lie was enough to betray him. Sophie's mouth dropped in disbelief.

"I don't want to get him in trouble, Sophie."

"Tell Sergeant Harris whatever you know. For God's sake!" She marched back towards the house.

"How about we all go in together?" Luke called after her. "We can go for a nice coffee in town and I can get that light bulb and some petrol for these things. I'll just push this stuff inside the shed in case it rains."

Inside the shed, Luke listened to Declan's voice, whispery and urgent, tell him to keep him abreast of developments and not say they'd been talking.

CHAPTER TWENTY-FOUR

After taking that line of coke in Tommy's kitchen with Declan and her brother, Cliona was struck with a pang of guilt. She told Declan she didn't want any more and he put his hand on her stomach and kissed her neck and said, "I understand." But that didn't stop him from finishing the bag with Tommy and having another two bottles of beer. The flat started to get claustrophobic. "I'm going out," she said. "I'm hungry."

"I have some food here," said Tommy.

"What have you got?"

"I'm not sure exactly."

"I want to go out. I want to get something proper to eat in a proper cafe and get out of this dead air. Are you two going to come with me or not?"

Declan's feet fidgeted on his stool like he was doing a little tap-dance. He kept checking his phone.

"I don't know, baby. I get a feeling I should be keeping a low profile just at the moment. There's a lot of people looking for me by the evidence of all these calls and messages and I don't really fancy running into any of them."

"So, are you going to hide out here forever or just until Tommy's supply runs out?"

"Relax, Cliona. We're going to get out of here, remember. Out of this shithole town and this shithole country. I just need a little time to get my head together. When it gets dark, I'll go back to my house and grab my passport and a few things. Book the first flights out of here."

"Just like that?"

"Just like that. We'll go straight to the airport from there. You have no ties. You're just bouncing from gaff to gaff. You said last night that you could leave with just the clothes you have in this place."

"You'll just whisk me away, will you?" she said.

"Come here."

He put his arms on her shoulders without getting up from his stool and gave her a long kiss. "Bring me back something nice to eat, will you?"

Cliona removed herself from his clinch.

"Tommy has food here for you," she said and marched out of the flat.

Cliona liked the café off the main street with the old stone steps but it was absolutely rammed and there was a couple struggling with a buggy that struck her as too ominous a sign for her present mood. There was a bagel place in the town shopping centre. That would have to do instead. Once there, she ordered a tuna bagel and salad with a black coffee and took a table in the open-plan dining area. The shopping centre was thronged with people and she shielded her face a couple of times when she thought she saw heads she knew, people she recognised from school whose faces had either fattened or harrowed with the intervening decade. She didn't eat much of the bagel, poked at the salad but she enjoyed the coffee and she enjoyed being on her own. Even among the noise and jumble of shoppers she was able to think.

Cliona had left London last year after spending five years there. Those five years had seemed like somebody else's life. She wasn't entirely sure that she wanted to go back there now but she had to get out of Cromuck. Living back here was like being in an audience while a cast of ghosts tried to drag her on stage with them. None of them had any lines to say or any actions to perform, they just wanted her to stand up there, pointless and dumb with them, until the curtains eventually fell. London at least could set her up for her next step in life, whatever that might be. She would just have to try to avoid her ex-boyfriend, the main reason she left there in the first place. She would definitely have to make sure that he and Declan didn't meet. There was no outcome where that could possibly be a good thing. She stirred the coffee-silt at the bottom of her cup to dissolve it in the remaining liquid.

They were actually quite similar, Declan and her ex. Did she have a type? An unreliable, slightly criminal type? Though, the fact that Declan was a Garda actually made him worse. He was cleverer and sneakier. Even the fact of where he parked his car when he came into town to meet her was clandestine. He always parked it down the back of a second-hand car lot whose owner he had some kind of hold over and who had given him a set of keys to let himself in and out as he pleased. He had even brought her there one night to have sex in the grimy prefab that acted as an office. She had a funny feeling that that's where her current predicament came into existence. He hadn't bothered to use a condom that time.

It was funny that this was her town—where she was born, grew up, went to school—but she had no importance in it at all, no recognition apart from being that girl who liked to party and then went to London. Declan was only really here a few years and yet his tentacles reached everywhere in Cromuck. It's like he was able to root out weaknesses in people and mould them to do what he wanted. What did that say about her? He saw her weaknesses, her lack of direction, her suggestibility. He had her where he wanted her for a long time; the bit on the side who didn't hassle him and didn't ask for more, who was always ready for a good time because she didn't have anything better to do anyway. Well, that had all changed now. Now he owed her. He owed her for the callous way he assumed she would have an abortion.

Of course, that had been her first inclination as well but, as the concept of a child sat within her, she grew to think that it might be a good thing. It could change her. She had spent her life flitting from job to job without any dedication. She tried various hobbies and sports but none of them stuck for more than a couple of months. The only real constant in her life was clubbing but she had seen how some of her old clubbing companions in London had changed when they had children. They became like earth mother types. They seemed more stressed and less fun to be around than before they had kids but they also projected a sense of purpose. She had never experienced the need for a sense of purpose before but maybe now was the time, whether Declan was involved in it or not.

They'd have to knock the drugs on the head and stop going out as much, apart from on special occasions. She would just have to be very wary of Declan over there. He couldn't be counted on. The fact he was going to leave his wife and son to go to London with her was telling. Having that first child hadn't changed him. Though she knew the type that Denise was. She knew that type from going out in Cromuck. She could understand why Declan would want out of that.

When Cliona got back to the flat, Declan was crashed out on the couch. She could see in his crunched eyebrows that when he woke, he was going to have a bastard of a headache. Tommy was playing a game on his Xbox but he had the sound turned down respectfully low.

"Do you have any tablets?" she asked him.

"Tablet tablets?"

"No, don't be stupid. Headache tablets. For him, when he wakes up."

"There's some in the bathroom cabinet."

"Thanks."

"You really going with him?"

"I guess so. You never know, Tommy, things might work out for me."

She squeezed her brother's shoulder as a pasty beam of sunlight anointed the squalor of the room.

"Cliona." Tommy put down his game console. "I've known him for a few years now. I've seen what he can be like. Just be careful, ok?"

CHAPTER TWENTY-FIVE

It didn't look like it was going to rain ever again. It was one of those crisp, bright September days you often got in Ireland that made you forgive the country for its erratic summer. Sophie wore her sunglasses while she drove and Luke pulled the visor down. Her annoyance with him only faded after repeated assurances that he wasn't going to tell stupid lies for Declan.

"But surely you don't believe he has anything to do with it?" Luke protested.

"No. I don't. And that's all the more reason not to lie for him. Whatever other mischief he's up to, it pales to nothing compared to what's going on."

At the Twisted Tree, a squad car held vigil with a young Garda sitting on the bonnet. Luke recognised him from being with Harris the night before. They slowed to a crawl. They could see into the field beyond the tree. Three men in pale jumpsuits drifted like ghosts examining the ground while a large white van attracted them sporadically to its open side door. The Garda waved with a friendly smile and Luke raised his hand in reply.

"Don't stop to talk," he said to Sophie. "I can't bear to look at that tree. I can still see blood on the branches."

"I'm surprised they don't have the road closed," said Sophie.

"I wish they'd chop that fucking tree down and burn it. I dread having to see it every time we leave the house from now on."

"Unless we're going in the other direction."

"There's sweet fuck all in the other direction," he replied.

When they got to the station Sophie took Elliott for a walk around town while Luke spoke with Sergeant Harris. They went over and over the same story he had given the night before. How many different ways could he describe it? Harris pressed him for anything he might have noticed before seeing the head. Had he seen anyone else at the scene or running away from it? No. Had he heard from Declan? Had Declan had ever spoken to him about Roisin Kelly?

"No, he never did. Was she the other body then?"

"It appears so, although we haven't found all of her yet."

"And the eye and the bits that my wife brought home?"

"Yes, we think they were part of her."

Luke's stomach turned. He wasn't sure if he should try and keep that news from Sophie or not.

"And there was a man, you said. A man's parts?"

"Yes," said Harris. "We're looking into who that might be." He eyed Luke slyly. "It's not Declan."

"Oh great. I mean, it's good that it's not him. Not good for whoever it is, of course."

He pondered whether he should mention finding Noel Quirke's car, but he thought he'd better wait until he spoke to Declan. No point in opening up a can of worms. Hadn't Declan told him he didn't need to worry about that?

"If you think of anything else," said Sergeant Harris.

"Sure."

Luke sloped out of the station. Sophie and Elliott were waiting outside for him.

"How was that?" she asked.

Luke took a heavy breath. "Just going over what I said last night."

"And you told them that Declan was in touch?"

"Yup."

"And have they discovered anything new?"

Luke decided that Sophie was strong enough for this truth and he also didn't have the energy to keep another lie going. "The other body parts were Roisin Kelly's."

"Oh." Her eyes fell.

"And so were the parts in the pot you brought home."

"Ugh." She shivered. "Well, I guess I knew that but it's still disgusting to think about it. I picked them up with my bare hands."

"I don't even want to think about it anymore." He took her hand in his and squeezed it. "Come on, let's go and get a coffee and try to take our minds off it."

They found a little cafe with small stone steps and a narrow door that almost deterred Elliott's buggy. They managed to manoeuvre it inside and, with some rearranging of chairs, tucked it in beside their table under the glare of the middle-aged lady behind the counter. The place was tight and noisy with the chatter of customers. There were no menus on the tables, just a chalk board behind the counter. Luke went up to it and looked past the lady's sour expression to decipher the handwritten offerings. She grumpily took his order and then pointed to a sign on the window that said 'No buggies'.

"Right, sorry, I didn't notice that. We'll leave then. Is there anywhere nearby that does allow buggies?"

"Well, it's too late now, I suppose. You're already inside. I'll bring down your coffees when they're ready."

Luke considered leaving anyway, he knew that was what Sophie would do, but he was looking forward to the coffee and he fancied a piece of the carrot cake behind the glass counter. "Gimme two pieces of that as well, please."

He sat back down and Sophie nodded towards the window. "No buggies," she said.

Rather than try to forget about their recent grisly experiences they found themselves exploring them in detail. Sharing and speaking about them together took away some of the horror.

"Now at least if we wake up screaming, we'll wake up screaming together, and about the same things," said Sophie.

They located a hardware store on the outskirts of the town and bought spare light bulbs, motor oil for the lawnmower and two-stroke mixture for the other machines. They also bought a petrol can and stopped at the filling station on the way home. When they got back to the house Sophie said, "Oh shit, we should have gotten the spare tyre fixed."

"I'll go back in tomorrow and get it done somewhere," said Luke.

"So, are you not going to work tomorrow?"

"Nah, Professor Stafford said to take as much time as I feel I need, so I reckon there's no point in going in until next Monday. We could do with the time to settle in. I should have taken some days off for that anyway, I didn't realise it would be such a stressful move."

"I don't think moving is usually quite like this," said Sophie.

For the rest of the day, Luke got stuck into doing things around the house. He replaced the bulb in the attic and under the restored light, found that the cable coming from the TV aerial had corroded. Rooting around in their unpacked boxes, he unearthed an old coaxial cable and some connectors. A good hour of snipping and twisting and botching bits together in the cramped roof space finally resulted in him replacing the corroded piece. The privacy up there also gave him the chance to call Declan with an update. They both sounded like kids telling secrets over walkie-talkies past bedtime but Declan wasn't giving a whole lot of detail in return.

"I still have stuff to sort out. I'll be seeing you soon. Don't worry."

Luke came down covered in dust and smiles.

"I'm like fucking MacGyver," he said to Sophie. "Your daddy is like MacGyver, little man," to Elliott.

After that he went outside and cleaned up the lawnmower. He filled it up, started it and tried to cut the lawn, but the length of the grass kept making the machine cut out. He turned his attention to the strimmer and the brush cutter instead. The line of the strimmer was almost gone and, anyway, as much as he tried, he wasn't able to start it. The brush cutter was in better condition. He pushed the little bulb on the side until it filled with fuel, tried a few positions of the throttle and got the engine to purr on the third pull. There was a harness hanging from a nail in the shed which he assumed belonged to it. He brushed the cobwebs and a dead spider from it, adjusted the straps and put it on. The straps pinched the skin under his armpits so he loosened it before clipping it to the rumbling machine. It was heavy and hard to balance. He pressed a button on the handle and the rumble turned to a roar. Smirking with excitement, he tore into the long grass. It was only when something clipped his cheek that he realised that he should be wearing goggles. He scythed through a bit more of the seed headed growth, then switched it off. He was sweating already from the weight of it. He would have to buy goggles and ear protectors tomorrow when he was out getting a new spare tyre and then he'd take a good cut at the garden. The next hour was spent rearranging and tidying the shed, making space to get at the garden tools easily. He was getting a feel for this gardening lark.

"Come here and look at this," he called into Sophie. She came out and watched him fire up his new toy and slice up a bunch of nettles that had colonised a corner of the flower bed.

"Put that away." She laughed. "You'll chop your dick off."

"I like it out here," he said. "I think we could make this into a great place. There's enough room to make a whole playground for Elliott and whoever else might come after him."

They took a few minutes to walk around the space, stepping out vague measurements for swing sets and slides, vegetable patches and herb gardens. Then they went inside and made dinner together while Elliott rolled around on a big soft playmat on the kitchen floor. The sun was sinking into the horizon when they sat down to eat. Luke observed the two of them and almost wanted to hold their hands and say grace, like a happy Christian pilgrim thankful for another day with his family. Instead, he gazed at his wife and said, "Thank you, Sophie."

"For what? The dinner? You helped me make it."

"Just, for everything. For you, for Elliott."

Her cheeks pinkened. "Shut up," she said.

Luke picked Elliott out of his high chair and brought his bowl over with him.

"Come on, young man. You can have dinner sitting on your daddy's knee."

He fed him a few spoons of mashed sweet potato and turned him around so he could get a good look at him. Elliott got the food nice and slimy with saliva then let it drool all over his father's T-Shirt.

After dinner they cooed over their son for a while before putting him to bed. They sat down in the sitting room and enjoyed the novelty of having terrestrial TV again, although the only thing worth watching was the nine o'clock news. Luke pulled across the curtains as the last hints of dusk were gulped up by the night.

Then Denise arrived.

She hammered at the front door until Sophie let her in. Until that night, Luke had never really thought much about Denise one way or the other. Declan didn't really talk to him in detail about her and she didn't seem to have changed his friend to any substantial extent. Luke thought she was attractive in a bland, popstar sort of way. She could pass herself off as the grumpy one in a girl band. He knew Sophie found her both dull and demanding but she was always polite to him, though he had probably never had a proper, in-depth conversation with her about anything. He just accepted the fact that she was present now at any formal occasion that involved him and Declan but she didn't really affect him and if someone didn't affect him then he tended not to think about them that much.

Before now though, he had never experienced her in full attack mode.

She stormed in through the door in a frenzy, holding Bill firmly by the hand, as if he were a weapon she was about to deploy. The boy had a manic, eager smile on his face, the kind of expression that knew it was about to witness someone else get into serious trouble. Luke was familiar with that smile; Bill had inherited it from his father.

"Luke," shouted Denise. "Come on, you're coming with me now. That bastard friend of yours is in O'Shea's pub and the prick has his slut with him."

Luke stepped back from Denise as if pushed by the force of her words.

"In O'Shea's?" said Sophie. "So, he's finally turned up. We should call Sergeant Harris. He's looking for him."

Denise and Luke both shouted together: "No!"

"Not yet, Sophie. Luke, you're going to drive me up there and I'm going to shame him in front of the whole place. I'm going to bring little Willy and he can look his son in the eye and choose between him and that bitch and if he won't come back willingly then you can help me drag him back."

"Denise, Denise, calm down," said Sophie. "Luke will drive you there alright, that's not a problem, but I don't think it's such a good idea to bring Willy. Look at him, the poor little fellow is confused by all this."

The boy was twitching hyperactively, as if a sugar bomb had gone off in his head.

"I know this must be awful for you," Sophie went on. "You can leave Willy with me. I'll mind him while Luke goes with you."

Denise glared warily at her, as if this were a trap of some sort. Then she knelt down in front of her son. "Is this upsetting you, Willy? Are you ok?"

The boy's eyes couldn't focus on his mother, they kept darting around like their sockets wouldn't be able to contain them for much longer.

"Right," said Denise, "I'll leave him here with you. This isn't right what Declan is doing to me and to his son. He's humiliating me. You two had better be on my side."

Luke turned to Sophie as if to plead for help before addressing Denise.

"Are you sure you want to go there? It's late. There's no good that can come from causing a scene. I'll talk to him tomorrow and try to get his side of the story."

"He has no side of the story!" Denise roared. "The story is that he's a lying, cheating bastard and that's the end of the story. Now hurry up and let's go before they escape."

Luke's eyes dropped to his chest. "Just let me change my T-Shirt," he said, backing out of the room. "Elliott dribbled on it. I should change it, and I have to get my jacket."

He went upstairs to their bedroom with Denise's voice calling after him to get a move on. He fumbled with his phone as soon as he was out of sight and started writing a warning text to Declan. He didn't dare ring him within earshot of Denise. He just hoped that his friend would read the text before he had delivered his wife's rage to him.

Chapter Twenty-Six

In Declan's car, Cliona kept thinking of Tommy's words, or rather of his concerned expression when he spoke them. Tommy was rarely concerned about anything. Declan had slept until the early evening and when he got up, he had two more beers and another line of coke before they went to get his car from the used car lot. He was pleased she was accompanying him, said it was fitting that they began this new adventure together, said he was doing it all for her. But as they left Cromuck and got on the country roads, the cocaine confidence wore off him and he started acting nervously.

She didn't like the erratic way he was driving. She had driven on these roads a few days ago. Although they now appeared unfamiliar in the dusk, she remembered they were narrow, twisting and unforgiving of speed. That had been the day she discovered that she was pregnant.

It summed up the way things always seemed to fall for her that on the day she learned of a new life inside her she was showing up in a daze at a stranger's funeral to announce it to another woman's husband. Even then she couldn't even bring herself to go up to him when she clocked him there in his suit, looking like a respectable member of the community. He wasn't so respectable now though, wiping at his nose and turning the radio on, then off, loud then low.

"I'm not too sure how this is going to go, Cliona," he said.

"What do you mean?"

"She's not going to react well. You don't know what she can be like."

"So, what are you saying, Declan? Are you saying you don't want to leave her? Just tell me if that's what's happening, ok, so I can make other plans for my life." Her voice was calm and resigned. She realised she had been expecting to be let down all along, the only surprise was that Declan was still fooling himself.

"No, it's not that. Maybe I just need to steel myself. I need to leave her, fuck I want to leave her. I just wish it was already done." She could see lights up ahead of them as he spoke. "If I could just click my fingers and get my stuff from the house without having to even see her … Let's just pull up here for a while."

Declan steered the car towards the lights illuminating the car park of that village pub he lived near. "I need a drink," he said. "I'll be able to do it after a drink, or else maybe I can work out some other way to get in and out without having to face her."

They entered the dull lounge and Cliona sat down at a table in the corner. Declan stood in the middle of the floor before he went up to the bar and he twirled around with wildness in his eyes, as if expecting to be pounced on by somebody, baring his claws in defence. Cliona tucked herself right into the corner of the seat and her fingers scratched at its drab, green upholstery. The lounge was half populated with drinkers but not too noisy yet. There was no music coming from the tatty speakers on the walls and most people were just muttering away in pairs. They all stared at Declan but nobody acknowledged him with a greeting apart from one spindly-limbed old man on his way back from the toilets. Declan ordered two bottles of lager and brought them down to the table. He knocked back the first one before saying anything and went back up to buy two more and a whiskey chaser.

"Can't wait to get out of this fucking hole," he said. "London will be full-on, won't it, Cliona?"

"Yes," she said. "It can be whatever you want it to be, I guess. I'll need to have a different life than the one I had there before, if we have this baby. You know that?"

"Yeah, the baby," he said. "It'll be good to get away though. Good for me. Leave all this shit behind."

They sat there for a while, watching the people who came in. Some of the younger ones came up to talk to Declan but he was too much in his own head to make any sense of them and Cliona couldn't make out what they said. The speakers came to life with music, some old compilation album of Irish rock that raised the volume of everyone's conversation. She drank another bottle of beer and Declan knocked back two more whiskeys. She wasn't sure anymore if there was any possible direction for this evening to take except oblivion for Declan and probably a taxi home for her. She didn't care. There was no point in expecting anything from him in this state. When he wasn't glowering at the other customers he was squinting at his mobile.

Then, all of a sudden, as if a different entity had taken possession of his body, he became forthright and determined.

"Ok," he said. "Let's do it." His eyes were circling in their sockets like a flyweight in a boxing ring. "Let's go there and get it over with. I'll get what I need and tell her it's over. Clean break. I'll need you to drive, Cliona. I'm probably not alright to drive."

"I shouldn't be driving either. I've been drinking too."

Declan pulled a face. "What? Two beers?"

"I still feel a bit spaced out from earlier, come on, Declan, forget it. We'll just have another drink and then call for a taxi back to Cromuck. Get the car tomorrow and get your passport and do whatever else you need to do then."

"Fuck that shit, Cliona. It's now or never. I'm doing this for you."

Cliona reckoned Declan had never in his life done anything for anyone but himself but she didn't argue. She was being pushed along in whatever direction he pointed her in. She knew he wasn't a safe or reliable navigator but she didn't care anymore. Her arguments against him were always half-hearted. It was like if he made the decisions then she could enjoy doing the wrong thing without taking responsibility for it. Leaving her beer, they pushed their way through the huddle of drinkers out to the car park. She adjusted the seat to her petite frame and turned the mirrors to suit.

Cliona liked driving but she rarely drove in the dark. When it was dark, she usually wasn't sober enough to drive. Another car flashed their headlights at them as she pulled out of the car park.

"You have your full beams on," said Declan.

"Yeah, I know. Leave me alone."

She drove cautiously. The moon brightened the surroundings slightly when they got away from the lights of the pub but everything was still encased in a misty grey as if the air had been infused by damp black mould.

"You'll have to give me directions," she said.

"Just keep going straight down this road."

A minute later she slowed to a stop.

"What's the matter?" he asked.

"See that up ahead?"

He sat up straight in his seat.

"That's a police car, isn't it?" said Cliona. "If they stop me, I'm fucked. They must be breathalysing. Why else would they be there?"

Declan squinted out the windscreen. Up ahead, pulled in beside the Twisted Tree was a squad car. Its lights were off but their headlights caught the side of it enough them to make out a fluorescent and blue stripe along its white side.

"Shit," he said. "Ok. Turn off your lights. Don't let them see us."

"Why do you keep checking your phone?" She twisted the headlights to the off position and a soft glow rose from the mobile in his hand.

"I have a plan. It might be someone I know. They won't breathalyse me if I'm on my own but it could be awkward if I have a passenger. You'll have to get out and hide in the ditch."

"Fuck it, I knew I shouldn't have driven."

Cliona studied the scene before her, waiting for any movement, expecting a tall blue uniform to step out of the stillness.

"I'm not sure if there's anyone with the car, though," she ventured. "There doesn't look to be anyone there. Surely he should have his lights on."

She put the car in gear and crawled forward like a cat getting ready to pass a sleeping dog. "I could sneak by them."

"No, don't do that."

Before she had crept more than a few metres down the road, Declan's phone bleated and he took his hand away from it to squeeze her arm. "Stop, wait," he said.

"What is it? What's wrong?"

"It's from Luke. Ah fuck."

"Luke?"

"Denise is on the warpath. They're going to look for us in the pub."

"What does that mean?"

"I shouldn't have brought you with me. This could get ugly if she sees you."

Cliona turned on the overhead light in the car and fished inside her bag for some chewing gum.

"What are you doing?" asked Declan. "Turn that off."

"I want some gum in case they breathalyse me."

"Gum is no good. You have to hide. Why won't you fucking listen to me?"

A set of invasive headlights appeared in the road ahead.

"Ah shit," said Declan. "That's them. That's Denise and Luke."

As the car passed, Cliona glimpsed two inquisitive heads turn towards the illuminated interior of their car.

"Shut that off," Declan cried. The Renault travelled about a hundred metres further on and then its bright, red brake lights glowed as fiercely as devil's eyes.

"Right," he said, grabbing Cliona by the shoulder. "You'll have to get out. You have to hide. Don't let them see you and don't let the Guards see you. I'd better go with Luke and Denise. Hide in the fields behind the Twisted Tree once we're gone. I'll come back for you in a bit after I deal with them and get my stuff. Quick now, get out."

He leaned across her and unbuckled her belt, yanked at the handle of the door, almost pushing her out with the motion.

Cliona slid out of the car, making sure he saw her expression of disgust. The door shut, nearly clipping her hand. She couldn't help herself from spitting vehemently at his disregard and her saliva trailed miserably down the window.

The reverse lights of the Renault lit up and it started to back up towards them. Cliona went round the other side of the car and stooped down in the ditch. She sighed as the wetness of the long grass seeped through her jeans. A nettle stung her hand and she cursed, feeling like just giving up on Declan and everything else to do with this shitty country. She crossed her arms on the damp ground, trying to find a spot that didn't scratch or sting and she lay her head down on her sleeve and gritted her teeth. Here she was, half-drunk, pregnant, abandoned, lying in a cold ditch at the side of a miserable country road. There had been some shitty situations in her life. She knew, without having to dredge up too many others to compare it to, that this wasn't the worst of them. What made her despair so much now was that when she left London, she had hoped she had grown out of getting into such predicaments. But she could feel in her heart that this wasn't the last of them, or the bleakest.

CHAPTER TWENTY-SEVEN

"That was them back there, stop the car, go back!" Denise bashed the dashboard and Luke slammed on the brakes. He gripped the wheel as he turned to her. He was sick of her incessant shouting. He was sick of being forced to hunt down his friend like a bold pup.

"Are you sure it was them? It could just be a couple parked up. I don't want to walk in on some weird dogging locals who think we want to join them."

"What? What are you talking about? Of course it was them. Their light was on, I could see into the car. Did you not see them?"

"I was trying to keep my eyes on the road, Denise," said Luke. Actually, he'd been distracted by the squad car parked up on the other side of the road, beside the Twisted Tree. He had been feeling sorry for the poor Garda still stationed out there and wondered why he didn't have any lights on. Then he decided that the Garda must be asleep in the back of his car instead of being on guard and he started to feel jealous of him. He was still feeling the effects of the last few days. A sleep in the back of a car, or anywhere for that matter, would be bliss compared to driving his friend's vengeful wife around.

"Well, what are you waiting for?" she said. "Go back before they drive away."

Luke turned the car around, mindful of the soft verge. The last thing he needed was to get stuck. With five awkward manoeuvres he managed to face the other way, under the pressure of Denise's harassment, and drove up alongside the car. He knew from the number plate it was Declan's but Denise shouted the fact at him a few times in case he wasn't aware of it. He rolled down the window and a beady-eyed Declan did the same.

"Hey buddy," Declan said to him.

"Hey Deccie."

"Where the fuck is she, you prick?" yelled Denise across Luke. "I saw her sitting in there with you. She was driving the car. You weren't in that seat a minute ago. Where did she go?"

"What are you talking about, Denise?" said Declan flatly, as if reading lines he himself was unconvinced by and didn't expect them to fool anyone else either. "Where did who go?"

"You know who. How can you do this to me? Do you hate me that much? Do you hate your son?"

"Come on, Deccie," said Luke. "It's time to go home. Will you follow us back?"

"He can't drive," said Denise. "Look at the state of him. He wasn't driving that car. I saw her in it."

"Can you drive, Deccie?"

"I may have had a few too many, I suppose," he slurred.

"I'll drive him back," said Denise. "I wouldn't trust him to follow us anyway."

"No," snapped Declan. "I'll travel with Luke. You can take this car back but I'm going with Luke."

Denise opened her door and sprang out of the car. Declan did the same with an agility that belied his drunkenness. He sidestepped around the car like he was playing a game of cat and mouse with her, then darted over to the other side of the road to put extra distance between them. She threw her hands in the air then got into his car and slammed the door.

"Fuck you, Declan," she said and started the car.

Only when she drove off ahead of them did Declan get in beside Luke and smile sheepishly at him. Luke let off the handbrake and drove slowly after Denise. There was still no sign of life from the squad car.

"I'm in trouble there," said Declan.

"Jesus Christ, Declan. What are you doing? This is no time to be playing silly games. People have been murdered on this very road. Everyone was wondering where you were. Your boss keeps asking me questions about you."

"You're a good pal, Luke. Keeping me in the loop. I just had to stay out of things here for a bit. It's all good now."

"Good? That fucking tree back there. They hung bits of their bodies off the branches. I found it, Declan, it was disgusting. It was the worst thing I've ever seen in my life. Roisin Kelly, that girl Mary who was always on her bicycle. Remember I told you there's a male victim as well. I bet it's that boy in the Honda Civic. They cut them up into bits. My God, when I think how Sophie found bits of Roisin Kelly. She found her eyeball taken out of her head. I can still see Mary's decapitated head staring up at me from the ground. Why didn't you tell me that she had a complaint in against you, Declan?"

"Ah that was nothing. It was a misunderstanding, that's all. The bitch just wanted to get me into trouble for some reason, I don't know why."

"I hate lying for you. Why did you not just come home, show up to work?"

Declan flipped down the visor and held his own gaze in the vanity mirror, rubbed a palm across the rough stubble of his cheek.

I had some things to sort out."

"With this Cliona girl."

"Yup."

Luke could smell the alcohol turned stale on Declan's breath.

"And?"

Declan pushed the visor back up with one slow finger. "And that should be all sorted by now," he said.

They weren't far from their houses. In front of them, the other car slowed to navigate a tight bend.

"Where is she now," asked Luke. "Back in the pub? No, don't tell me. I don't want to know. It's better if I don't know anymore. Ha, Denise was so angry, she was convinced that Cliona was in the car with you."

Even in the darkness, even with his eyes on the road ahead, Luke could sense that Declan was smirking.

"Declan," he said. "Tell me she wasn't in the car. Tell me you didn't leave her in the dark, back there, at the tree? Declan, people are being killed. It's dangerous out there."

"Well, yeah! That's the whole fucking point. I'm not stupid, Luke. I know there's something evil around here. I don't know what the fuck they are but I've seen what they can do. I'm just using them to clear up a mess."

"We have to … we have to go back for her."

Up ahead Denise turned the car into Luke's driveway.

"What's she going to your house for?" asked Declan.

"She left Willy with Sophie."

"Bill," replied Declan. "Listen. It's too late to go back for anyone. Just go back in there and take care of Sophie and your kid. There's some real bad fuckers prowling around the countryside in the middle of the night. A good husband like you should be at home protecting his family."

Luke grimaced. "Fuck you, Deccie. I have to go back. I can't just do nothing." He pulled the car up behind where Denise had parked and kept the engine running. Declan didn't move. Luke gripped his shoulder.

"Get out! And make sure nothing bad happens here until I get back."

Chapter Twenty-Eight

Conor Gallagher pursed his lips and pouted at the mirror in his bedroom. He held the shotgun like a guitar and he lunged towards his reflection when he strummed it along with the blaring chords of Iggy Pop's 'Raw Power'. They were outside still.

He had seen their silhouettes darting across his kitchen window when he was making a cup of tea earlier. Shortly after that he heard rattling at the back door, so he went round the house to make sure all the windows were shut and all the doors were locked. It was a traditional farmhouse with old style doors and single glazed windows that didn't keep the warmth in and allowed dampness to settle in the walls. After he had shuttered himself in, he stopped drinking tea and opened a bottle of Jameson. He just needed a couple of glasses to settle the nerves. Then he heard laughter outside his sitting room window, which wasn't any better at keeping out sounds than the cold, so he went upstairs to his bedroom with the shotgun and the whiskey and had a few more glasses. The stereo drowned out the laughter.

He stopped posing in the mirror at the end of the song and switched off the stereo to have a listen outside. He opened the curtains and pressed his face against the window. Something thudded against the glass and he jumped back. A headless crow. Jesus, was he seeing things? A headless crow? How did it fly into the window? There was a crack in the glass. He stepped cautiously towards it. Down below a figure hunched over, struggling with something. It was twisting and yanking the squirming thing in its hands. There was a terrible squawk, then the figure sprung back and hurled a black feathered object at the window. Conor was fixated by the second crow as its decapitated torso smashed against the window and lengthened the crack.

As if attached to a puppeteer's strings, he picked up his phone from his bed then put it back down again. He wished he hadn't made that second call to the Gardaí. The first one had been ok. He said there was someone prowling outside his house and they said they'd send a car round as soon as one was free. The second call, though, was after he'd had a joint and some of the whiskey. He couldn't remember exactly what he said but he knew he garbled about *them* being outside laughing at him and he was fairly sure he mentioned goblins and demons. They weren't going to send a car round now, that was for sure.

"Fuck the phone, I don't need the phone," he said. Then he thought again.

"The phone is a torch," and he stuck it in his pocket.

He put his denim jacket on and buttoned it up. Practiced loading the shotgun again. He had the hang of it now, could do it fairly quickly. He stuffed a bunch of cartridges into any pockets he had available between jacket and jeans and sidled towards the window with the shotgun pointing upwards, like he had seen SWAT teams do on television. He could see the figure with its back bent, tearing the head from another bird. Conor reached over, unlatched the window, and tried to push it up with one hand, but it wouldn't rise smoothly and it got stuck halfway up. Gently, he put down the shotgun then grabbed the window frame with both hands. As he reefed it upwards, he could hear that mean laughter again. By the time he took up the shotgun and fired, the figure had released its missile and was lurching away from the light of the house. The shot echoed across the darkened fields and there was an explosion of black feathers in front of Conor's face. Deafened by the blast, he stumbled backwards onto his bed and shook his head to try to clear it.

He took a deep breath of the cool air from the open window then he pounded down the stairs.

Downstairs, the back door was rattling vehemently so he took aim at it and blasted. A hole appeared in the wood and, when his ears stopped ringing, he heard that laughter again. He drew a kick at the door but the splintered frame stayed on his hinges so he had to unlatch and open it. A shadow scurried away down the driveway. Then it was joined by another. Conor jumped on his quad and started the engine. The headlights made him feel like he had an extra weapon against these filthy creatures and he drove out the gate after them.

They fled down the road away from him before scurrying over the fence of his nearest neighbour. Conor pursued with an initial blast of anger but he hesitated when he reached his neighbour's gate. He was reluctant to get off his quad. He felt safe on it, with the light it threw out and the reassurance of a quick getaway. Then he started to get anxious about things creeping up behind him. How many of them were there? He had seen two; what if there were more? They were quick; what if they had doubled back behind him?

He heard the pained roar of one of his neighbour's bullocks and watched wide-eyed as the black-coated beast hurtled towards the gate with something lying across its back, leaning into its neck. The bullock rammed it head-on and the gate burst open. The animal froze for a moment, faced with the blaring headlights of the quad. Conor could make out a clamber of limbs on its back. Both of the creatures he had chased were up there. The one at the front leaned in close to the bullock's neck as it stampeded down the road away from him. He aimed the shotgun and fired. The bullock galloped off with its terrible riders urging it on.

Conor followed. He kept it in his headlights and could see the creatures constantly squirming on its back, wildly guiding it forward until it swerved off the road out of his lights and disappeared.

He slowed down the quad, confused and agitated. He tried to drive at an angle so he could aim his lights at the ditch, awkwardly holding the shotgun at the ready in case they jumped out at him. When he got to where they had disappeared from his sight, he found a point in the ditch low enough for the bullock to have leapt over. On the quad he couldn't make it through but he knew there was a gate into that field a little further down so he sped on towards it.

Only when he was opening that gate did he stop to rationalize what he was doing. Why was he following them? He could go back to his house and barricade himself in until morning. He could ride on to O'Shea's, warn everyone there and batten down the hatches with a load of drink to pass the time. But a murderous, hateful urge boiled up inside him when he thought of these creatures, a sickening feeling that the sense and fleeting glimpses of them had churned up in his heart. He had to get rid of them, he had to kill them tonight. He pushed the gate open wide and only discovered the electric fence behind it when the shock travelled through the metal frame and up his arm. He yelped like a dog and let go of the gate. The shock wasn't bad but he didn't want to touch it again, so he hopped back on the quad and rammed the gate forward until it snapped the wire, then he opened up the throttle and ploughed down the field, bumping madly over its uneven terrain.

Conor zigzagged as he travelled forward so his lights spread across the widest area possible and eventually, up ahead, he saw some movement. The bullock was trotting around in a small circle as if tethered by an invisible rope. There was nothing straddling its back. He drove nearer, slowly. The ditch behind the animal was teeming with activity, shapes moving around in the darkness. They were hunched and creeping, flitting in and out of the beam of his headlights. They were the same breed as the beings he had seen outside his house, the same that had spooked him at the Twisted Tree; oversized heads, unnatural jerking movements. He couldn't tell how many there were, they dove in and out of the gloom. It made his skin tingle with fear to see them loose and active. The bullock was getting more agitated. All of a sudden, one of the creatures dived at it and hacked its tail off. The poor animal bellowed across the field while its skinny, misshapen abuser whirled the tail above its head.

Conor shuddered at the thought that others might be sneaking up on him in the shadows. He knew this local land so well. He recognised where this part of the field was. On the other side was the road where the Twisted Tree stood. Before he could decide whether to hightail out of there, a scream came from the direction of the road. A human scream. It forced him to action. He got off the quad taking care to keep himself out of its lights as he searched for its source. It was a woman's scream, panicked and terrified:

"Nooooo!" she screamed again.

Three figures lurched through the thick ditch from the roadside back into the field. They were directly in front of him now, they were in his sights, even in this murky visibility he could hit them from here. He fired twice and one fell to the ground. The other two figures scampered back through the ditch and onto the road.

Conor leapt back on his quad and drove along the perimeter of the field, catching glimpses of their movement through any gaps in the trees and growth that bordered it. Above the noise of his engine, he could hear an animalistic roaring of pain entwined with a sick laughter. He must have hit one of these ones running away. He'd finish the fuckers off. With the ditch acting like a screen between him and them, he pursued by sense as much as sight. He knew the road was branching off at a junction around here and they could steer away from the field he was in and he would lose them. Their wretched noises were growing distant. There was a low point in the ditch near the corner of the field. If he didn't get out to the road then they would get away from him altogether, so he accelerated hard towards the ditch and the quad crashed through it. The front wheel hit a bank of clay. He came tumbling forward off the front of the quad and hit the ground. In a panic he realised he still had a hold of the shotgun. He couldn't believe it hadn't gone off. His hands and face burned with scrapes from the brambles but he got up and could just about see them up ahead, clambering away along the verge of the road. Afraid they might cross into another field and away from him, he aimed to fire at them again. Steady. One of them was lame. It limped and jerked but he had it in his sights. A set of headlights blinded him just as his finger squeezed the trigger. He missed his target but the sound of his shot steered them away from the ditch and kept them running down the road. The car blared its horn and sped past. Up ahead was Weldon's old house. Luke's place. He had to keep them from getting to Luke's family.

Chapter Twenty-Nine

The boy was transfixed by something outside the window.

"Willy," said Sophie. "Willy, come over here. Do you want to play with some of Elliott's toys?" She half-heartedly rattled a cloth dragonfly with plastic wings and antennae. "Come on, Willy, your mammy's not out there yet but she'll be home soon. And she might have Daddy with her." Sophie regretted saying that as soon as the words were spoken and added a "maybe", but Willy didn't seem to be too concerned by fatherly comings and goings. He pointed out into the darkness.

"Not Mammy," he said. "Monsters."

Sophie chilled at the matter-of-fact way it came out of his mouth. She wanted to shake him, to turn him away from the window.

"No. No, Willy, there's no monsters out there."

"Monsters," he confirmed.

She stood up from the couch and went over to him.

"I'm going to close these curtains now. We'll have a nice play and wait for Mammy. Shall we get something to drink too, a nice glass of milk?"

She reached up to pull the curtains and caught sight of a dark shape moving near the low wall at the end of the front lawn. It stopped and sank down into the shadows where the wall met the grass.

"Is there an animal out there, Willy? Is it a doggy?"

"Monsters."

There was an apple tree on their lawn, further up from the wall.

Something moved by the base of its trunk and caught her eye. There was something there, keeping low down to the ground and crawling towards the house. Sophie tried to speak but words weren't coming out. She put her hand on the boy's shoulder and squeezed it. There was a dart of motion from over at the wall and she thought she saw a figure on two legs running fast over to the side of the house.

"Elliott." The word dribbled from her lips and she stepped backwards from the window. "Willy, sit down on the couch, get away from the window."

The boy didn't move but she cared so much less about that than about going upstairs to check on her own son. She ran up the stairs and hit the light switch in his room, rushed to the cot and picked him up out of it. He started to cry at being woken so suddenly. Her eyes scanned the room to make sure there was nothing in it that shouldn't be there, that the windows were shut. She hugged him as he cried and, through his wails, she just about heard the click downstairs of the front door opening.

"Oh no," she cried.

Holding her child tight in her arms, she went back out to the landing and over to the top of the stairs. Willy was standing in front of the front door. The door was open.

"Willy," she screamed. "Get away from there."

Sophie edged down the stairs, taking the steps sideways as if she wanted to make a smaller target of herself and her son, but somehow, in her heart, she knew that whatever was outside wasn't interested in firing things at them from a distance. They wanted to get up close to inflict their damage. She got to the bottom of the stairs and reached out to grab Willy's hand. The boy didn't turn around, he just kept staring out into the darkness. Something dashed past the doorstep outside and Sophie shrieked. Willy turned around to her now and she dragged him back down the hallway into the kitchen and shut the door.

She put Elliott down on the floor and pushed the table up against the kitchen door. The back door. Was it locked? She dashed across the kitchen to the outside door, thankful that they had left the key in it and made sure it was secure. A large, long face appeared in the window of that door and she screamed. It ducked back down. She had seen eyes, red eyes, hateful eyes. Sophie searched all around the kitchen countertops but even as she did so, her despair told her she had left her phone in the sitting room. She wished she had spent just two seconds extra in the hallway, the two seconds it would have taken to reach out and shut the front door. An image shuddered through her of whatever was out there coming brazenly into the house and wandering through the rooms until they decided to try to get into the kitchen.

Luke and Denise would be back soon. The thought was a relief at first, then it turned into a worry. She had to warn them it wasn't safe. Declan might be with them but what state would Declan be in? Any split second of a warning would help them. She edged over to the window of the back door, hoping to see who or what was out there. What exactly was she dealing with?

A thin, white object, like a bleached stick. rose up in front of the glass. The point of it was sharpened. Tap, tap. She peered closer. It was a bone. Sophie groaned. The point of it tapped off the glass again and she tottered back away from it with a sickness swirling in her stomach. Elliott whimpered where he sat on the floor. Willy was hypnotised by the teasing white bone at the door. It moved from there to the main kitchen window, tapping a steady beat. Sophie shuffled over to the interior door of the kitchen. She considered pulling the table away from it and dashing into the sitting room to grab her phone. That would mean leaving the kitchen unprotected for … how long? How long would it take her to grab her phone and get back and push the table up against the door again? She had seen how fast those things moved. The phone was on the couch, she was sure it was on the couch, she wouldn't even have to think, she would just speed in and grab it.

The tapping of the bone on the window ceased. Elliott stopped whimpering. Into the new silence rose the noise of a car and Sophie recognised the boisterous rattle of their Renault. Luke! She had to warn him. Forget the phone, just a warning shout would make all the difference, it would put them on their guard. All she had to do was get within earshot and shout "danger" or "intruders" or "murderers". That would give them a chance. They could hit them with the car or something. She spied out the kitchen window and saw nothing. She looked out the back door window for another view. It was risky. She hated the thought of leaving the children for even a second but if she did nothing then Luke and the others would get ambushed and killed then she and Elliot and Willy would be next. She gripped the key. No sign of danger to be seen out there. All she needed was a few clear seconds. Lock the door from the other side to keep the kids safe, run round the side of the house, scream her warning and run back inside.

"Sshhh." She raised her finger to her lips, hoping to settle the children, then unlocked the door, opened it just enough to get out and slipped into the night. She fumbled with the key, trying to get it into the keyhole on the other side. It suddenly felt fat and huge and the keyhole seemed a tiny sliver. It was too dark. The key rammed off frustrating metal as she tried to get it in. She had to stoop right down to the level of the handle and guide it until finally, it locked.

Outside, she could hear two cars round the front of the house. Then one of the engines stopped but she recognised the sound of their Renault still running. She sprinted round the side of the house. Something rushed past her as she rounded the corner and she sensed the briefest hesitation in its charge, as if it would have stopped to deal with her if it hadn't been moving so fast. She got a smell of raw meat and sweat from it. The skin beneath her ribs tingled as did the backs of her legs, like they were exposed and vulnerable to damage.

Two sets of headlights flooded the front yard. Declan's car was parked up but Declan wasn't in it. Denise was behind the wheel. Declan was getting out of their Renault. He manoeuvred himself unsteadily out of the passenger side, took a moment to make sure his legs were able to stand, then faced his own car as if he were bracing himself for attack. Sophie tried to shout her warning but her mouth fell slack, the air dried her tongue. The Renault's engine was still clacking away, its lights were on and it began to reverse away from the house. She could make out Luke's familiar shape behind the steering wheel and the hope sucked out of her as the car backed away.

The door of the other car opened and the interior light came on, illuminating Denise. Her face was filled with anger and her eyes were fixed on Declan. Denise didn't see the thing creeping into the car down by her legs through the open door, but Sophie could see it. One word entered her mind at the sight of it and that was the word she screamed.

"Monster!"

CHAPTER THIRTY

After Declan opened the door and clambered out, Luke looked over his shoulder and reversed back out the gate. The idea of someone, particularly a young woman, being out on her own on these roads was awful. The memory of Mary's decapitated head wormed its way to the front of his thoughts and made him hurry to put the car into first gear. Before he drove away, he glimpsed Sophie standing outside the house and he wished he had time to tell her where he was going but the sooner he got back to the tree and collected Cliona, the sooner he'd be back and safe with her at the house.

Over the noise of his acceleration, he fancied he heard a single word screamed out loud but it was hard to make out. He hoped it wasn't Denise screaming it at Declan, he hoped it was the cry of a night-time fox or just his imagination creating the sound of his inner panic. He put his foot down and sped on, even when he saw Conor crusading up the road on foot.

"What the fuck is he doing?"

There was movement in the opposite ditch too, dark figures, but he watched Conor instead. There was a wildness in the man's gait that drew Luke's attention and he realised the long object that he was holding in his arms was a gun. There was a thunderous shot and Luke jerked the wheel, banging the horn in fright. He would have to tell the Garda stationed out here in his car there was an unstable music fanatic running around the roads with a shotgun.

In a few heart-pounding minutes he was at the Twisted Tree. He pulled the car over to the side of the road, blaring his headlights at the squad car and revving his engine before shutting it off. That would wake him up if he was asleep in the car.

No door opened. No light came on. Surely there was somebody there. They wouldn't just leave a squad car in the middle of the countryside unattended. He got out and went over to it, rapped his knuckles on the driver's window. There was no sign of life inside.

"Hello," he shouted. He kept scanning the surroundings as he banged on the window. "Cliona? Guards? Anyone around?"

Luke pressed his face against the back window of the car and his foot brushed off something on the ground. A pair of shoes were sticking out from under the car. He could see the legs were intact as far as the ankles at least, but he didn't want to get down and investigate what the case might be further in. He held his head in his hands. If there was a worse place to be right now, he couldn't think of it. In this light, the roots of the Twisted Tree looked as if they were moving, writhing, opening like the lips of a dark and terrible mouth. He had to ring someone. He whipped out his phone and scrolled through the last dialled numbers until he got to Sergeant Harris.

"Please, please answer," he said out loud to himself. The phone rang once, twice, then he took it away from his ear and listened carefully. From behind the tree, down in the field, he could hear moaning.

Chapter Thirty-One

"Monster!"

Sophie's voice drilled through Declan's cloudy head. He hadn't even noticed her at the side of the house until she screamed. He had been looking over towards his own driveway. The sensor lights had come on. Through the mesh fence he could see their dog crashing into his locked gate. It clattered its small, wiry frame against it three times before it collapsed. Then it resorted to bloodily digging into the hard ground like it was trying to tunnel its way free. Declan could just about make out its frightened whine until Sophie's shriek drowned it out.

She was crouched over like she had a pain in her stomach and one hand was held to her mouth, as if she was trying to put her scream back in. The other hand was raised, the forefinger outstretched. Declan was so shocked by the sound that came out of her it took him a moment to realise she was pointing at something. She was pointing at his car. She was pointing at the dark figure crawling into his car beside Denise. The anger in Denise's face was aimed at him and it was so fierce it lasted for a second longer than it should. It should have changed to an expression of fear earlier than it did. It should have changed to fear as soon as she heard Sophie's scream and saw her finger point at the space beside her; the space being filled by something horrible and vicious. It turned to an expression of pain before the fear got a chance to materialize. It turned to an expression of pain when those long fingernails inserted themselves into her ear and the teeth tore into her cheek.

Declan couldn't believe what he was seeing. The car door closed gently, the locking lights of the car pulsed once and he heard the thing inside laughing alongside Denise's agonised crying. The interior light stayed on, oh fuck, why did it stay on? A wrinkled hand reached up to the rear-view mirror and directed it down towards his wife's eyes so she could see her own face as it performed its mutilations on it. Declan looked away to where Sophie had been but she was gone now. He ran his hands loosely over his clothes like he expected to find a weapon there, a gun, a baton. His mind was circling in shock. He should be in uniform at times like this. He should have something with him to stop what was happening.

Then, as if he had wished it into being, he saw a shotgun approaching him. It was being held by someone else but he felt like it was part of him as he watched it raise up to shoulder height. He watched it advance and draw level with him. He reached out to touch it but the man holding it shoved him away. Conor Gallagher strode past him, aiming his gun at the car. In the car the creature had wrapped itself around Denise and a long nose sniffed her bleeding face.

"Shoot," he said.

Conor Gallagher kept stalking towards the car with the shotgun pointed at it.

"Shoot it," Declan said. "Shoot it."

Conor walked closer and closer until he was almost at the car, until the barrel of the gun was almost touching the driver's window. The creature was tearing her to pieces. Blood sprayed onto the inside of the glass.

"Shoot," said Declan again, nearly a whisper now, as if he was saying it to the universe rather than as a command to the man with the gun.

Conor took one final step forward and fired the gun. Two heads erupted in a mess of bone and glass and skin and hair.

Chapter Thirty-Two

Sophie heard the gunshot as she ran back around the house. She had shouted her warning to them. She should have gotten it out of her mouth quicker, she knew that, but she couldn't dwell on it now.

The gunshot had to be a good sign. Those things weren't carrying guns. It must have been a human that fired the gun, must have been Declan. She was sure that thing had gotten inside the car with Denise but she had to concentrate on getting back to the kids. She couldn't afford to hesitate over anything again.

But then she did hesitate, or rather come to a shocked stop at the corner of the house. Someone, *something*, was almost at the back door. Its hunched and scrawny back was turned to her. The way it moved, elbows twitching with delight and menace, the wrong size of its head, its stench of sweat and violence in the air, all brought a rotten taste to her mouth. A whimper too, at the thought of it getting through that door to her baby, came to her throat but she trapped it there—*hush*. That bone was in its hand, the one it had been rapping on the window earlier. Sophie scoured the area for something to attack it with. It hadn't realised she was behind it yet. It was too busy straining its neck to get a sideways look in through the window of the door. The shed door was open. There had to be something in there. She remembered all the tools that Luke had been sorting through earlier. There would be something sharp, something lethal. She crept over to the shed and tried to adjust her eyes to the darkness inside. The creature was fixated with what was inside the house, sneering and gurgling in the window, scraping the bone along the glass as she searched around in the gloom. Her hands met a long object on the floor, close to the door, and she immediately knew what it was. She wondered if she should even bother with it. Could she start it? Would it be any use if she couldn't? Hesitating again. Breaking glass tinkled its terrible melody. It had broken out one of the small panes of glass in the door. Stop hesitating! Two tiny voices cried from inside the house. A horrible laugh followed its hand in through the glass and Sophie heard the rattle of the locked door handle.

She dragged the brush cutter out of the shed, grabbed the cord and pulled. It wouldn't yield to her. She pushed a button on the handle and tried again but it refused to start. The monster was cackling now in answer to the children's distress. Shit, how had Luke started it earlier? Her hands and fingers were working at a speed she didn't know was possible as they ran all around the head of the machine fumbling for bits to switch or press. A small rubber bulb softened under her touch. This was familiar. This was something. She remembered using a lawnmower as a teenager at home, being shown how to start it by her father. She pressed the bulb rapidly until it filled with fuel and her hand found a lever and flicked it as the word 'throttle' formed silently on her lips. The creature banged its fists against the door. She pulled the starter cord again and the engine spluttered.

The banging of the door stopped. She didn't even look up. She pulled again and the engine coughed then paused, like it had been politely clearing its throat. That rotten laugh. She pulled a third time and pressed the trigger on the handle. The engine gave a healthy roar and, this time maintained it. The blades spun ferociously.

She looked up now. The creature had turned its attention away from the door and was moving towards her. It was advancing crookedly, like it was trying to stay out of the light cast from the kitchen window, but she could make out a long nose and a wide smile across its huge, ugly head. She lifted up the brush cutter. The weight was more than she expected and the balance felt all wrong. It pulled away from her. The blades scraped off the shed wall and squealed, sending sparks and grit at her face but she kept her grip and swung it round in front of her. The creature ducked away. Its eyes narrowed wickedly beneath the frown of its heavy brow. It tried to get behind her so she staggered backwards to put her back against the wall of the shed. The brush cutter was so heavy; it lurched to the side as she retreated and she couldn't hold it upright any longer. The blades stuttered in the soft ground. Stuck! The monster sidled round to the side of her. She pressed the trigger frantically, heard raspy, hungry panting over the stifled sound of the sunken cutter. The thing smiled and drooled as it crouched down and prepared to dive at her. At the very second it launched, she managed to swing the handle of the cutter upwards and out of the ground. Her grip juddered as it hit something hard and screeched through it. The creature hit the ground, releasing a wretched noise like a tuberculosis death cough met with the caw of a crow. It squawked again and again, sounding like it was going to tear its own throat out. As it squirmed and writhed on the grass before her, Sophie could see that she had taken off one of its legs just below the knee and the other dangled loose and jagged around the bone. Fury blazed in its eyes. Vicious fingers stretched out. It was still trying to get up and attack her. It was as if it hadn't attributed its pain to the loss of its legs. Sophie breathed in and out heavily, slowly. She rested the cutter down, just keeping the blades angled off the ground and pointed them towards the creature. Her face felt wet.

Then, with a roar, the monster leapt upright onto its stump, buckling the half-cut leg beneath it, and bared its teeth at her. The smell from its mouth was disgusting but she didn't recoil or turn away. She pressed the trigger of the cutter and the blades sang as they spun. She raised it up and all her strength returned. Nothing would harm her family, certainly not this demon of spite and mindless cruelty. She swayed with the motion of the tool as it cut and sliced and ripped the hateful creature apart.

Chapter Thirty-Three

Luke didn't know what to do. He knelt down on the ground beside Cliona and kept her propped up but he had never learned any first aid so wasn't sure if moving her would be ok. Thank God Sergeant Harris had picked up. Luke had been too scared to raise his voice above a whisper, but Harris heard enough to reassure him help would be there fairly soon. But once the laughter had started in the darkness around him, Luke was sure it wouldn't arrive soon enough.

Cliona waftedin and out of consciousness. He had followed her moans of pain across the ditch into the field behind the Twisted Tree. When he first found her, by the torchlight of his phone, she was able to mumble the words 'shoulder', 'shot' and 'chest'. Since then, she had opened her eyes a few more times and attempted to speak but just managed to release drool and a groan. There wasn't much left of her shoulder that wasn't ragged skin and sinew. He didn't know how bad her chest was but there were lots of holes in her clothes and blood was seeping through them.

He took off his jacket, wishing he'd worn more than a T-Shirt beneath, and put it around her. Hoping it might help hold her together as well as stop her shivering, he held her tight and whispered to her it would be ok and help was on its way. Then that sordid laugh, almost like an animal. She shuddered awake at the first one.

"Nooo." The word racked her body like an electric shock. He could feel her terror in the grasp of her fingers on his arm. That chilled him as much as the wicked laughter.

It came from behind him, from back at the Twisted Tree. It was joined by another laugh and then he heard other noises, further back towards where the squad car was parked, and what sounded like something being dragged along the ground. *Now might be a good time to make his escape*, he thought, *if he wanted to stay alive*. If he could lift her and run back to the car. If it was ok to move her, that was. A bustle of movement erupted through the ditch and a collection of dark shapes gathered together in the field, like pigs at a trough. Luke heard a sucking sound like a hand was being punched into something inflatable and then pulled out. Then he heard a crack and an awful slurping noise and that made up his mind. They were only a stone's throw away but while they were occupied, he had a chance. He gathered the girl in his arms as securely as he could and got his legs into a position to lift. He heard a man's voice in among the other noises, a sad, dying groan, and he almost wept. The Garda had still been alive.

Luke tensed his legs and rose carefully from the ground. Cliona was light but so limp it was hard to keep her in his arms. If those things heard him, he was dead. He tried to move as quietly as he could but, with his first two steps, the swish of his feet through the grass seemed as loud as storm-winds through a chimney. He forced himself to lift his feet higher, straining with the effort. Low chuckling and grunting, noises of evil contentment, rose from the feasting mob. Cliona's head suddenly jerked up towards Luke. He stopped and stood still, staring at her, hoping she wouldn't make a sound. Her eyes didn't open and her neck flopped loosely back over his arm. He stepped forward again, high careful steps that came down gently, and the effort sent fire through his leg muscles. It was only ten metres from the ditch but it was taking him so long to advance each of those metres. His chest tightened and it took him a moment to realise he had been holding his breath since he'd stood up with Cliona in his arms. He exhaled slowly, sneaking out his breath, as if releasing too much of it might poison the world.

He knew he wouldn't be able to get over the ditch quietly. It was sloped back up to the roadside. Long, dead grass and dry branches were strewn on the slope. They might be hiding divots that could turn his ankle as well as add a soundtrack to his progression. If he could manage to get close enough to the ditch without being detected, he could run and burst through it, get to his car before anything could catch him, even carrying Cliona, no matter how fast they were. About eight metres from the ditch now. He flexed the muscles of his arms and legs in advance of the dash he would soon take. The chuckling from over in the darkness was low and relaxed. He took another of his exaggerated high steps, but when he brought his foot down it was onto a rounded stone. His heel slipped and he stumbled slightly. Cliona slipped in his arms and moaned. The chuckling stopped. He heard shuffling in the grass. They were coming for him.

Luke bolted for the ditch, struggling with his injured cargo. He trundled up the slope, briars catching his clothes. Cliona fell forward from his arms but he managed to scoop her up through the undergrowth and get her onto the verge of the road. His car was just there. He hadn't locked it.

A swift, gangly shape scuttled in front of him. Just as it began to stand upright and face him, he instinctively threw a fist at it and it skidded back down the ditch. His knuckles burned with pain, it was like he had thumped a punching bag made of barbed wire. With his other hand he dragged Cliona by the neckline of her top. He yanked open the door of the Renault, shoved her in and dived in on top of her. He pulled the door shut just before a dark body bashed up against the window. His keys were in his pocket and he reefed them out with his sore hand still throbbing from the pain of delivering the punch. When he pressed the central locking button, the lifesaving clunk sounded sweeter than any music he'd ever listened to.

With his next movement the car alarm went off. Cliona stirred at the noise, bringing him both surprise and gratitude that she was still alive. The dashes of amber lights from the alarm created fleeting illuminations of the figure circling the car. It slammed itself against the rear window and Luke scrambled into the front seat. He put the keys in the ignition and started the engine. The creature came round to the driver's window and pummelled its clawed fists against it. Luke put his foot to the floor and roared away, the alarm still screaming.

A mile up the road he took a sharp bend too quickly and Cliona rolled off the back seat and onto the floor. Luke turned around at the sound of her tumble, afraid that something had gotten into the car and, in taking his eyes off the road, he drove into the ditch. The front tyre dipped into the verge and he fought the steering wheel for a violent second, dragging the vehicle back onto the tarmac. He slammed on the brakes and the car sat in the middle of the road facing sideways. He took a deep breath. He had to be careful, there was no need to drive so recklessly. He was away from them now, a good distance away. He could drive normally; they were on foot.

In the distant darkness he saw the flashing of blue lights getting closer to the area he had just escaped from and heard an ambulance's siren. Then the lights stilled and the siren muted.

"No," he said out loud. "Don't get out. We're not there anymore."

He raised himself up out of his seat to take out his phone. It wasn't in his pocket. He turned on the light and stuck his hand under Cliona to see if it was there but he couldn't find it.

"Shit, shit, there's no time anyway."

He had to go back to warn them. If he drove back towards them beeping his horn that would work. That would make them stay in the vehicle. He had to do something. He started to drive but straight away the steering wheel dragged to the left and he heard an awful flapping sound. The smell of abused rubber permeated the car.

"Ah shit."

Luke surveyed the area to make sure nothing was outside then he opened the passenger door and leaned out to see the torn, flattened tyre that had dipped into the ditch.

He put his head in his hands and sank back into the driver's seat. He couldn't warn the ambulance now. Who knew what would happen to them as they searched in the dark field for a wounded woman who wasn't there? He banged the steering wheel as he realised he hadn't gotten the spare wheel repaired. He couldn't even drive himself to safety. His options had shrunk to cowering in the dubious protection of the Renault or venture out unprotected on the road. He opened the window and listened for screams. Surely the Guards wouldn't be much further behind. The paramedics wouldn't get out until the Guards got there, would they? The blue pulsing light shone into the sky. He probably wouldn't hear the screams from this far away.

There was still time to get away, to run away, if those things were occupied with trying to take new victims. Cliona was crumpled on the floor. He would have to move fast. He couldn't carry her. She would have to be left here. He tried to move her as gently as he could onto the floor of the car, into something resembling what he thought the recovery position might be. They might not see her down there if they came this way. If he locked the doors, she might be safe. They might leave her alone.

He drove the car out of the middle of the road, hearing the grinding of the busted wheel as it struggled to move. It clunked over to the widest part of the road and he edged it as far as he could to the side. Luke put his hand on Cliona's head, brushed the hair from out of her eyes and told her he was sorry over and over. He opened the driver's window just a little, not enough to get a hand through, then he got out, locked the car and slid the keys through the gap. He hoped that she would wake up and find them there and that she would be in a situation where she could unlock the car to a helper, not shrink in terror from an attacker. Then he ran.

He ran faster than he could ever remember doing. He'd never run this fast on a treadmill in the gym or playing sports and it amazed him that it didn't hurt. He was weightless. He felt like he could run even faster than this and he kept pushing himself harder. His body was experiencing pain but his mind wasn't registering it because it was comparing it to the pain it would experience if he got caught. He barely registered the impact of his feet touching the tarmac and he fled until he got to his own driveway and there, on the front lawn, he saw Declan down on his knees in front of his car.

Conor was on the lawn too, dashing around like he was searching for somebody or something. Conor had the shotgun in his hands and was poking through bushes with it. Luke realised that there was something unusual about the way he was dancing around. Whichever way he circled around the lawn he kept his back to Declan's car. He wouldn't face it even if it meant shuffling around sideways or jogging backwards. It was like he was performing a pantomime skit with the car as the villain behind him.

As Luke neared the car, he could see the mess of blood and fragments of bodies splattered around its insides. A hand still gripped the steering wheel which led back to a shoulder and a bit of a neck but not much of one. There was a wedding ring on the hand. It actually surprised him to see that Denise still wore her wedding ring with the anger she held towards her husband. He didn't stop to comfort Declan. Declan was rocking back and forward slowly, not even aware that his friend had arrived. Luke kept a wide berth from Conor.

"You shouldn't stay out here," he shouted to them both. "They might be following me."

His energy had all but left him as soon as he had gotten to the driveway and now it felt like he was wading through water but he kept pushing himself forward towards the house. His legs were about to buckle underneath him. They might just disintegrate and float away into the night air. He didn't allow himself to think about what might be inside the house. He just kept repeating their names in his head like a mantra.

"Sophie and Elliott, Sophie and Elliott."

The open door, the empty hallway. There was nobody in the sitting room. Nothing looked out of place or damaged. His mantra travelled from his thoughts to his throat.

"Sophie," he called. "Elliott."

The kitchen door was closed. Luke pushed down the handle but there was something blocking it on the other side.

"Sophie, Elliott!" he wailed.

Her voice croaked from inside the kitchen.

"In here. We're in here."

He heaved against the door and heard the floor tiles being scraped until he created a gap big enough to squeeze through. Every moveable object in the kitchen had been pushed up against the door: the table, all the chairs, even the fridge had been unplugged and dragged into the blockade. The tall, wide food cupboard was shoved up against the back door. It had been pushed as tight as possible against the door but the handle sticking out created a small gap. Luke could see that the glass in the window had been smashed. Sophie was kneeling down on the floor in the middle of the kitchen holding Elliott and Bill tightly as the two children sobbed. Her clothes, her hands, her face were completely covered in dark, sticky blood. He held her face in his hands and his lips quivered as he tried to speak.

"It's ok," she said. "It's ok. It's not my blood."

CHAPTER THIRTY-FOUR

Declan rose from his knees and retreated to the front door of Luke and Sophie's house. The backdrop to Conor's dance of distress was shifting and morphing. A swarm of dark shapes was closing in from the road at the same time as mistruths and conveniences filled Declan's mind like fluid. He edged inside the door and eased it shut just as Conor turned to face him.

"Wait," croaked Conor and he shuffled forward, one hand outstretched, the realisation that he was being sacrificed widening his eyes as Declan locked the door.

Cackles of laughter filled the lawn. Inside, Declan moved to the same window his son had stared out earlier at the monsters crawling through the shadows. But this time there were so many more of them and this time, instead of coming for the house they were all advancing on the broken man with the shotgun in his hands. The curtains allowed Declan a cold secrecy to his observation. A low figure broke from pack, snapping teeth in its outsized head, and took a chunk from Conor's thigh before he could bash its misshapen skull with the stock of his gun. Tears streamed down his face as he fumbled to reload.

A thick tendril of a briar was lassoed around Conor's neck and they hauled him to the ground. The thorns ripped and tightened on his throat. All accompanied by a chorus of cruel, sneering mirth. Conor's legs kicked out frantically as they dragged him on his back across the rough concrete driveway towards the road. The shotgun was prised from his fingers and discarded beside the car upon which it had wreaked such damage. A thick gang of the creatures marched down the road with their captive like some sadistic work detail, barks of terror finding occasional escape from their doomed captive's throat.

Declan maintained his watch. A few pairs of eyes remained, glinting in the cool night air, examining the area like historians of terror. One of them snarled at the house and Declan's grip tensed on the fabric of the curtains. But the snarl wasn't a prelude to attack. The few that stayed behind set to the task of gathering the remains of their kind that had died. Hunched and crooked figures scoured the grass. They picked bits from the car and then they scampered round to the back of the house.

Declan ran through to the kitchen, blind to his traumatised friends comforting each other until he had peered out the window. Out the back, the spindly bodies worked quickly to remove the splattered pieces of the one that Sophie had shredded. They communicated with each other through grunts and squawks, a melody of nastiness and hate. Two of them produced sacks to contain the gathered gore. One of those ancient, creased faces stared in at Declan, as the others worked behind him, as if it were drilling a warning into his mind through the mean pits of its eyes. Soon they were all gone.

"Alright," he said, snapping his fingers in front of Luke. "We have to get our stories straight. The less we say we know the better. Plead ignorance. Conor shot Denise, that's as much as we saw. Sophie, get yourself cleaned up. And nobody mentions monsters or demons or whatever the fuck those things were or we'll be spending the rest of our lives in a mental institution and these boys will be taken away from us."

CHAPTER THIRTY-FIVE

"Luke, I'm sorry to ask, I know you like to leave early to get on the right side of the traffic."

Luke finished positioning an information card below a dull brown, deformed callipers from the early 1800s and closed the display case.

"Well, it's about more than getting stuck in traffic, Professor Stafford. I thought I had explained all this before I came back to work. It's actually not safe for me to travel the roads near my house after dark."

Stafford's nose wrinkled with annoyance. He glanced at Luke's laptop sitting on a nearby table. Its open browser window displayed a property rental website.

"It's just that we were initially hoping to have this collection ready for the public by tomorrow. I know you've been through a lot recently but you haven't really been giving me the hours I need from you, even when you're physically here. How about making an exception for this evening and staying on for a while?"

"I'm sorry, Professor. That's just not an option. I have to get back to Sophie and Elliot. Look, I'll get rightly stuck into it tomorrow but, as you've always taught me, you can't rush these things. These items have been around for hundreds of years, another few days out of the limelight isn't going to make much difference in the long run."

"No, I know that, but we are already behind schedule and I don't have anyone else on staff at the moment who can take up your slack. Perhaps we may have to think about a different arrangement. Perhaps I should hire someone to job-share with you."

"I don't think I could afford to job-share, Professor."

"Then perhaps we'll have to discuss your position here entirely."

Luke's phone rang and he frowned at the number. "I'm sorry, I have to take this."

Stafford glared at Luke as he pulled off his gloves and answered the phone. The older man blinked in disbelief and flustered out of the room.

Luke paced incessantly as he spoke into the phone.

"Why are you ringing me, Sergeant Harris? Has something happened?"

"I was hoping you'd drop into the station this evening on your way back from Dublin. Just to answer a few more questions, tie up a few loose ends."

"But I've told you everything I know."

"There are bodies missing, Luke. We can't just stop looking for them. Good men who disappeared while trying to assist you and Miss Casey, not to mention a member of the force. Don't forget Conor Gallagher still hasn't been apprehended. That was some vanishing act he pulled. You were right in the middle of it. I can't believe he didn't tell you something that will help us. There must be something else you can remember."

"Conor … Conor's probably dead, like I keep saying. He was very disturbed."

Luke packed away his laptop, a nervous eye on the time.

"I hear you've received some threatening emails, Luke."

"How do you … I mean, what do you … um, no."

"From friends of Mr. Gallagher."

"So?"

"Accusing you and Declan of telling lies. We don't want that, now. We don't want there to be lies or doubts."

"I can't call in on the way home, Sergeant. It'll be too dark to drive home after I finish with you. You can come out to our house if you're determined to talk to me today. Just don't drive out there on your own."

"Don't worry about me, Luke."

***

Driving home, Luke forsook music so he could listen to two subjects. Once again in his life he was obsessed with the property market. Buying, selling, renting. It was a mess out there. The other subject was just as troublesome. Traffic.

Unexpected tailbacks from an accident near the edge of the city panicked him for a while with a ten-minute delay, but he had given himself plenty of time to avoid the onset of darkness. Dusk was still holding off until nearly seven in the evening and he was leaving work every day at four. Any later would run the risk of getting caught in heavy traffic. He would rather suffer Professor Stafford's admonishments than have the end of his commute being enveloped in shade. The clocks changing would soon steal more sunlight from him. Hopefully that by then, he could manage to find somewhere to rent in Dublin. The streets were still safe there compared to the country roads. He would walk past any amount of junkies or adolescent gangs without fear after the things he had seen. If he had to sell the car for a rental deposit on a flat and walk to work or get public transport, he would. He wanted to put the house on the market already but there were complications because of the investigation and the estate agents he had spoken to weren't confident about getting a decent asking price with the new history the place had acquired. He would sell at a loss, he didn't care, they would work it out.

Sophie rang.

"Are you on the way?" she asked.

"Yup. I'll be back well before dark."

***

By half past five he was home. Sophie met him out of his car with a kiss. Over at Declan's house, the Jack Russell sat in a basket outside and whined. Willy sat at the top of a plastic green slide, head downcast, hands in his lap.

"He just sits there," said Sophie. "Declan puts him outside and he just sits on that slide until he's lifted off and brought back in. Doesn't slide down, doesn't run around, doesn't make a sound."

The front door of the Maguire house opened and Declan filled the frame.

"Hello, Luke, old friend," he hollered across the fence.

Luke didn't reply.

"We never talk anymore, Luke."

"Just ignore him," Sophie told Luke as Declan kept talking.

"Maybe it's best, old pal. Not talking. People do too much talking these days."

Luke kept his eyes averted and his lips tight.

"I'm keeping an eye on them, just so you know," called Declan before they got to their door. "I'm keeping an eye on Sophie and Elliot. Making sure that no harm comes to them while you're at work."

"I hate him," Sophie muttered as they stepped inside. "Any joy with apartments? Anything at all out there?"

"No, not that we can afford while still have this place. We'll be gone soon, I promise. I'll find somewhere." Luke turned and took in the uncomfortable stillness of the scene set beneath the sullen sky: the frightened dog, the broken boy and the dark threatening grin on the man who was once his friend. "I'm just worried about the boy."

"Surely, he wouldn't hurt his own son." Sophie locked the door behind them.

"By the way, Sergeant Harris is calling here in a while."

Sophie raised her eyebrows.

"He's calling here after dark?"

"He said he wouldn't travel alone."

"Nobody else in the locality will go out in the dark."

"Who said that?"

"I was talking to Denise's friend, Sinead. She called round to see how I was getting on. She said that nobody knows what to believe but everyone is staying inside at night. O'Shea's is closed up; they have no business anymore. She and her husband can hear noises in the distance some evenings, across the fields. It might be laughter, but they don't know whether to report it or not."

"What's the point, I guess? Who'd believe it?"

They went into the sitting room where Elliott was sequestered in a playpen with a bunch of toys. Outside, the sky began to muddy and Luke closed the curtains, first checking that all the latches were shut tight. Then he picked up his son and bounced him gently in his arms. The growl of an idling engine beckoned him to the door.

"That must be Harris."

But when he stepped out—Elliot still in his arms, Sophie following—it wasn't a Garda car they saw and it hadn't pulled into their driveway. A blue minivan, the name of a local taxi firm plastered across its side, was parked outside Declan's house. The silhouette of a woman was visible, hunched in the rear seats with the spiritless pose of the condemned. The driver lumbered out and opened the back door to hand a single bag out to Declan before offering his arm to the passenger.

Just then the Garda car did arrive. Harris and a tall, younger Garda with a nervous lip got out and joined the Sheridans in their observation.

"Your new neighbour has arrived then," said Harris. "I'm sure that'll set the tongues wagging around here. She's a very lucky girl though, with Declan willing to take care of her while she recovers."

Cliona moved in slow motion out of the taxi, as if stepping barefoot through a field of thorns. Her left side, shoulder and arm, seemed frozen in place beneath the dark layers covering her upper body.

"Why ... why is she here?" asked Luke.

"I didn't think he'd offer to take on the responsibility like he did," said the sergeant. "Fair play to him. She was in a bad state for a while in the hospital. Spouting all sorts of nonsense. Nightmarish stuff."

"Crazy talk," added the young Garda.

"Declan managed to put her at ease when he got to visit, calmed her down. Losing the baby must have made the whole ordeal so much worse for her," Harris said.

Declan paid the driver and guided Cliona towards the threshold. She flinched at his touch but shuffled inside with her head downcast like she was hiding from the sky and the fields and the trees.

"Come on inside and we'll get this over with," said Sophie. "I don't know what else you think we can tell you but you shouldn't be out on those roads any later than you have to be."

In the sitting room, the two Gardaí dredged up old questions they hoped might lead them to the remains of bodies that would never be found. Luke and Sophie gave empty answers with blank expressions and Elliot cried at the strange stiffness that had infused his parents. Outside in the failing light, behind the house and deep in the fields, a faint laughter hung in the air like a contamination, freezing the birds in the trees, driving small animals underground, chilling the blood of the people in their homes. The ancient hawthorn tree, its branches stripped now of anything they ever held, looked in a certain light to pulse and shift; those gaps between its twisted roots like cruel mouths threatening to open.

ACKNOWLEDGEMENTS

My parents have always been supportive of the creative pursuits of their kids (weren't we the lucky devils) and now my own little family are just as encouraging of each other.

Thanks to Heather, Steve and all at Brigids Gate Press for their hard work and kindness in publishing my debut novel. I hope you make it over to Ireland for a visit sometime.

I was fortunate to have Nicola Cassidy as a mentor through the Meath Libraries Getting Published Mentorship when I was submitting Country Roads.

Elle Turpitt and Stephanie Ellis were the book's excellent editors. Elizabeth Leggett conjured up the wonderful cover.

ABOUT THE AUTHOR

Some grotesque creatures lurk in the ancient countryside of County Meath. Colin Leonard is one of them.

He writes horror fiction mostly set in Ireland and his short stories have appeared in a number of anthologies and online venues including Horror Library Volume 7, It Calls From The Veil, Eyes, The Vampiricon and Fudoki Magazine.

Country Roads is his debut novel.

You can find more details and connect with him through his website www.collyleonard.com or on twitter @collyleonard.

Content Warnings

Violence

Animal cruelty

MORE FROM BRIGIDS GATE PRESS

According to Dante, a sin is the misdirection of love—the human will, or essentially, the direction of our beings. Love the Sinner is an examination of just how those sins can kaleidoscope into horrific consequences creating a distorted and deadly landscape. These stories stand stark before you in full glaring misstep and macabre to show the human psyche in all its twisted reality.

From grief and its rage to medical meddling to ensure a new world order to bloody revenge within a quantum leap, these stories seek to solidify one absolute truth: man is the scariest monster.